BLACK JACK

BLACK JACK

Lora Leigh

St. Martin's Griffin
New York

This is a work of fiction. All of the characters, organizations, and events portrayed in this novel are either products of the author's imagination or are used fictitiously.

www.stmartins.com

ISBN 978-1-250-03667-4 (trade paperback)
ISBN 978-1-4299-5513-3 (e-book)

St. Martin's Griffin books may be purchased for educational, business, or promotional use. For information on bulk purchases, please contact Macmillan Corporate and Premium Sales Department at 1-800-221-7945 extension 5442 or write specialmarkets@macmillan.com.

First St. Martin's Griffin Edition: May 2013

10 9 8 7 6 5 4 3 2 1

Dedicated most thankfully and with the utmost love to my daughter, Holly, and my son, Bret, who are growing up much too fast.

You are two of the most enduring and most special lights in my life. You bring me laughter, joy, and love, and I thank God for the very special gifts he sent me when he sent to me my babies.

ACKNOWLEDGMENTS

Special thanks to CO2 Donna, a nearby correctional officer, for the information on the modified Glocks. Any mistakes I've made in the translation are my own.

Special thanks as well to Randy, the owner of Friendly's Sports Bar at Franklin and Walnut Streets in Hagerstown, Maryland, for the use of his bar. Good friends and good bars are wonderful research sources, and he has one of the best. And the food is out of this world.

Try the Chicken Wings.

PROLOGUE

IT WAS AN ANNIVERSARY of sorts. The anniversary of her death.

Lilly Belle, code-named Night Hawk, maneuvered the streamlined Ninja into the dimly lit parking lot of the bar at which she had been ordered to meet her contact, and fought not to reflect on life and death. There lay a whole pit of problems best not poked at. There lay madness, and she preferred not to invite more madness into her life.

It wasn't as though her former life had been perfect, she told herself. There had been problems and dangers there. But it had held all she had known of safety and love. She had known the rules, she had understood the intricacies of living within it.

She had her mother, her brother, a niece and nephew, and once she had had a father who had loved her, who had protected her.

Once, there had been more to life than survival.

Parking, she lifted the customized, electronically enhanced helmet from her head and secured it to the chest rest of the bike before dismounting. She stared at the building, heard the laughter and music drifting from inside.

This was a hell of a place to celebrate such a momentous occasion as dying. Even more problematic was the man she was meeting.

Her weakness.

She smiled at the thought as she fluffed her dark hair around her face, attempting to restore a bit of body to it before entering the bar. She'd even used makeup tonight. Something she rarely did for a mission this simple.

The last meeting with this man had culminated in a kiss, though. A kiss that had fried every synapse in her mind and tingled her nerve endings clear to the soles of her feet. It was a kiss that had fueled her fantasies and her imagination ever since.

The memory of that kiss was guaranteed to shred her self-control when she met with him once more. She knew it. She looked forward to it. And hoped that tonight would be the night.

Thankfully, the information she had brought to America was something that could be taken care of quickly. The disk she carried in the inside pocket of her jacket contained information on several individuals who had been known European associates of the person known as Warbucks, an American who had stolen and attempted to sell sensitive military weapons several weeks before.

The information would help develop a plan to wipe out the network Warbucks had begun creating that dealt in thefts, transportation, and sales of highly classified items.

Running her hands quickly down the snug leather that covered her hips, Lilly let a self-mocking smile touch her lips.

Travis Caine, code-named Black Jack, the man she was meeting, was a man of mystery. The identity he had taken with his induction into the Elite Ops was that of "facilitator," a man who negogiated agreements between rival companies or organizations. He thought nothing of working opposite sides of the law, and he didn't care if he spilled blood if need be.

The *real* Travis Caine had met an unfortunate and very secret demise, which had allowed *this* Travis to take the deceased man's identity. The original Travis Caine had been a cesspool of depravity. But then the original Lilly Belle had been no angel either.

Drawing in a deep breath, Lilly walked through the parking lot toward the side entrance of Friendly's Sports Bar. A weekend crowd filled the place nearly to capacity, with alcohol fueling the joviality and carefree laughter.

It was one of those bars where friends met after work and on the weekends to drink, shoot pool, or just talk. Comfortable, almost homey, and just run-down enough to make it feel well loved.

She caught sight of Travis within seconds after she entered the bar. There, lounging in the shadows, was Black Jack. Dark blond hair fell over his brow and the hint of a beard and mustache shadowed the lower part of his face. Predatory brown eyes with a hint of green gleamed within his darkly tanned face, expressing well-honed strength and pure arrogance.

Brooding awareness filled his rough-hewn features, and for a second, just the barest second, her breath caught in her throat at the flicker of pure male arousal that gleamed in his gaze.

He didn't bother to hide it. His gaze took in the leather over-the-knee boots, and in the second it lingered there she wished she had worn her high-heeled boots rather than the ones that allowed her easier movement.

His gaze moved on to the leather pants, pausing for a breath of time at her thighs, before lifting again. An impish recklessness invaded her and had her unzipping the short leather riding jacket she wore to reveal the snug white shirt that clung to her breasts and rode high above the waistband of her pants.

Her nipples tightened, pressing against the material of the shirt and doing everything but waving for his attention. Not that he missed them. His eyes narrowed on them as his lips quirked with a hint of smile. She propped her hands on her hips, tilted her head, and arched her brow.

This was a fine way to treat a mission. She was certain her commander would have had something to say about her hormones clouding her judgment.

But what the hell, she was already supposed to be dead, it wasn't as though she were going to lose more than she already had. Unless she counted really dying.

Moving across the room, striding slow and easy, Lilly had to fight to remember that she was here for a mission rather than the good time she was dying for.

"You're late." His voice was like midnight sex. It rasped across her nerve endings and sent her hormones screaming in response.

Her nipples were spike hard and dying for more than

her own touch. Her sex felt hot, swollen, her clit rubbing against the silk lining of the leather pants as she slid into the booth across from him.

"So report me," she drawled as she sat back in the seat and reminded herself that she was here for much more than the man.

"What makes you think I haven't already taken care of that?" He turned in the seat, one of his long legs moving under the table rather than stretched out on the bench seat as it had been.

"Then I have time to come up with an excuse." She shrugged. "My boss is across the ocean, darling, not looking over my shoulder."

His lips tightened, though the corners lifted as he shook his head and a chuckle left his lips.

"Lucky you," he stated as his shoulders shifted beneath the leather jacket he wore. "When did you get in?"

"A few hours ago." She was tired. She'd realized that as the plane landed. Tired of so much, and wondering if the price she had paid would ever feel worth the pain she endured.

"Hungry?" He nodded to the bar. "The chicken wings were exceptional."

Lilly shook her head. She wasn't hungry for food, she was hungry for touch. So hungry that at times it felt as though the need were gnawing a hole inside her soul.

This man made that need burn brighter, hotter. As though he alone held the key to her arousal and her satisfaction.

He stared around the bar for long moments before turning back to her.

His gaze was more intent now, darker.

"Are we going to keep pretending?" he finally asked.

The question shocked her. She'd had the impression he was fighting the attraction harder than she was, that he would be the last one to give in. She hadn't expected him to make this first move.

"Pretending's safer," she finally said, but the aching need couldn't be disguised. She heard it herself, she knew he could hear it as well.

"It's safer," he agreed as he slid across the seat and rose to his feet.

Leather pants as well, leather bomber jacket, a white shirt beneath, the loosened buttons revealing the strong column of his neck. The jacket emphasized the lean strength of his chest and shoulders. His arms, she knew, were powerful, corded with muscle and warm, so very warm, when they wrapped around her.

This man had trained her when she had joined the Ops, covered her on missions and led her through the strange new world of the agency she had been a part of for the past six years.

"Let's go." He held his hand out to her, the strong palm and fingers inviting, his expression intense and bordering on total male hunger.

It sent the strangest surge of adrenaline racing through her. Akin to fear, or danger, it raced to her heart, sent it pounding, then raked across her clit before tearing into her vagina and sending her juices flowing.

He wasn't waiting, and she was tired of waiting.

Good Lord. It should be criminal. She was certain, in her former world, it was against the rules. And hormones certainly had no place in the Elite Ops. Sexual need, emotions, hungers, they were all to be ignored, especially during a mission.

Lilly had managed to obey those rules, until it came to Travis Caine.

Lifting her hand to him, she felt his fingers curl around hers, felt the heat of his skin, and had to restrain a shiver of pure reaction as she allowed him to help her to her feet.

She hadn't expected this, not from Black Jack, the need and the hunger reflected in his eyes, transferring to her in the heat of his palm against hers.

It reminded her of another time, another man, a life that had existed before her "death."

It was the oddest sensation. As though that warmth were physically sinking inside her, rushing through her veins, caressing sensitive nerve endings. Breathless anticipation began rising inside her, chills racing up her arms despite the warmth of the bar and the leather she wore.

"What are you doing?" Staring up at him, suddenly wary of what she saw in his eyes, what she felt racing through her own body, she couldn't help the question as it slipped past her lips.

"What do you want me to do, Belle?"

Belle. It wasn't a name he used often, but each time he used it, the sound of it on his lips sent reaction racing through her. It never failed to make her wet.

What did she want him to do?

"We don't have enough time for what I want." She wanted all of him. The touch, the taste, the dreams she had been forced to give up.

His expression became heavier, more sensual. The

green in his eyes seemed to brighten, to flicker. It made her wonder what color his eyes had been before the Elite Ops. Before he had "died."

Blue, she thought. His eyes had been blue. The convergence of the green, the golden brown, and then the darker brown was so oddly aligned that it almost appeared as though the separate colors had broken into their own small groupings. The laser surgery that had been done to change his identity had come close to the color required, but Travis's eyes were so much more than a simple hazel.

"We'll make time."

She followed him from the bar, her lips parted as she fought to breathe, to believe this was more than a dream, or a fantasy that she had lost herself within.

As she left the bar she had to fight not to pinch herself to be certain she was definitely awake.

She had been a member of the world's social elite at one time. She was a trained Elite Ops agent now. She had killed. She had lied. But at the moment she felt like a teenager again, and she had managed to snare the most handsome, the most popular guy in the world.

Her hands would have shook if she hadn't forced them to be still. Her knees felt weak, and the night, which had seemed too cool earlier, now felt steamy with sensuality as they stepped outside the building.

Traffic surged along the street, anyone could be watching them. But all her senses knew, all they responded to now, was Travis.

"What did you drive?" she asked as she glanced around the parking lot, looking for the Harley he had ridden months before when they met in St. Louis.

"I had a cab drop me off." He paused, glancing back at her, his expression heavy with sensuality. "We'll use your cycle."

Her cycle.

She went as he drew her to it, checked it quickly for tampering before swinging his leg over the seat and pulling her to him.

Lilly went willingly, straddling the narrow pad behind Travis and leaning forward, her breasts pressing against his back as the cycle rumbled to life.

Travis felt the gentle warm weight of the woman as he made his way through Hagerstown's streets to the hotel he'd checked into earlier.

What the hell was he doing? No doubt thinking with his dick rather than his brain. But at the moment, his dick was holding sway and there wasn't a damned thing Travis could do about it.

He knew better than this. He'd known the treachery of one woman. Hadn't that been enough? But this woman, she had slipped past his guard years ago as he had trained her. She had covered his back, wormed her way into his trust, and through it all, he had ached for her.

She was the epitome of every dream he'd ever had, even at a time when he'd had no business dreaming of another woman. She had even overshadowed the dream of innocence and laughter that had filled him before his "death."

His marriage had been hell. His life as Lord Xavier Travis Dermont had been a double life. As an agent for MI6, and a husband fighting to keep a rein on his willful, cheating wife, he'd learned that the job was a hell of a lot more dependable.

Until Lilly.

Lilly made him wonder what he had been missing. She made him wonder what he had thrown away when he had left that life so easily after his wife had betrayed him and her country.

Pulling into the back parking lot of the Homewood Suites, Travis checked the area carefully before pulling the cycle into the darkened corner at the edge of the lot.

He'd pay for this, he knew. Somewhere, sometime, this one night would rise up and bite him in the ass. And still, he couldn't help but follow through.

His wife was a part of the past, a life that no longer existed. He was no longer Lord Xavier Travis Dermont. He was Travis Caine, a facilitator between disagreeing parties, criminal or legal.

He was a man with an unsavory past now. A man that others feared. And he had no life to offer Lilly. They had nothing to offer each other, but this night.

As the motor cut off, Travis let his hands grip hers where they pressed against his abs, her small fingers warm, trembling before helping her dismount behind him.

He had every intention of getting her to the room, getting her into a bed before he touched her. He knew how shaky his own self-control was.

As he turned to her, though, and stared into those brilliant green eyes, suddenly nothing mattered but tasting her again, feeling the heat and the warmth of her fragile body.

One hand wrapped around her neck while he pulled her to him with the other. Still straddling the cycle, he had no trouble lifting her to him, guiding her leg over his, and settling her into his body as his lips took hers and he lost himself in her kiss.

His cock pressed into the junction of her thighs, the heated softness of it beneath the thin leather she wore made him think of sweet summer nights.

Damn, she was going to be that good, that slick and wet for him. He knew it. He could sense it.

Tangling the fingers of one hand into her hair, he held her in place as his lips and tongue ravished hers. Lilly gave as good as she got. Her fingers speared into his hair, tight and desperate, and a mewling little moan tore from her lips as her tongue licked at his, stroking, caressing with desperate hunger.

He shouldn't have started this out here. He should never have allowed himself to touch her yet, to taste her. He knew the taste of her. It had tormented him for months. He knew the feel of her, but not enough. Not yet.

Jerking back from her, Travis did the only thing he could think of to keep from being arrested for lewd and indecent acts in a public place.

He lifted her from him, ignoring her protesting cry as he unwrapped one of her legs from around his waist and helped her back to her feet. Swinging his leg over the seat, he wrapped his arm around her waist and all but dragged her to the side entrance of the motel.

Sliding the key card through the security reader, he waited for the subtle click, then pushed the door open and led her to the elevator.

It took only minutes to reach the fourth floor and the room he'd rented for his stay there. He paused a moment to ensure that the hair he'd lain over the top of the reader was still there before he swiped the card, then pulled Lilly into the darkened room.

There was no thinking after that. There was only the taste of her, the feel of her. Stripping her of the clothes that kept the satin softness of her body from him, then tearing his own from his body to allow his flesh to stroke against hers, and still, he couldn't make it past the small sitting area to the bed that was only a few steps away.

He was dying for her. God help him, he couldn't stand another moment away from her, so much as a second without their flesh touching. Never in his life had a woman affected him this way. Never had he known such a powerful hunger, such a driving need to touch, to taste, to forever imprint the feel of another's flesh inside his mind.

Until Lilly Belle.

Pulling his head back to string kisses down her neck, he was surprised as she began stringing them down his chest instead. Held in a vise of pure sensual sensation, Travis could only feel, could only watch as her lips and tongue painted a trail of agonizing pleasure to the thick, heavy erection that pulsed in need.

Never had he seen anything so beautiful as the sight of her going to her knees in front of him, naked, her breasts swollen, her nipples hard. Her fingers attempted to wrap around the width of his cock, but they couldn't quite make it. That didn't stop her from leaning forward and licking a white-hot trail of sensation over the sensitive crest.

"You don't have to do this," he groaned, but damn, he wanted her to.

A siren's smile curved her lips before they parted

over the wide head of his cock, and slowly, tantaliz-ingly, she sucked it into the silken heat of her mouth.

Travis's fingers bunched in the heavy strands of her hair. His head tilted back as the muscles in his body tightened, bulged with the effort to survive the extrem-ity of the pleasure now washing through him.

The heated dampness swirled around the head of his cock, seared over nerve endings so sensitive now that each draw of her mouth, each lash of her tongue, was an agony of pleasure.

Bending his head once again, he forced his eyes open, forced himself to watch the most erotic sight he had ever seen. It was enough to make his balls clench in agony. The sight of her lips parted over his cock, taking him in, sucking him with reckless greed as the fingers of one hand stroked the shaft, and the other, sweet heaven, the fingers of her other hand curled around his balls, her nails scraping the flesh as he felt her moan vibrating around the too-sensitive head.

Each draw of her mouth drove him closer to the breaking point. Each lick of her tongue had his nerve endings screaming with need.

Until he couldn't take any more.

Gripping her shoulders, he drew her to her feet de-spite her protests, a tight grimace contorting his fea-tures as the hard flesh slipped free of the hot ecstasy surrounding it.

He'd wanted so much more than he would be able to give her this first time. He wanted to touch her for hours, stroke her, taste her. He'd wanted to gorge him-self on her and pray it would finally sate the hunger tormenting him.

Instead, he could do nothing but lift her to him, turn, and sit her on the desk beside them. He reached down, grabbed his pants, fished a condom out of his pocket, sheathed himself, and stepped between her thighs. As her legs wrapped around his hips he stared into the wild green of her eyes, and knew he would never have enough.

"I have to," he groaned as he pressed the head of his cock against the snug, heated entrance of her slick pussy.

The slick dampness coated his flesh as he pressed against her, easing with agonizing slowness inside the tight entrance.

"I waited." Her whisper tore into his soul. "Tell me it's not a dream."

What she did to him was probably illegal. It might very well get him killed.

"It's a dream." He had to clench his teeth against the rapture enclosing his cock as her sweet pussy began to suck him inside. "Tell yourself that, Belle. Believe it. It's just a dream."

It had to be a dream, because anything else at this moment could destroy them.

He heard the hitch of her voice and couldn't bear her pain, her regret. He felt her hands tighten on his shoulders and knew that he couldn't allow the night to be anything more than that. Just a dream.

Working against the ultrasnug grip of the sweet, heated muscles gripping his cock, Travis began to press deeper inside her, to take more of her. His muscles tightened as his entire body seemed to spasm with the pleasure that raked through him, burning through his body and imprinting her into areas of his soul that he knew he should never allow her into.

"I don't want to wake up then." The lost, lonely sound of her voice tore at his heart. "Don't let me wake up, Travis. Let me sleep forever—" A cry ended the plea as Travis surged those last inches inside her, pushing past that fragile barrier. His cock throbbing in agony, pulsing with a white-hot demand for release as the heat of her pussy surrounded it, milked it, gripped it like the sweetest vise, and stole the last of the control he had possessed.

Gripping a hip with one hand, Travis let his fingers curl around the firm weight of a breast as his head lowered. His hips moved, shifted, taking shallow thrusts that had her pussy tightening further as his lips covered the tight, velvety peak of a nipple.

He sucked it inside, laved it with his tongue, and listened to her attempt to hold back her cries. She failed. He began thrusting inside her, then pulled back until just the crest of his cock remained before powering inside her once again only to draw back quickly, thrust in hard. It was a brutal, ecstatic cycle that had perspiration slickening both their bodies as he felt her begin to tighten further.

Her pussy rippled around his dick, tightened, heated. He felt as if his cock were fucking into a vise of pure hot silk covered with rich syrup.

Her legs were tight around his hips as she moved with him, taking each thrust and returning it as she slowly lay back on the desk, forcing him to release the sweet taste of her nipple.

But it gave him so much more to touch. Stretched out before him, she stared up at him as he gripped her hips, and his gaze dropped to where he possessed her, his jaw tightening as he fought to hold back his release.

Sweet, soft, bare flesh hugged his cock, glistened with the heavy layer of her juices, and encased his flesh with every hard stroke that separated them. Her clit was swollen, a pale pink gem peeking out at him, tempting him until he lowered a hand from her hip to stroke the tiny pearl gently, quickly.

Timing each caress to the strokes that were only gaining in speed, fucking her with all the desperate hunger riding inside him, Travis felt himself unraveling in the sheer pleasure of the act of taking her.

His thumb moved faster over her clit, stroking it, her muted cries gaining in depth until he felt her coming around him. Her pussy became so tight it was agony stroking through the clenched muscles. They sucked at the heavy crest, flexed around the throbbing shaft, and between one heartbeat and the next, Travis felt her orgasm.

The power of it drew her body tight. It lifted her back from the desk, widened her eyes, and began to jerk through her body as pure ecstasy possessed her. Thrusting in harder, one stroke, two, Travis gave in to the tortured pleasure wrapping around his balls and buried himself to the hilt to fill her with the hard, steady blasts of release that poured from him.

His head fell back on his shoulders. His fucking knees were shaking, weakening. Sweat ran down his face in rivulets, adding to the sensations that racked through him, tore up his spine, and exploded in his brain with a rapture he knew he would never recover from.

Collapsing over her long minutes later, he fought to catch his breath, to get his bearings. His flesh was still buried inside her, he was still hard, and he wanted more.

He wanted to consume her. He wanted to possess her until nothing mattered but the sheer white-hot pleasure that surrounded them.

"Don't wake up," he whispered as he felt her shudder against him once more. "Dream with me, Belle. Sweet Belle, just dream with me."

Lilly felt sad as she drove to the warehouse that housed the headquarters of Elite Two. Returning to the life she lived now, rather than the life she had lived six years ago, or the one she wished she could live in Travis's arms, was one of the hardest things she had ever done.

Lilly had given Travis the information she had been sent to deliver before leaving, but leaving had been nearly impossible. She had wanted to stay there, to linger, to hold onto the warmth of the man who had held her for as long as possible.

She'd had to make a choice. Stay with Travis or grab what little time she would have to see her family.

She had walked away from her family. There was no changing that fact. Or rather, she had been forced to do so by whoever had killed her father and had attempted to kill her on a wintry night six years before.

She was dead to her family, but despite her difficult relationship with them when she was "alive," they weren't dead to her.

And really her mother had been the difficult one.

Angelica Harrington was volatile and slightly neurotic, to say the least, Lilly thought with a tight smile. Consumed with appearances, arrogant at every opportunity, and convinced her way was the only way, her mother had ruled the Harrington household with an iron fist. Her father and brother had shielded her from most of it, but no one could completely escape her mother's often disapproving regard. Even so, Lilly loved her mother. As Jared used to say often, "She loves us, Lilly." And then he would laugh. "Even if she has a funny way of showing it."

Lilly smiled, thinking of her brother. They had been so close when they were younger, but they had drifted apart a bit after he had gone to law school, then graduated, married, and started a family of his own. Still, her heart clenched when she thought about how her brother and her mother must have felt to lose both her and her father at the same time.

Lilly's smile faded as she remembered the night her father had died. She remembered walking into his study and seeing him lying there in his own blood. She remembered feeling like it had to be a nightmare, but she was unable to wake up. She had been about to run to her father and then nothing . . .

The next thing she knew she was waking up in a hospital, bandaged practically from head to toe, and in so much pain that she had wanted to die if she wasn't dead already. She remembered hearing Jordan's voice through the pain.

"Do you want to live, Lady Victoria, or die forever?"

The satellite phone on the seat beside her rang insistently, breaking her train of thought.

Glancing quickly at the display, Lilly couldn't help but bite her lip in indecision. She had a feeling she knew what was coming.

Sighing loudly, she reached to her ear and activated the bluetooth.

"I'm on my way, Raisa," she told the other woman.

"Yeah, like we'll get to talk when you get here, bitch," Raisa laughed good-naturedly. The other girl's explicit language no longer fazed Lilly.

The exotic Afghani girl had taken to defying all the rules she had been raised to live by when she had watched her parents die before her eyes, then had "died" herself in a war that had destroyed every dream she had ever known, she had told Lilly.

"We'll find time," Lilly promised her.

"Like hell," Raisa said. "I want the scoop now. Did you get you some? Because I swear if anyone ever needed a little sack time with a tall sexy man, then it's you."

Lilly flushed, suddenly thankful that this conversation was on the phone rather than face to face. Raisa was terribly intuitive, and Lilly knew the other girl would see all the things she wanted to hide.

Things Lilly wanted to hide even from herself.

"I had a mission to finish, not sack time to accomplish," Lilly informed her, fighting to keep her voice even. "Damn, Raisa, maybe you're the one needing the sack time with a tall, dark and handsome."

"Only if I have my knife at his throat and he's tied to the bed," Raisa snorted. "Anyway, we're discussing your sack time, not mine."

Striking and darkly beautiful, Raisa was the one agent Lilly considered least likely to go looking for a one-night stand. It wouldn't surprise her in the slightest to learn that the other girl was a virgin.

She had "died" at age sixteen and the horror of the hours she had spent at the hands of the enemy still brought Raisa awake screaming from the nightmares.

"No sack time, Raisa," Lilly lied. "Sorry."

"Damn, you're no fun." Raisa sighed. "I miss those bad boys, Lilly. They make life interesting."

And Elite One did make life fun. sometimes. Whenever she or the other girls were sent to gather information before Elite One went in to complete a mission, there was always a few days spent briefing them on what they had learned.

It was days spent going over the intel, eating pizza and sometimes a few practical jokes played by Wild Card or Heat Seeker. At times, there had been stolen moments of sensual teasing between Lilly and Travis. Raisa had walked in one of those times.

She hadn't stopped teasing Lilly since.

"I'm almost home," Lilly finally told her. "Put on a pot of coffee and a snack of some sort. I'm starved."

"Already working on it," Raisa promised her. "And you're right on time. We have several missions coming through. A few of them actually look interesting."

None of them were interesting. They were all dangerous, they were all soul-tiring.

"Be there in five then," Lilly said.

"We're watching for you. See you soon." The line disconnected as Lilly reached up and deactived the link before pulling into the warehouse district that housed Elite Two's headquarters close to London's docks.

The long drive back to the warehouse had passed quickly. Stepping from the SUV, Lilly paused and looked around. She took in the brick buildings that surrounded the Elite Two's headquarters, the darkened windows, the almost sinister feel of the area, as heavy storm clouds rolled in overhead.

She suddenly felt on guard. She could almost swear she felt the scope of a sniper's rifle aimed at her own head. Her commander had once stated that when you'd been the hunter long enough, you would know when you had become the prey.

Suddenly, she definitely felt like prey.

Reaching inside the SUV, she pressed the activation on the steering wheel as she quickly bent and reached for the weapon lying on the passenger seat.

It happened then. As she moved. As she heard her commander's voice through the communications patch, the explosion of a gunshot came barely a second after agony engulfed her head.

She felt, not for the first time, images of her life tearing through her mind. This time, it wasn't the memories of a child's laughter, or a father's voice that she heard.

This time, it was the voice of a lover who should never have been her lover. A man who had stolen her heart. His voice whispered in her ear, and the feel of his lips caressing her flesh almost washed through the pain as she felt her body fall.

In that millisecond true regret wasn't for the life she had lost before, but for the man she couldn't return to.

She saw eyes the color of gold and brown and flecked with green. She saw his face, felt him against her, and wished she had done things differently. As darkness closed around her, a single word slipped past her lips, rife with regret, pain, and an aching sense of loneliness.

"Travis."

CHAPTER 1

Two months later

A STEADY, RAIN-FILLED wind whipped around the dark helmet covering Travis Caine's head, sang around the leather pants and jacket he wore, and whispered a caress over the full, face-shielding helmet he wore. Heavy boots covered his feet, protecting him against the elements as rain poured down from the skies, and lightning lit the darkness with jagged forks of power.

The Harley he rode roared down the open highway, throbbing with the increased power it had been customized with. The display beneath the handlebars was lit with a muted glow indicating speed, time, and location. The embedded electronics in the night-vision shield of the helmet provided other readouts considered imperative in his line of work.

According to that information, he was growing closer to his destination and a mission he still wasn't certain he was prepared to be a part of, because of the woman he was partnered with, because of a night they shouldn't have shared.

He shouldn't have loved her.

No, he shouldn't have fucked her, he corrected himself. He immediately felt an edge of distaste at his attempt to make that night into something unemotional. Something less powerful than it had been.

It was a night he hadn't been able to forget. In the past two months it had tormented him, torn at him, and left him hungry for more of her in ways he had never hungered for another woman before. She was the last woman he should have ever touched.

What the hell was she doing to him?

Elite Two and the women that were a part of that team were a hidden, rarely mentioned section of Elite Ops.

The Ops was more than the one team Jordan commanded, Travis had learned. For years he and the other agents under Jordan's command had believed that Elite One was the only sanctioned operation and that the women they had helped train were meant to be backup, nothing more.

They hadn't realized just how good those women were.

Elite Two had hidden even the slightest sign that they, too, were agents. No one had told Elite One what those women's true purpose was, nor had anyone explained the full extent of the Elite Ops and the units that comprised it until after the Warbucks mission months before.

Warbucks had been stealing and selling top-secret military weapons as well as agents' identities. He'd managed to infiltrate government agencies as well as the companies his father had had interest in to acquire the stolen resources.

Elite Two had gathered the information that had led them to Warbucks because of their covers as very exclusive, well-trained escorts.

Once the mission had revealed Warbucks' identity, Elite Two had also managed to reveal his associates, his buyers, and his silent partners in many of the sales.

It was then he and the other agents had begun questioning the organization that had taken them in, that had saved them, and created new lives for them.

They'd learned it was much more extensive than they could have imagined. And the missions were drawing together slowly, linked by a thread of information here, a suspect there. Travis could feel it edging toward a single denominator, which made him begin questioning all the missions they were given.

This latest one had him questioning even himself.

It was a damned dangerous game he was getting ready to participate in, and thinking about it left a sour taste in his mouth. Despite all the good it was doing, there were times the Elite Ops had little tact and even less taste. To use a woman in the manner they were prepared to use her had his back teeth clenching in anger and a sense of injustice rising inside him.

The fact they were using his woman, despite her agent status, only pissed him off more.

And he was damned if he could figure out why he was letting it bother him. It wasn't as though he hadn't learned the hard way how easily a woman could betray a man. He'd "died" with that lesson pounding in his head years ago, and when he'd been reborn, he'd sworn to himself that he wouldn't forget it.

He'd lost everything in his life because he'd trusted a

woman and it wasn't a lesson he cared to repeat. It was one he had sworn time and time again he wouldn't repeat. But the minute he'd learned how the Elite Ops was forcing this woman to face her past, he'd become enraged.

Lilly was different, his heart swore, though his mind fought that instinctive knowledge.

He shouldn't have been surprised, though. He should have expected it at some point once he'd managed to uncover her former identity. She was the perfect asset to use to find the individual or individuals involved in the death of the powerful, influential Lord Harold Harrington, Lilly's father.

But they were prepared to use her in a way that Travis feared would end up destroying her. Returning her to her old life, to the family she had left behind, wouldn't be a cakewalk for her.

Sure, Lilly had already been training to follow in her father's footsteps as an MI5 agent before her "death." But even then, she had been a Harrington and had been entrenched in that blue-blood life. She had been raised to be a lady and to assume all the responsibilities that entailed. However, once she had joined the Elite Ops, she left all of that behind and had become someone else entirely. An outsider, a rebel . . . a lost soul who had seen and done things others only saw in their nightmares. Like him, she no longer belonged in that rarefied world. And making her face what she had been forced to leave behind was damn cruel.

Facing it himself wouldn't be easy. There was an added painful element for Lilly, though. They were returning to investigate the death of Lilly's father and the attempt on her own life when she had been Lady Victoria Harrington. Lilly remembered very little about that final night of her old life. She remembered seeing her father lying in a pool of blood when she entered his study, and nothing more.

The next day Lord Harrington's body had been pulled from his car, which had gone over a cliff. The fuel line had cracked upon impact, and in a matter of minutes the car exploded. Harrington's body had been burned beyond recognition. They'd had to identify him by his dental records. Lilly's body had never been found. It was believed that she had been thrown from the car upon impact and that her body washed out to the sea at the bottom of the cliff.

They believed that whoever shot Lord Harrington had tried to cover up the crime by making it look like he and his daughter had gotten into a horrible car accident. And because he had been wealthy and titled, and because MI5 would have preferred not to have anyone looking too closely into why Lord Harrington might have died, he had been laid to rest quickly and Lilly had been declared dead. Unfortunately, the ones responsible still had not been identified.

As a covert agent for MI5, Lord Harrington had been investigating the electronic theft of thousands of pounds from trust funds and legitimate companies in England. The situation came to his attention when he had launched a probe into his own company when funds had gone missing.

Those funds had been diverted to accounts overseas, transferred again and again until they disappeared entirely in dummy accounts. That's when Elite Ops had become interested in the case.

No one could track who was doing it, how they were doing it, or who would be targeted next. Until Lord Harrington had sent a message to MI5 that he had figured it out. Before the agency could send anyone out to his estate to pull him in, he had turned up dead, and his daughter had disappeared. However, money was still disappearing, and they had finally managed to track it to several terrorist accounts and it looked like someone among England's very wealthy was involved, which made it a delicate situation for MI5. And though they might hesitate to investigate England's upper crust, Elite Ops had no such compunction.

Pulling beneath the wide receiving area of the Marriott, Travis cut the power to the Harley, unclipped his helmet, and swung his leg over the seat before striding through the electronic doors to the reception desk.

The tired young woman who checked him in paid a little too much attention to the wet leather he was wearing. The glint of lust in her eyes assured him that if he needed any company when she got off her shift, he only had to let her know.

Hell, he should take her up on it, he thought as he strode to the elevator. He would have, if he wasn't damned sure that he'd end up disgusting himself. Once a man saw heaven in one woman's arms, then nothing else would do. And that scared the shit out of him, the thought that no other woman but Lilly would do.

Sliding the security key card into the electronic slot, Travis waited for the green light before stepping carefully into the room, his fingers curled around the butt of the gun holstered beneath his shirt.

The room was empty. The sense of vacancy that filled

it wrapped around him. It was pure loneliness. Hell, he would have almost preferred an assassin.

Closing the door behind him, Travis tossed his leather bag to the empty chair beside the bed and stared around the darkened room for long moments before moving to the lamp and flipping it on.

Turning, he came to a hard stop at the sight that met him in the shadowed corner on the far side of the room.

"Hell, I didn't even sense you." Travis raked his fingers through his hair as Jordan uncurled himself from the chair next to the small round table. "I thought we were meeting later."

Jordan was an enigma to him, as well as to the rest of the team. Even his nephew, Noah Blake, admitted that his uncle was damned complicated. Travis knew he had never worked with another man as dangerous, nor as completely icy, as Jordan Malone.

"We need to talk before we meet with the commanders from Elite Two. You'll be accompanying them to Switzerland, and I wanted to brief you first," Jordan informed him as he moved to the tiny kitchen station in the corner and pulled open the door to the box refrigerator.

"I could have used a nap first," Travis grunted.

Why the hell Switzerland? The last he heard he was heading to England.

He could have used some time to think about this one.

"You want the nap or full disclosure?" Jordan asked as he pulled free two beers, uncapped them, and handed one to Travis before returning to his chair.

Full disclosure from Commander Tight-ass? Now that would sure as hell be a change.

Setting the bottle on the dresser behind him, Travis threw the helmet to the bed before peeling off his wet jacket and throwing Jordan a dark glare.

"Since when do you give full disclosure?" he asked.

Bright blue eyes flashed with a hint of anger as Jordan lifted the bottle and took a long drink of the beer. When he set the beer back on the table, his expression was once again cool, composed.

"Since we're using a noncombatant," Jordan stated, his voice harder than normal.

Travis watched him carefully now. "Night Hawk isn't a noncombatant, Jordan," he reminded him. "She's an agent."

Jordan took a long sip of his beer, his expression thoughtful before saying, "Not any longer."

Travis froze. He'd never heard of an Elite Ops agent being released from duty. It was a life sentence. Try to run, try to hide, even dare to think of revealing the truth about your life, and it was fatal.

"What do you mean, not any longer?"

The only way she could have managed release was death. And she couldn't be dead. She couldn't.

Leaning forward, Jordan braced his elbows on his knees and stared back at him, his expression remote, but Travis felt the tension emanating from the other man.

"We believe Night Hawk has been compromised," Jordan said. "Two months ago she was shot outside of Elite Two's headquarters. She was struck in the head."

Two months ago. She would have just been returning to England. Two months and he was just now learning what had happened to her.

Travis felt ice form in his veins. For one everlasting

moment bleak darkness seemed to flow through him, to slice into the hardened shield he'd placed around his heart.

Night Hawk. She was tiny as hell, fragile, slender. There were times she appeared almost broken inside. She was the type of woman that a man wanted to protect, to wrap in cotton batting and hold close to his heart forever.

The fact that she was a trained sniper with a rating that other snipers would envy never failed to amaze him. She didn't look strong enough to carry the rifle he knew had been customized for her. She sure as hell didn't look merciless enough to use it, though he knew she was.

She was filled with regret, with bitterness. There was a dark, overwhelming agony that lived in her eyes, and a hunger that went far beyond the lust he knew she felt for him.

And now, there was a chance he would never again touch her, never taste her, never know the culmination of the need that filled her gaze each time she looked at him.

He could only imagine the damage, and the horrific results of those images flashed through his mind, sending a shaft of pain through his soul that he should have been immune to.

"Status?" He could barely force the words past his lips as he suspected the worst.

Jordan had stated she was compromised, not dead. That left hope. God, he needed hope. He couldn't imagine his Night Hawk gone forever, the tiny glimmer of hope that always lingered in her gaze extinguished.

"Recovering. She moved at the last second, so the bullet just grazed her. She has a damned hard head, but there are complications." There was no emotion in Jordan's tone. He could have been discussing the weather rather than a person's life.

Travis had to do something. If he continued to stand there, then he might end up losing his grip on reality.

Jerking fresh, dry jeans from his pack and ignoring Jordan, he removed the leather riding pants before pulling the jeans over his legs and securing them quickly. Pulling the damp jacket from his shoulders, he tossed it negligently to the floor before stripping the moist T-shirt from his body and tossing it to the floor with the jacket.

Jordan wasn't talking.

Travis pulled a T-shirt over his head, then turned, lifted the beer, and finished it in one drink.

"What are the complications?" he finally asked, knowing Jordan was going to draw this out, to force him to ask, to reveal any emotions he might feel. Any feelings that could compromise the assignment or Travis's ability to use Night Hawk however Jordan intended to use her.

When he spoke, he was deadly serious.

"Amnesia. She's completely forgotten the past six years. That includes her father's death. For all intents and purposes, she's become a liability, Travis."

Amnesia. She was once again the woman she had been rather than the woman she had been trained to be. For a moment, a sense of joy threatened to swell within him, because he remembered the young woman she had been rather than the agent she had been forced to become. One he knew suffered from the loss of the life she had left behind.

"Then the operation has changed?" She was alive. She was alive. The words played through his mind, his heart, as he fought to get his bearings upon realizing that she hadn't been killed, that at least he could hold on to the fact that she still breathed.

"The operation's focus is still the same. But the reasons behind the mission have . . . expanded a bit," Jordan informed him. "And we're still going to use her. You're still going to use her."

Knowing it and hearing it were two different things. Having that knowledge affirmed with such cool confidence, such lack of regret or mercy, had the power to piss Travis off more than it should have.

"Now why the fuck doesn't that surprise me?" Travis bit out, his voice rough, emotion slipping through his control despite his attempts to hold it back. "Fuck, Jordan, over the years, has it occurred to you that you've turned into nothing more than a governmental fucking robot?"

He knew the original operation that had been planned. It would have been hard enough for her to go back to her old life. Doing it with no memory of who she had been for the past six years would make her a danger to herself, to himself, and to the mission, and that wasn't acceptable.

"We suspect that whoever tried to kill her six years ago has somehow found her again. The Elite Ops could be jeopardized if this is true, Travis. If they found her, then every agent in the program could now be at risk. We have to find this bastard and find out just how much he knows."

"You'll get her killed if you try to use her now," Travis warned him, only barely managing to maintain an air of unconcern now that the initial shock had passed. "If she's unaware of her training, then she's unaware of the danger as well."

He was surprised at the slow nod of assent he was given in reply.

"We've considered this," Jordan informed him. "Myself and Night Hawk's commanders have come up with a viable alternative for the situation. She's changed, Travis, just as the rest of you have. She won't be the same woman no matter what her memories are. However, you were more involved in her training and she's closer to you. We suspect she'll trust you no matter the situation. You'll have to guide her through the mission without revealing your true reason for being there, or her previous agent status."

"Really?" His lips twisted cynically. "Is that all?"

Jordan gave him a mirthless grin.

"Her closeness with me may not help," Travis told him. "Actually, it could hurt."

Jordan watched him closely for long moments.

"I'm confident you can handle it," Jordan finally stated. "Especially considering the night the two of you spent together."

Travis remained silent at the comment. His night with Lilly was between him and Lilly. It had nothing to do with Jordan or with the Elite Ops. "What do you know about the attempt on her?" he asked instead.

"The plastic surgeon listed as her doctor was killed in a fire in his office the day before she was shot," Jordan revealed. "And Raisa has reports that in the past month someone had been questioning Lilly's contacts in Berlin and Afghanistan. We have to find out if they know about the Ops as well."

Dragging his fingers through his hair, Travis sat down on the edge of the bed and stared back at his commander. "What are the chances of her memories returning?"

Jordan shrugged. "Our doctors say no chance. There was too much damage. She's damned lucky to be breathing on her own.

"Elite Command is willing to let her go, to allow her to return to her old life as long as her memories stay buried. She'll never be safe, though, until her would-be assassin is caught. This is the second attempt on her life. We have to know if Elite Ops is at risk as well, how she was found, and who Lord Harrington suspected was electronically stealing and transferring those funds. It's all tied together. Find Lilly's attempted murderer and we'll solve the rest of the mysteries."

"Do we have any suspects?" Travis questioned, his voice rough.

"A whole society full," Jordan informed him grimly. "Lady Victoria Lillian Harrington and her father were incredibly social, as her family still is. At this point we haven't pinpointed who it isn't, so it could be anyone."

"What does your gut say?" Travis demanded.

"Her uncle, Desmond Harrington. He married her mother the second year after Lord Harrington's death. He's my best guess."

Breathing in roughly, Travis fought to push back the anger that was fraying his control. He'd learned over the years that it rarely paid to give in to his emotions. The plain and simple fact was that he had signed up for this willingly, and he had known the rules when he had done so.

"Any indication Elite Ops has really been compromised?" It was all he could do to force the words past his lips, to keep his anger at bay that Lilly would now be so damned vulnerable.

"Several." Jordan's jaws clenched together. "There were inquiries into several agencies questioning any covert status she might have with them. In Afghanistan one of her contacts reported and forwarded several anonymous e-mails he received requesting any known agents she may have worked with."

"That list is long," Travis bit out, his voice cold. "Lilly Belle was trained for just such work."

"And it's well documented within those agencies that she provided security as well as contacts," Jordan agreed. "But we believe her cover will hold."

Travis nodded thoughtfully. He kept his anger contained for the moment and forced his mind to consider the angles of this new, far more dangerous operation.

"How will I re-establish myself in her life?" he asked.

"Directly would be the most efficient," Jordan said. "Her Elite Ops cover as a professional escort will be in place. If anyone goes digging into the past six years, that's what they'll find. We'll also stick close to the truth about your past association with her—that you trained her. But in addition to that, you were one of her more frequent clients, as well as her lover. That should give you more than enough cover to get close to her. She'll want to know about those missing years. Who better to tell her about them than her lover, Travis Caine?"

Travis clenched his teeth and refrained from warning Jordan that this might not be as easy as he and the others were assuming.

He knew Lilly. She would never accept that she had been a professional escort. She would know better, and he fully expected she would eventually remember the truth. Lilly was too stubborn not to remember.

"It's as if you had this planned from the beginning. It's laying in smooth as hell, isn't it, Jordan?" Travis mused sarcastically.

"Nothing about this has been smooth," Jordan informed him. "You were the one who rescued her that night. If you hadn't been there, she would have died six years ago. It's unfortunate we weren't fast enough to save Lord Harrington though or to identify the killers."

Travis regretted that as well. And sometimes it shook him to think that it had been mere luck that had saved Lilly's life that night. He and Noah had been there hoping to steal the information Lord Harrington was going to turn over to MI5.

"So is MI5 in on this?" Travis asked.

Jordan shook his head. "We've been involved with this one since the beginning and it concerns one of our own agents, so they're handing it over to us completely. Besides, you know they'd prefer not to have to go after one of England's most privileged themselves, and that's exactly where this thing is pointing."

Jordan sighed. "As for Lilly, this is her chance to go home, Travis. We both know she's missed it, despite the fact that she never mentions it."

"Even if she doesn't belong there anymore?" Travis ran a hand through his hair.

"Yes," Jordan said with a joyless smile, "even if."

Travis paced to the large window, though he didn't pull the curtain aside to stare into the night beyond.

Lady Victoria Lillian Harrington.

Victoria Harrington had been quiet, filled with laughter, and as polite as hell. She had been all woman, though.

He remembered dancing with her before his own "death." He had been very married at the time. He had also been very aware of his wife's infidelities. He'd danced with Lilly and fought his arousal as he saw the very innocent, very feminine hunger in her eyes. He'd seen her regret, too, just as sharply as he had felt his own.

"Do you think it's truly possible for her to go home after the life she's lived the past six years?" Travis mused. "She's not that innocent, idealistic young woman any longer, Jordan."

Was it really possible to return to innocence no matter the memories lost?

Jordan breathed out roughly at the question.

"Who knows?" He finally shrugged. "Either way, we have a mission to complete and a very dangerous person to find. Lord Harrington was a very specialized, well-trained agent. Whoever killed him knew what the hell they were doing.

"MI5 focused on the new lord. Desmond Harrington, Harold Harrington's half-brother from their father's second marriage. He's caretaker of the Harrington title now."

"I'm surprised Lady Harrington remarried so quickly." Travis knew Angelica as well. There were few things that mattered as much to her as appearances did.

Jordan sat back in his chair and finished his beer before speaking. His expression was thoughtful, suspicious.

"If she hadn't, the title would have been lost to her son. If Desmond Harrington married and had other children, Jared would have no chance of inheriting it." He looked at Travis. "Speaking of Angelica, it seems she tried to have Lilly sent to a psychiatric clinic in France to cure her of obstinacy."

Travis grimaced at the information. "It's a very nasty but common occurrence in some of the titled families," he responded. "It's kept quiet, considered a shameful secret, but highly relied upon to control the actions and decisions of the younger generations."

Jordan was staring at him as though he were crazed.

Travis sat down heavily on the bottom of the bed and stared back at his commander in resignation. "Did you read my wife's file?"

Jordan frowned. "There was nothing there about psychiatric problems or hospitalization."

"There wouldn't be," Travis agreed. "It's kept quiet, as I said. Very quiet. Even I was unaware of Patricia's 'stay' in France until after her death. It was then her father informed me of her psychiatric problems. The fear of going back ensured that Patricia kept any activities her father or I would disagree with carefully hidden."

Not that Travis would have allowed her to be hospitalized again.

"Hell." Jordan shook his head in amazement. "Will Lilly be at risk?"

Travis's lips thinned. "It's possible. If Lilly associates with Travis Caine, Lady Harrington might try. However, when she discovers her daughter's past as a paid escort, one day she may simply disappear, and then we'll be looking at a mess."

Jordan's expression hardened. "A mistake Lady Harrington doesn't want to make."

Travis's smile was mocking. "Lady Harrington doesn't make mistakes. She's always right. Always perfect. And she'll be a pain in our collective asses."

CHAPTER 2

Two months later
Hagerstown, Maryland

HE WAS THERE AGAIN.

Lady Victoria Lillian Harrington glanced out of the corner of her eye as she pretended to survey the dresses in the shop window while she and her mother strolled down the crowded sidewalk of historic Hagerstown, Maryland.

She could see him, there in her periphery, standing dangerous and tall, his gaze narrowed on her, watching her with almost complete absorption.

She should be terrified. She should be fighting against the dark shadows, the terrors that rose inside her at night and the visions that haunted her even when she was awake. He brought to mind the one vision she couldn't get away from even when she slept. The figure standing by her bed, watching her with such intensity, holding her with gentleness and compassion as agony screamed through her brain.

It was a vision her mother had sworn time and time again couldn't have been real. It was one she knew *had* to be real. It was too intense, the echo of that pain too agonizing.

She didn't fight her mother over it, though. Lady Angelica Harrington was too determined, too certain of herself and her own rules to admit she could be wrong.

Lilly rarely argued with her mother.

No, Lady Victoria Lillian Harrington rarely argued with her mother. But *Lilly* was finding it harder and harder to keep from doing just that.

"Darling, you're too quiet again." Her mother reached out, her fingers trembling as they still did whenever she touched her daughter, as though she couldn't quite believe she was there.

"Sorry, Mother, I was thinking about that dress." Glancing back to where she had glimpsed the aloof figure moments before, she felt disappointment tear through her.

He was gone. Dark blond hair, or was it light brown? Those eyes, what color were they? she wondered as she turned back to the window of the shop. Brown. They had to be brown. A raptor brown. Mixed with green. Intent and brooding. Eyes that could fire a woman's arousal and her imagination. Not to mention her confusion why she would know that.

"We could go in and try it on," her mother urged her, the soft lilt of her English accent drawing gazes from the couple that passed by them. "I'm certain it would look positively gorgeous on you."

Would it?

She looked beyond the dresses to the other attire the store offered. Jeans, close-fitting, and shirts that would have her mother gasping in shock, she was certain. Not because they were revealing, but because they were common. Her mother strictly detested whatever she believed was common.

"Victoria, we could look at the dresses."

Victoria.

She frowned at the image that greeted her in the glass.

She didn't see Victoria there. She saw an unfamiliar image, a woman she was comfortable with, yet those weren't the features—the face, the eyes, or the hair—of the woman she'd been before. Lady Victoria Lillian Harrington of the London Harringtons. She was related to royalty, though admittedly, the kinship was a distant one at best. Still, she couldn't quite acclimate herself to who she knew she was, the person she knew she was supposed to be.

"Victoria." Her mother's voice echoed with exasperation now.

"I don't think I need another dress, Mother," she stated absently as she moved for the door of the shop. "I see something else I might like, though."

Where the hell was her British accent? She remembered having one. She remembered once being proud of that accent. It didn't exist now, though. Her voice was smooth and cultured, but it lacked any accent, any inflection, that could have identified her as a member of any particular country or indicated her social status.

"Victoria, you're acting rather odd." There was a note of fear in her mother's voice as she entered the shop and moved beyond the dresses.

Was she acting odd? She was sure as hell feeling

damned odd, she thought, before a brief moment of shock hit her. More and more often she found herself cursing. There were moments it was all she could do to hold back the earthy vulgarity when she was talking.

"I'm fine, Mother," she assured her again as they moved through the small store.

She was going to obey the dictates of what she wanted rather than what her mother would consider acceptable. It was a dangerous urge to follow. At least, six years ago it would have been.

And there they were. Snug, low-slung jeans. There were low boots made of soft, supple leather on a stand beside them. Boots that looked sexy and stylish while being practical and easy to run in. Which made her wonder. What would she be running from?

"Victoria, we've discussed this denim fetish you seem to have acquired," her mother stated worriedly as she moved closer and fingered the denim jeans. Tension seemed to thicken the atmosphere. "Really, Victoria. The dresses are much nicer."

Lilly had to clench her teeth in irritation.

Lilly, she thought. Her name shouldn't be Victoria, she had always disliked being called Victoria. She was Lilly. But she couldn't recall a single time that her parents had called her Lilly.

She was Lilly. Lilly . . . something. She tilted her head and stared at the material as she rubbed the pocket between her thumb and forefinger. Lilly. Not Lady Victoria Lillian Harrington. Not even Lilly Harrington. But who?

"Can I help you?" the saleslady asked just behind her.

"The jeans," she told the red-head as she moved to

where they hung. "I'd like to try these, please, as well as the boots." She moved to the boots and chose the correct size before stepping to a particular rack of blouses.

"Oh my God, you wouldn't dare! Victoria, Desmond would have a stroke if he caught you dressed in such clothing." Her mother was outraged, as she stared at the flat-heeled, sinfully black leather over-the-knee boots and snug jeans.

No, it wasn't Desmond who had a problem with the clothes. It was her mother. Angelica Harrington demanded a certain image be presented at all times. Jeans did not fit that image, nor were they allowed in her mother's presence.

Ignoring her, Lilly walked over to the nearby shirt, reached out and ran her fingers over the soft, expensive olive-green Egyptian cotton.

"Desmond will not appreciate this," her mother warned, her voice tight.

Desmond was her stepfather now. In the six years she couldn't remember, she had managed to lose her father, and her mother had married his younger half-brother.

"This blouse, please." The dull olive-green cotton would fit tightly, conform to her body and shape her breasts enticingly. She wasn't certain why she was suddenly drawn to the color, though.

She turned to the polite saleslady trailing them. The other woman smiled gently. Long red-gold hair fell to her shoulders and an understanding smile crossed her face.

In the meantime Angelica fussed in the background about the jeans and the drab color of the blouse.

"Victoria, really. The dresses are much nicer." Angelica continued to object as her daughter moved toward the dressing room.

She glanced back at the door. There was a spot just between her shoulder blades that refused to stop itching. She could feel the eyes on her. His eyes. Somehow, he was still watching her, still waiting for her. Would he be as surprised by the jeans as her mother seemed to be?

As Lilly entered the dressing room she breathed a sigh of relief and leaned wearily against the wall, closing her eyes and taking a hard, deep breath.

She opened her eyes and stared back at the woman in the mirror.

She wasn't Victoria any longer.

Who the hell was she, really? And why wasn't she comfortable with the knowledge of her own identity, her own looks?

The soft cotton material of the short gray dress skimmed over her breasts and hips, ending at a barely decent length just below her thighs. The soft gray material didn't seem appropriate somehow. Just as the green eyes staring back at her didn't seem right.

She had once had hazel eyes. She had always had hazel eyes.

Her hair was a dark red now. It had once been a rich deep brown. Her doctors were amazed at the fact that somehow her eye and hair color had been permanently changed.

She was different. Her looks were different. Something inside her was different. There was something that didn't seem quite right about the life she was living now, and the woman she remembered being.

"Darling, are you all right?" Angelica's voice came

through the thin walls of the dressing room. Lilly could hear the concern, the confusion in her mother's voice. But she also heard the forced patience and edge of irritation.

"I'm fine, Mother. I'll just be a moment," Lilly told her.

"Desmond is going to be utterly upset if you return to the house in jeans." There was a note of amused affection in her mother's voice when she spoke of her husband that had Lilly almost cringing in distaste. There was a warning there as well. "He may even fuss at you, dear."

Lilly stared at the denim, the boots, and the blouse. She stared back at herself in the mirror, then turned away. She loved it. She could move in this clothing. She could run, she could fight . . . who?

Dark flashes surged through her mind, electric images of gunfire, blood and death flashed like vibrant lies amid a midnight landscape.

Hurriedly stripping the new clothes from her body, Lilly pulled the dress back on, slid her feet into the heels that she knew she could never run in, then gathered up the articles she had tried on.

Stepping from the dressing room, she gave her mother a careful, cool smile in response to the frown on Angelica's face. She knew better than to upset her mother. At least, she had known better six years ago. There was a part of her now that balked at giving into another's dictates or the threat of the consequences.

"I'll take these." She handed the clothing to the saleslady, while trying to ignore the irritation in her mother's eyes. Perhaps it was best that she remain the daughter Angelica thought she was, but another part of her demanded that she be something else, something more, and that she be prepared.

She had to maintain the illusion, she thought. Survival depended upon blending into this life she was living now. Even the smartest prey understood the value of playing dumb. And a killer well understood the hunt.

Lilly almost came to an abrupt halt at the thought. Shock was a bitter taste in her mouth as she fought not to sink into the shadows and the memories that were just out of reach.

She wasn't a killer! She was a social butterfly; a scheming little debutante, her father had once accused affectionately. She knew well how to blend into this life, she had learned at an early age. She wasn't a killer. But the blood in her dreams indicated otherwise.

She resisted the urge to stare at her hands, a part of her desperate to ensure no blood stained them.

Who the hell was she and why did the memories of the past six years seem so elusive while the nightmares seemed more real?

She was indeed Victoria Harrington. DNA had proven it. Her blood was a perfect match for the DNA that had been taken from the Harrington children a decade ago to ensure they could always be identified, no matter the circumstances.

She knew who she was, yet she felt like an imposter. Whatever had happened in the past six years she had lost had changed her in ways she couldn't explain. It had ensured she no longer fit in with her family, her friends, where once before she had blended into this life seamlessly.

She had memories of her life up until the night before the car crash that had killed her father and left her struggling for life six years ago. The memories of the past six years eluded her, though.

And why was she searching for a face in the crowd, anticipation surging through her at the thought of one brief glimpse of a man she didn't know? A man who felt more familiar to her than her own face. The man she had caught watching her earlier.

"You're acting very strange, Victoria." Angelica sighed as they left the shop and moved back to the tree-shaded sidewalk and the shops that Angelica insisted on visiting.

Lilly could hear the edge of anger in her mother's tone and she knew she should be wary of it. Angelica Harrington had a hard, sharp edge when angry. One that cut with brutal strength. And she had no problem slicing into one of her children if she felt the need.

"I'm well, Mother." She watched the crowd intently, careful to keep her mother's body shielded as they continued the impromptu shopping spree they had decided on that morning.

She couldn't understand why she was doing that. Why did she suddenly know how to protect her mother, and what was she trying to protect her from?

"I didn't ask if you were well," her mother said, exasperated. "I said you're acting strange."

"So, I look strange and I feel strange, as well." Lilly snorted. "And could you please just call me Lilly?"

They both stopped.

Lilly tried to look everywhere but at her mother, before she was finally forced to meet Angelica's dark brown gaze. The anger was still there, but also a hint of

fearful confusion. Lilly well understood. Perhaps Angelica truly had lost her daughter.

"Lilly," Angelica finally said softly then, staring
back at her as though she saw more than even Lilly
could guess at. "That's what your grandmother called
you, you know."

No, she hadn't known that. Her grandmother had
died when Lilly was no more than a child.

As though by silent accord they turned and began
moving down the sidewalk again. There was a silence
between them now that wasn't exactly comfortable.

"I don't remember her calling me Lilly," she said,
trying to calm her racing heart and to ease the tension.

"You were very young," her mother said. "It doesn't
surprise me that when you disappeared you chose that
name to use. Your grandmother always claimed you
were more a Lilly than a Victoria. But your father insisted on Victoria."

She had been Victoria six years before. She had
been the belle of every ball. She had been powerful
in her own right. She had had lunch with the Queen
more than once, she'd known the Prime Minister, she
had danced with many members of Parliament. She had
conspired—

The memory slammed shut, just that quickly. It was
there, then gone as though it had never been. Frustration ate at her. The memories were there, just out of
reach, haunting her, daring her to do what, she wasn't
certain.

"You know, there's the nicest little antiques store just
ahead." Her mother changed the subject with forced
brightness as they passed a small café whose tempting

scents wafted out to her. "I thought it would be nice to see what they have. I found several flatware pieces there the last time I visited. It was quite unique."

Coffee. She would kill for a cup of hot coffee.

She would kill . . .

For the barest second the sight and scent of blood filled her senses, and it wasn't the first time. She didn't freeze this time. She barely paused at the memory, and, like the first time, it disappeared just as quickly as it had come.

She didn't stumble, she continued walking, balancing perfectly on the high heels even as she thought that if she had to run, it would take precious seconds to shed the impractical footwear.

"Desmond usually comes on these little forays with me." Her mother continued chatting. "It's too bad he had that meeting this afternoon in D.C. He could have accompanied us."

Lilly had breathed a sigh of relief when Desmond had announced he couldn't take the trip with them. For some reason, she no longer felt as though she could trust the uncle she had once cherished. That feeling left her off balance as if she couldn't trust anyone anymore.

It was locked in her memories. All the answers she needed were locked behind the veil of shadows that had wiped out the past six years of her life.

What had happened the night her father's car had gone over that cliff with her in it? Had they argued? Had they been in danger? Why had they left the party that night without telling anyone or making their excuses?

None of the explanations she had been given when

she awoke in the hospital nearly four months ago made sense. She had lost more than just memories. Lilly felt as though she had lost herself as well.

She had lost her life, her father. Her mother and uncle felt like strangers, and where was the brother who had always tried to protect her? When he had come to see her in the hospital, he had disowned her as a lying, scheming tramp attempting to steal his sister's identity.

And perhaps that hurt most of all. She had idolized Jared. To have him turn on her had broken her heart in ways she feared would never heal.

"You're too quiet, Lilly. How do you hope to ever acclimate if you refuse to try?" Her mother's voice was hard now, censorious. "I still think you needed time to heal further. The clinic in France . . ."

"Mother, really." Lilly smiled gently, consolingly. "I'm acclimating fine. I'm just getting my bearings, I promise."

"And you would tell me if it were otherwise?" her mother questioned, concern softening the hardness in her tone.

"I promise I will," Lilly lied.

"The dress becomes you."

Lilly froze at the sound of the voice at her ear, slightly husky, rich and dark, like the finest black velvet rubbing against the senses.

She knew that voice. It sank inside her, caressed against memories that chafed beneath the shadows and eased a sense of fear that had been riding inside her for the past months.

She hadn't realized how frightened she had been until that clenched, tight part of her soul seemed to relax marginally.

"I think I prefer the jeans, boots, and thigh holsters you wore in Afghanistan better, though."

She felt his cheek against her hair as her heart began to race, to pound erratically with fierce anticipation. Her body suddenly became too sensitive, too warm, as a distantly remembered heat began to flare inside her.

"Et." The halting sound delayed her attempt to turn around. "Stay still, no need to turn around yet." There was an edge of darkness in his voice as he gripped her hip with one hand and held her in place.

There were too many sensations racing through her body now, too much heat and too many pinpoints of emotion that she couldn't make sense of.

"Who are you?" she hissed as she gazed around desperately, wondering where her mother had gone off to, wondering what she would think of the man standing much too close to her daughter.

"You don't remember me?" There was an odd note in his tone, one she couldn't decipher quickly. "As much trouble as we've instigated together? I think I'm offended, Belle."

A sense of vertigo assaulted her at the chiding tone.

"Evidently I don't." She fought to still her racing heart, to ease the harshness of her breathing.

"I heard you'd been wounded. Evidently the rumors of lost memories is true." The comforting tone to his voice did nothing to still the alternating emotions that were suddenly tearing through her. "Trust me, baby, you know me."

She believed it. She knew it. She could feel that knowledge heating her body.

"Then I can look at you." She kept her voice low, as he did, her gaze continually scouring the interior of the shadowed store for anyone that could be watching or listening.

"Not yet. Turn around and I won't be able to help myself. Your mother would find you in a very compromising position. She doesn't seem the type to look the other way if she caught her daughter being seduced in a back corner of an antiques store."

Her mother would be absolutely mortified. Furious.

"Do you remember Friendly's Sports Bar?" he asked then.

She shook her head slowly, though a ghost of a memory surfaced. A large dim room, a jukebox playing, the crack of pool balls and spirited laughter.

"The corner of Franklin and Walnut Street," he told her.

"We've met there before?" She heard the uncertainty in her voice, the neediness, the hunger for information. Finally a prayer had been answered. Someone who knew who she was rather than who she had been.

"Several times," he assured her. "Tell me, Belle, how severe is the amnesia?"

She couldn't decipher the underlying emotion in his voice. Part concern, part something else that had her wondering not just who this man was, but what he was to her.

"The past six years are gone," she answered truthfully, though she wasn't certain why she had. This man had her guard up, yet a part of her was reaching out to him, desperate to trust him. "Did you know me well?"

His hands tightened at her hips. "I'll let you decide that. Meet me tonight at the tavern, alone. No mother, no driver. You could ride that racy little motorcycle you looked so good on. The one you keep in storage here in Hagerstown."

She rode a motorcycle? Since when did she ride a motorcycle?

She shook her head almost instinctively, rejecting the idea that she would, that she could ride, even as she remembered the wind in her hair and the power pulsing between her thighs.

"I'll be there at eleven." His fingers caressed her hips. "Will you be there, Lilly?"

"I'll be there." The decision was made so quickly, so instinctively, that she almost called the words back.

"Good girl." Were those his lips brushing against the shell of her ear?

Lilly shivered at the exquisite sensation of warmth, almost a kiss, as she took in a hard, shocked breath.

"I've missed you, Lilly." Was that a note of regret in his voice?

Lilly fought the overwhelming urge to turn and confront him, to demand the answers she was certain he had. There was no doubt he had known her during those lost years. There was no doubt he may have possibly known her intimately.

"Who am I?" The words slipped past her lips, the emotion in her voice undisguised, the fear that she fought to keep hidden revealing itself in the husky, plaintive tone of her voice.

Behind her, the warm male body bracketing hers was

still for a long moment before she felt the silent sigh ripple across his chest.

"We'll discuss that tonight." There was a promise in his voice and, a part of her feared, a warning.

A warning about what? The truth perhaps?

The truth could be a double-edged sword, her uncle had warned her several times when she questioned if he had had the past six years of her life investigated once he learned she was alive. Surely he had, yet he refused to give her a straight answer.

The evasiveness had been driving her insane. Perhaps, this time, someone would give her a straight answer.

"And if I don't show up?"

His hands eased away from her slowly as the sound of her mother's voice discussing the merits of a particular porcelain plate filtered through the dim room.

"Then I guess you don't show up," he murmured. "Perhaps, Lilly, there're things about yourself that you don't really want to know."

As she tried to understand that comment he slipped away from her, the warmth of his body no more than a dream as she turned quickly to try and catch a glimpse of the man who had held her so intimately.

Was he the one following her? Was he the one that filled her fantasies as well as her nightmares?

However, all she saw was his back as he slipped out the door and moved quickly past the long, narrow window of the shop.

Lilly began to race after him. Waiting until tonight for answers suddenly seemed less than feasible. She wanted those answers now.

"Lilly, Mrs. Longstrom has the most gorgeous lace tablecloth in the back room." Her mother's voice stopped her as she took the first step. "You simply have to come back here and see it. I believe it would be perfect for the breakfast room at the manor."

Lilly turned quickly back to her mother, a question forming on her lips, a demand to know if her mother had seen the man speaking to her. If she knew him.

In the moment that the words would have slipped past her lips, she snapped her teeth quickly together. Her mother hadn't seen him, or she would have already posed the same questions to Lilly.

Angelica suddenly paused, her gaze sharpening as though she sensed or saw something in Lilly's face that concerned her or perhaps angered her.

"I believe it's time we go." Angelica moved quickly across the room despite the height of the heels she wore with her alabaster slacks and matching sleeveless blouse.

Lilly protested as her mother's fingers curled gently around her arm and urged her toward the door. "Really, Mother, we don't need to leave."

She had to get her bearings, had to make sense of what was suddenly happening. What she was feeling.

She should never have had such a reaction to a man she couldn't see, only hear. A man who seemed more familiar to her than her own body.

She followed her mother from the antiques shop, back to the busy tree-lined street. Pausing, Angelica Harrington made a quick call to the chauffeur, gave him their location, then turned to her daughter with a worried frown.

"I tried to do too much at once," Angelica said, the

apology in her voice pricking at Lilly's conscience. "I should have allowed you to rest a little longer."

"You're going to have to get used to this, Mother," Lilly informed her firmly as she let her gaze survey the busy street with narrowed eyes behind her dark sunglasses. "Just as I have to get used to myself."

Lilly didn't catch her mother's look of consternation. The older woman watched her daughter as one might watch an alien, waiting, watching for any signs of danger. But together with the wariness there was also pain.

A mother's dream had come true. The daughter she had thought she had lost forever had returned home. Her child lived and breathed. She was given the chance few parents who had lost children were given. A chance to say all the things she hadn't taken the time to say before. A chance to kiss her daughter good night. A chance to see her smile. Hear her laughter.

Perhaps.

Travis wondered if Lilly had learned to laugh again. He knew the few times he had managed to pull laughter from her it was like seeing sunshine for the first time.

He wondered if her mother saw sunshine when she saw her daughter's smile, or heard her laughter. He wondered if she'd seen that smile or that laughter since her daughter had been home. God knew, Lilly deserved at least a few moments of happiness before the world went crazy on her again. And before her mother possibly lost her daughter all over.

One thing was certain, beneath the impatience and flashes of irritation Angelica Harrington's heart was also breaking as she watched the young woman she had been told was her daughter.

There was no doubt Lilly was definitely Victoria Lillian Harrington. DNA proved it, her dental records proved it, but there were no fingerprints to back it up. Her fingerprints had been removed the day she signed on with the Elite Ops. With her return the blame had been lain on the fiery car crash.

Standing well out of her line of vision, he watched her closely, a smile tugging at his lips as she slid her sunglasses on and continued to watch the street with what he knew were eagle-sharp eyes.

She'd caught him following her several times throughout the afternoon. Each time she had stopped, arrowed in on him, and watched him with a familiarity he knew did nothing but confuse her.

He'd seen that confusion. He'd felt it. He'd nearly tasted it as he stood behind her and breathed in her scent.

She was fighting to make sense of the world she was in and the memories she had lost, but she was still game to fight for the answers.

She would be there tonight. There wasn't a doubt in Travis's mind that she wouldn't find the bar in time to meet with him. He wondered if she would make it there alone, or if her shadow, the bodyguard her uncle had hired, would manage to follow her.

Lilly Belle, code-named Night Hawk, would never have allowed herself to be tracked to a meeting. She would have ensured she arrived alone, and if she didn't, then she would ensure the one following her regretted it.

That was his Lilly. She could be merciless, but in being so, he'd watched, year by year, another piece of her soul erode.

Those wounds were still there, in her eyes, along with her confusion, her wariness.

"What do you think?"

Travis glanced over his shoulder at the towering former Russian who stood carefully back from the edge of the building.

Nik Steele watched Lilly and her mother, his icy blue eyes lasered in on them intently.

"I think we need to plan for when all hell breaks loose," Travis grunted as a limo drew to a stop in front of the two women.

The chauffeur jumped out, and Travis couldn't help the amused twitch of his lips. He had to admit, Wild Card made a hell of a chauffeur.

"Looks slick in that perky little hat, huh?" Nik said. "Maybe we should send pictures to his wife."

Travis snickered at the thought. Wild Card's wife was a hell of a woman; he had no doubt she wouldn't ooh and aah over how cute she thought he looked. It was enough to make a single man shudder in fear. Or in envy.

"Save the pictures," Travis advised him. "Maybe we could throw darts at them instead."

Nik's amused grunt was a rough, broken sound, part amusement, part mockery. The man never laughed. He rarely smiled. But hell, Travis couldn't remember the last time he'd laughed himself.

"So what are we putting in our report to Live Wire?" Nik asked him as Wild Card helped Lilly and Angelica into the car.

What *was* he putting in his report to Jordan?

"She's viable," he stated.

"Really?" The skepticism in Nik's voice wasn't lost on Travis. "That's not how I saw things, Black Jack."

"Do you intend to report differently?" As the limo pulled away, Travis turned back to the mountain they now called Renegade.

Nik was the only one of the team that seemed to change code names like underwear. Jordan couldn't seem to make his mind up about the big, blond-haired giant.

"Not me." Nik shook his head firmly as he glanced back at Travis. "If I were you, I'd talk to Wild Card, though." He nodded in the direction the limo had taken. "Make sure he has the same report. Because I'm betting 'viable' isn't the word he would choose either."

But it was the one he would use in his report, Travis promised himself. He'd talk to Wild Card. Tonight, he'd meet with Night Hawk. The game was about to begin. That meant "viable" had to be the word they all used. Or Night Hawk would pay the price.

Under no circumstances could the Elite Ops be revealed. The damage it could cause, the danger it could represent to them all, was too high.

If Lilly wasn't considered viable and an asset to the operation, then she was a risk. And all risks had to be eliminated.

Immediately.

Chapter 3

LILLY HAD THOUGHT there would be no way to find a motorcycle she hadn't even known she owned. The idea of it intrigued her, though. The thought of riding wild and free with nothing but the wind surrounding her filled her with a sense of heady excitement.

Finding the damned thing would be the hard part. Or so she had thought.

Lilly didn't have memories of the past six years, but she had a strong sense of intuition.

As she rode through Hagerstown in the rented cab, her gaze narrowed on street signs and buildings, Lilly found herself pulling free bits of memory. She could remember riding through town in the dark, but she didn't remember why.

A certain street sign snagged a memory and she had the driver turn. A building pulled at a memory, a sense of familiarity struck her at an intersection, and soon she had the driver stopping in front of a lot filled with storage units.

She stared at the long lines of blue and white units. A

flashback tore through her mind, causing a sudden shaft of pain to seize her temples.

It was here. She knew the unit number and the code to the lock. Her temples throbbed with pain, but she *knew*. The memory of it was there, a little hazy, but present.

Paying the driver, Lilly left the car and entered the lot, walking quickly to the farthest line of units. She could feel the security cameras trained on her as she kept her face turned carefully from them.

The storage unit she moved to was a simple ten by ten with a combination key and digital code lock.

Lilly bent to the edge of the bottom frame, moving aside the thick layer of gravel carefully until she revealed the cement pad beneath the unit. There, a small depression had been hollowed out of the cement. The key rested there, wrapped in a protective, heavy plastic case.

Within seconds she had the unit unlocked and the key returned to its resting place.

Opening the door slowly, Lilly reached in, flipped the light on, and entered the unit as she closed the door behind her.

There was more than a motorcycle sitting there. Lilly felt her throat tighten, her heart racing out of control. Perspiration dotted her forehead, and for a moment she swore she would become ill. On one wall a series of shelves had been hung. A wide black case sat in the middle of the shelf, surrounded by smaller ones.

Stepping to it, she opened it carefully, her breath catching at the sight of the weapon packed carefully in black foam.

A sniper rifle. It was broken down, well oiled, and shining in the dim light. Reaching out to touch it with trembling fingers, Lilly fought back the realization that she had used it, more than once.

Moving to the smaller cases, she found handguns, and knew somehow that they were modified and highly illegal. There were empty clips and cases of ammunition.

There were clothes, maps, files that Lilly scanned as fear stole her breath.

What in the hell had she been involved in?

Shaking, she pulled a leather bag from a small cabinet and packed clothes, a Glock, ammunition, and several knives inside.

Storing the bag in the back compartment of the motorcycle, Lilly turned to the remainder of the clothes.

She dressed quickly in leather pants, t-shirt, and jacket. Flat leather boots pulled above the knee, and she found the key to the cycle hanging in the ignition.

Fear was ever present, but so was excitement. It pounded inside her, raced through her bloodstream, and sent adrenaline flying through her system.

She didn't remember who she had been.

She didn't remember what she had been.

But maybe those memories were now growing stronger, moving closer, and were almost within reach.

Friendly's Sports Bar sat in the perfect location for assignations such as the one Travis had set up with his favorite former Elite Ops counterpart.

It sat on a corner. Across the street were an assortment of closely built inner-city brick houses that served as apartments, homes, and offices.

Franklin Street was a busy area, especially on a Friday night, which allowed for greater anonymity, as well as plenty of traffic, both by vehicle and by foot, which could be used as a distraction as the other agents positioned themselves to watch every corner of the tavern.

They wanted to know who was following Lilly, how she was being followed, and who they could be traced back to.

Sitting at the bar, Travis nursed a beer, his gaze trained on the side entrance of the building from the short end of the L-shaped bar. At the other corner, Nik sat sideways on a bar stool as the red-haired Tehya, one of the team's communications experts, sat beside him and flirted outrageously.

Farther down the bar Clint McIntyre, a former Navy SEAL and now part of the Elite Ops independent backup team, sat with his wife and tried playing the drunken male on the make while his wife, Morganna, her long dark hair pulled back in a braid, pretended not to be amused.

The rest of the team, backup as well as the agents, were positioned outside along with Jordan and Santos Bahre, one of Lilly's commanders.

"She's not showing." Santos's voice came through the tiny earset that linked communications between the agents and the commanders. "I warned you she wasn't this predictable."

Travis glanced around the bar.

"She's here." She'd been here for a while, he suspected. He could feel her watching, those green eyes narrowed on him as she waited to see what he'd do.

"Doubtful." Reno Chavez, commander of the backup

team that had been with the Ops for years, now spoke into the link. "Macey and I both have the entrances covered. There's no way she slipped in there without us knowing it."

There was a way. Lilly always found a way.

Travis pushed back the warm beer he had been nursing and made to rise when he felt the small hand that pressed between his shoulder blades, indicating he should remain in place.

Settling back on the stool, he turned his head, restrained his smile, and watched as Lilly slid onto the bar stool that had been vacated beside him.

"I didn't think you were going to show." He motioned for the bartender to take her order.

Waving the man away, Lilly turned back to him, her gaze suspicious as she watched him closely.

She was wearing her riding leathers. Leather pants, boots, a short jacket, and a black silk shirt that bared her midriff if she moved just the right way.

"Neither did I." Her green eyes were dark in the shadows. "Tell me who you are and what do you have to do with me?"

There was something about him, something familiar, something she couldn't put her finger on. She should know him, but she couldn't remember him. She couldn't remember meeting him.

But her body seemed to know him. Each time she had seen him, this morning as well as tonight, her body had responded with heated warmth and that familiar sense of remembrance.

This man had touched her, he had kissed her. Her body remembered it and she ached for more. That ache had followed her through the day, the remembered feel of his body behind her, at the store, impossible to recover from.

"I've had many things to do with you." His smile was rakish, his brown eyes filled with sexual knowledge. A sexual knowledge of her.

Lilly looked up at the bartender as he set a cold beer in front of her.

"Good to see you back, Lilly." The grizzled bartender gave a wide smile and a wink. "I see your friend found you."

"That he did." She lifted the beer to her lips and took a long, cold drink.

The bartender moved away, leaving her with the man watching her now. She didn't even know his name.

"Travis Caine," he whispered at her ear as though reading her thoughts. "In case you were wondering."

She was doing more than wondering. It had been driving her crazy not knowing even that scrap of information. "I know your name then," she said quietly. "Who are you to me?"

"We met six years ago," he told her. "We've run together at odd times since."

Lilly pushed the fingers of one hand through her hair.

"We traveled together then?" Her heart was racing, her lungs starved for oxygen as she fought not to breathe too hard.

He nodded and Lilly tipped the beer to her lips, and finished it quickly before setting it rather hard on the bar and flicking her fingers at the bartender to the empty bottle.

He'd obviously been watching for her. Within seconds

there was another bottle in front of her. She wondered what tip she usually left him for such excellent service.

She finished half the beer, set the bottle on the bar, then glanced back at Travis.

"I fight?" she whispered back at him.

"Rather well." He gave her a strange half smile. Strange, because she felt she should know what that smile meant.

"What did I do when I fought?" she asked him. "Did I kill?"

She knew she had. She rubbed her finger and thumb together, knowing her fingerprints weren't there any longer and they weren't there for a reason.

"You don't remember anything about the past six years then?" he asked as he turned more fully to her, the backs of his fingers stroking down her lower arm.

Did she remember anything?

She remembered her nightmares. They were filled with pain, rage, and fear. She remembered a sense of drowning, of icy water closing over her head as she fought to breathe. She remembered a kiss, a touch and an underlying anger that made no sense.

She remembered the sharp retort of a gun, and then nothing.

"I don't remember anything." At least nothing that she was willing to discuss at the moment. Especially considering the fact she was presently being watched.

A long, slow turn of the stool seat gave her a clear view of the bar and within seconds she knew all she needed to know. A second later she was facing him once again.

"You have friends with you." She kept her voice low

enough that it wouldn't carry to any listening device, unless he was wearing one himself.

She felt herself paling at the thought and dropped her head to stare at the beer. Where had that suspicion come from? How could she look around once and see so much, pinpoint those who were there for fun and those she knew were there to watch her?

When her gaze met his again, she saw a warning in his eyes. A warning that she not see any more, or say any more?

"There's no one with me," he finally replied. "But you."

Yeah, right, no one was there with him. He was lying to her and they both knew it. But he was also warning her. To protect her? What the hell was going on here and what did this man want from her?

"Why am I here?" she asked him. "Are we going to talk or play games all night?"

"I rather enjoy playing with you." He grinned then.

"And I'm getting rather impatient." She got to her feet. "You want to talk, Mr. Caine, then you can come to me."

Lilly stood to pull her jacket on, only to have his fingers curl around her wrist to halt her.

"The same willful Lilly I've missed like hell," he murmured. "Tell me, how does your family handle your stubbornness? I've heard your mother rarely has the patience for it from anyone else."

Not anyone else, not from her, Lilly could have informed him. But he didn't need to know that.

"I'm her daughter." She arched her brow. "Of course I can get away with more."

"Of course you can," he agreed. "So tell me, Lilly, why did you sneak out of the house tonight rather than informing her that you were leaving?"

"The same reason I'm walking out of here now without answering your question," she retorted blithely. "Need to know."

At that, she turned and walked out.

He was following. She could feel him. Moving close behind her, the arousal that was so much a part of him spreading around her. Her thighs were tight, her pussy heated.

Her pussy.

She paused at the door, allowing the cold air to wrap around her and possibly cool her libido. He chose that moment to move closer, to step up to her until they were touching, the hard proof of his erection well defined beneath his leather pants as it pressed against her lower back.

Lilly gripped the door frame and held on tight. She wanted to rub against him, wanted to thrust back and feel the heady hunger rising harder and faster between them.

Right there, surrounded by dozens of bar customers and "friends" or perhaps "nonfriends" of Travis Caine's.

"Tell me where to meet you," he demanded. "Just the two of us."

"It was supposed to be just the two of us this time," she whispered breathlessly.

Taking a deep breath, Lilly stepped to the sidewalk, tried to brush away the need racing through her system, and headed for the parking lot. He was still behind her, walking silently, but she could feel the warmth of his body still surrounding her.

Moving to the motorcycle, she threw her leg over the raised seat effortlessly then unlocked her helmet, all the while too aware of him standing next to her, as though waiting for something, expecting something.

"What?" She turned to him, frowning, her heart racing.

His lips quirked. "You remembered the bike after all."

Lilly jerked her head down, her gaze focusing on the helmet straps she was playing with. She had remembered which storage unit it was parked in, she had remembered where she had hidden the keys.

She knew things that didn't make sense. Things that had no memories to back them, and that terrified her.

Such as the knowledge that this man could make her burn with hunger.

He had also taught her how to survive at one point. She was certain of it.

Why was she certain of it?

That question would drive her insane. Why? Why did she know? How? How did she know?

"Who am I?" Lifting her head, she tried to fight back the sense of loneliness and confusion racing through her. She felt lost.

Staring back at him, she watched as his hands lifted, his fingers stroking back the hair that had fallen across her face. As he tucked it behind her ear a small smile tipped one corner of his lips.

"You're wild and brave," he told her softly. "Over the past years I've sworn you'd get both of us killed."

And that only confused her more.

Travis watched the heaviness of her expression, the way her lips turned down, the sadness and loss in her gaze. He could read how lost she was, and for Lilly, that wasn't something he was familiar with. She didn't often show her emotions, no matter what they were. Unless it was passion. Damn if she hadn't burned the night down around them.

"Come with me, Lilly," he urged gently. "We'll talk, uncensored. I can tell you who you are."

He could tell her partial truths and half-lies. He could give her the explanations the agency had come up with. He couldn't let her know who she was entirely, only the cover the agency had given her. It was a piss-poor offering, but it would fill in some of the blanks at least. Maybe wipe that lost look from her face, at least for a little while.

"If you wanted to talk uncensored, then you shouldn't have brought your friends along for this meeting."

She moved to pull away from him, to put the helmet on her head and to ride away into the darkness. But he wasn't ready for her to leave quite yet.

Sliding his fingers under her hair, he gripped the back of her neck, catching her by surprise as he tipped her head back and lowered his own.

Travis caught the small gasp from her parted lips and took full advantage of the slight opening. His tongue brushed over her lips, then stroked inside in a teasing little thrust that had them both catching their breath when it deepened to much more than the gentle assault he'd planned.

Once his tongue touched her, tasted the trace of beer and feminine warmth, Travis was lost. He needed a hell of a lot more than a teasing taste.

As he held firm to her neck, his lips pressed down on

hers, sipping from her lips, driving his tongue deep inside the honeyed recess.

She set fire to him; there was no other way to describe it. She made him burn with need and a hunger to possess her unlike anything he'd ever known.

There was something unique about Lilly. There always had been, he had to ensure that there always would be.

As he felt her hands sliding up the leather covering his arms, the ragged need to have her naked against him tore through his senses. He'd been too long without her. Now that he knew the taste of her, the pleasure to be found with her, he wanted more. He wondered if he'd ever have enough of her.

"Come with me," he ordered against her lips before nipping at them seductively. "I promise, you won't regret it."

Lilly had a feeling it would be the one thing she ended up regretting more than anything else. But she didn't want to resist either. She wanted to be wild and free with this man.

She didn't remember the past six years, but she did remember the years before it. She'd lived her life according to others' expectations. Those of her parents, her friends, her associates.

Her father expected her to follow in his footsteps as a purveyor of information to British Intelligence and she had wanted that as well. She'd been trained young to step into the role, just as her mother had begun training her young daughter to take her place in English society. They had fought over that, she remembered. Her mother had no idea the work Lilly did with her father, but she had known her husband often advised Lilly not to marry, not to commit herself to another person.

She'd always done as she had been expected to do, as others had wanted her to do, as much as possible. She had never, that she remembered, lived within the moment. Taken a chance. Been wild and free. The woman Travis described wasn't the woman Lilly remembered herself being. She needed to know who that woman was.

"No censors?" she whispered, as his lips brushed over hers again.

"None." He demanded another kiss, another melding of lips, stoking the heat between them as Lilly gave into the pleasure.

It was incredible. No more than the touch of his lips on hers, his tongue stroking against hers. His heartbeat pounded against her breasts—how had he managed to pull her so close without her realizing?—his arms tight around her.

There was something about it that made her wonder if she had ever known passion before him.

Something warned her that she had known it with this man, and only this man.

Pulling back, Travis stared down at her shadowed features and knew she would follow him. He didn't say anything. Instead he lifted the keys from the pocket of his jacket and moved to his own motorcycle.

Straddling it, he pushed the key into the ignition. The two bikes started simultaneously. Within seconds they were pulling away from the bar and heading through town.

Damn Elite Ops and the mission. It would end up destroying him and possibly Lilly as well.

This was exactly what he hadn't wanted. To see the pain and confusion that filled her eyes, that was slowly tearing her apart.

There was instinct, suspicion, and what Travis knew was second nature. The fighter Lilly was was instinctive. It was as much a part of her as breathing. As being.

With such instinct, with such pure strength as he knew Lilly possessed, the memories would not be much further behind.

And now, they might well be closer than ever before.

The house he owned in Hagerstown was located in one of the more historic parts of the city. It was two stories, brick, completely remodeled on the inside, with almost an acre of land heavily bordered by a hedge of tall evergreen shrubs.

Hitting the remote programmed into the handle of the motorcycle, Travis slowed down for the rising of the garage door, then pulled the bike inside. Lilly rode in beside him, shut the engine to her own, and waited.

The door behind them slid closed with a squeak of the rubber seal against the cement.

"Nice." Pushing the kickstand into place, Lilly swung off the seat and pulled the helmet from her head as she looked around.

He knew what she saw beside the Jaguar sitting in the other bay. Travis Caine was wealthy, a man who worked with the most exclusive, the most powerful men and women on earth. His lifestyle reflected that. Beside the Jag sat a specially designed, security-upgraded Hummer. Beside that was another motorcycle, one known for its reputation of speed, power, and exclusivity. There were less than two hundred in the entire world.

"Very nice." She didn't touch it, not that Travis would have cared. The cycle had belonged to the first Travis Caine, as had the house, the vehicles, and the funds he lived on. Funds carefully monitored by the agency.

Travis was more interested in her shapely ass as she bent to look at the detailing of the hand-stitched seat.

"Would you like a drink?" He strode to the well-stocked bar on the other side of the garage. Hell, all he wanted to do was get her in the bedroom, and here he was, stuck, while she admired his bike rather than his dick. Wasn't that just his luck?

"No."

"Shall we go in then?" Opening the door that led to the house, Travis entered ahead of her and made for the kitchen.

Marble floors led from the small garage foyer to the kitchen and dining room.

The damned place must have been an exercise for that first Travis Caine in how much money he could spend on a residence while keeping the outside so modest-looking.

Opening the refrigerator, he pulled two cold beers free and tossed a bottle across the room to Lilly, watching her closely.

She caught it, without thinking, then stared at the beer in confusion before lifting her gaze back at him. What he saw there made him want to curse. Confusion. Anger. Fear.

"You knew I'd catch it," she whispered.

Unscrewing the cap with a deft twist, he tossed the metal disk to the counter before leaning against it casually.

He shrugged. "You like beer."

"I detest beer." Lilly stared at the bottle again, a bit surprised that her mouth was watering for the taste of it. Surprised that she actually wanted it.

"You learned to love it." She watched him. "You told me once that until you had been forced to drink it, you hadn't known how good it could taste."

"And how was I forced to drink it?" Lilly sighed wearily.

He chuckled. "We were in Mexico. It was my beer or their water. You chose my beer."

She just bet she had.

"Why was I there, Travis?" she asked, barely able to push the words past her lips. "Why wasn't I home?"

No one else seemed willing to answer that question. Would he?

"It had something to do with what you saw the night your father was killed."

Now, her surprise turned to shock.

She hadn't expected him to answer her. She blinked back at him, wondering at the quiet expression on his face as he continued to watch her closely.

"What happened that night?" She didn't remember it. The last thing she remembered was the party that night.

Travis stepped to the large, marble-topped kitchen island and stared back at her with a heavy frown. "You said your father suspected someone of embezzling money. You said he had been acting strangely that night and then he disappeared from the party. You went looking for him and when you walked into his study, he was already dead."

Lilly fisted her hands at her side and fought against the rage and the pain. Her father had died that night, and she had been unable to help him. Unable to do anything but run, apparently.

Shadows tangled together in her head. Like a fast-forward that went much too fast to make sense of, images raced through her mind.

"So I didn't see who killed him?" she asked. "I did nothing to save him?"

Travis shook his head. "We think you were knocked unconcious. And you suspected, but never told me either way. You had issues trusting people, especially with your secrets."

"I did nothing to prove my suspicions?" She heard her own voice roughen, felt the agony of failure tearing through her.

"I didn't say that, Lilly," he retorted gently. "You've investigated. At times I've helped you, but you always ran into a dead end. That doesn't mean you haven't tried."

She swung away from him, fighting her tears.

"You were working covertly with MI5 before that night," he continued. "You couldn't risk going to them, though. You trusted no one."

"But I trusted you enough to tell you that?" She swung back to him, the anger and fear eating at her now.

"We were close, Lilly," he stated softly. "There were many times you trusted me. And there were times you didn't."

At least he was admitting there were times she hadn't trusted him.

"Where did we meet?" The question was a whisper, as she fought to put together the puzzle of her life.

"We met in Israel. I was your trainer for a while." With that statement he turned, opened a lower cabinet door, and tossed the empty bottle away.

He moved with a predatory male grace, a sense of preparedness and yet casual laziness. She couldn't pinpoint the type of man he was, or even how trustworthy he was, and she considered herself a rather perceptive person when it came to others, but she couldn't read him well.

She watched as he moved across the room to her. Silently. He was even more silent than she was, and he was much heavier. There were muscles packed on that body.

"What sort of trainer?" she asked breathlessly as he came closer, brushing against her, staring down at her with his heated gaze.

What did she want? Information or that hard, hot body moving against her, over her? Her body was screaming for sex, her mind demanding answers and she was having trouble deciding exactly which she wanted to give in to first.

"Hand-to-hand combat and weapons." His head lowered, his lips brushed against her ear. "You were a very good student too." One hand gripped her hip and jerked her against the steel-hard wedge of his cock beneath his pants as his fingers tangled in her hair to draw her head back. "Teacher's pet, actually." His lips brushed hers.

Lilly caught her breath. She wasn't a virgin, and if

she had been this man's lover then she knew damned good and well she wasn't inexperienced. But she felt innocent, caught in a web of seduction and pleasure that was sensed rather than remembered, as she held her breath, waiting for his kiss.

"Why are you here, Lilly? Information, or this?" He asked the question that raged through her mind, but he gave her no chance to answer.

His lips pressed against hers, parted them, sipped from her as though arousal were an ambrosia and he was dying for more.

His tongue stroked over her lips then slipped inside, caressed her tongue, licked, tasted. A hum of pleasure left her as she felt her hands moving slowly up his hard arms. Over muscle and flesh, tough, invincible, as he pulled her closer and lifted her tighter against him.

The hard proof of his erection nudged at her pussy. It pressed against her clit, rubbed the material of her silk panties and the silk lining of her own leathers against the dampening folds between her thighs.

Sexual need, excitement, and a rush of emotions that made no sense crowded in on her. Her flesh heated, burned. Wherever he touched, wherever the warmth of his body caressed her, triggered such a rush of pleasure racing through her that she felt dizzy.

Her knees were weakening. Didn't that only happen in books and movies? Not in real life?

A moan whispered from her lips as her hands pushed into his hair, gripping the long strands, feeling the coarseness of it, the cool, achingly familiar touch of it.

So little in her life was familiar anymore. This, though,

this rocked through her system with an awareness that she had been here before, that she had missed this, needed it. There was also an assurance that she hadn't had enough of it. Not yet. Perhaps never.

His kiss was black magic, there was just no other word for it.

"Travis." She whispered his name as his lips slid to her cheek, the curve of her jaw, to her neck.

Nerve endings tingled with a rush of pure sensation, white hot and intense as it washed through her body.

Callused fingertips moved beneath the snug top she wore, caressed up, cupped . . . Jerking her head back, Lilly fought to hold on to a sense of balance as the pad of his thumb raked over her nipple while pressing beneath the lace of her bra.

It was exquisite.

As she arched against him her legs parted further for the hard thigh pressing between them, lifting her, forcing her to ride the hard contours of his thigh as she ground her pussy against him.

She ached. Oh God, she ached as though sex were more than a want, as though it were imperative to her very being. A cascade of heated sensations flooded her body, dampening her sex, clenching the intimate muscles as she fought to catch her breath.

Catching her breath wasn't that easy. Each time she tried, he did something else, something sexy and exciting. Something that burned over sensitive flesh and raced over her nerve endings.

Pulling the lace of her bra to the side, he exposed the

hard tip of her nipple to the cool air of the room, then to the incredible heat of his mouth.

Fighting to keep her eyes open, Lilly stared down at him, watching as his cheeks hollowed around the tight tip, the way his lashes shadowed his cheeks.

It was incredibly sexy. So sexy it made her heart thunder in her chest, made her breathing short.

The lash of his tongue had her eyelids fluttering, had sensation shooting straight to her clit and beyond as a wild, ragged cry left her lips. When his fingers moved to the snap and zipper of her pants, she was more than eager to help him with his own as well.

Her fingers tore at the metal tabs of his leather riding pants as the zipper of hers slid down. She gasped for air as he took her lips in a kiss, his tongue licking along hers as his fingers slid into the parted material, eased lower, and threaded through the silky curls between her thighs.

Lilly froze, tried to catch her breath. Her eyes widened, stared into his, and in the next second fluttered closed again as his fingers found and captured the tight little bud of her clitoris.

Callused fingertips circled, rubbed, and stimulated the sensitive bundle of flesh. Arcs of pleasure tore through her pussy as her juices rushed to coat the swollen folds beyond to tempt his fingers to touch lower, to stroke inside her.

"I dream about this," he growled against her lips as he gave her a moment to breathe. "Touching your sweet pussy again, feeling it quiver beneath my fingers, feeling your pretty clit swell with hunger."

Heat flushed her face at the explicit words while her pussy creamed harder. She wanted his fingers inside her. She wanted him to take her, to ease the hard knot of hunger tightening in her womb.

Her hips arched closer, forcing his fingers lower along the narrow slit he was caressing. Lifting her leg, she managed to get him a little closer.

He chuckled, a breath of male hunger and amusement, as his fingers rubbed over the clenched entrance.

"This what you want, Lilly?" he crooned against her ear as one finger slipped in just enough to tease, just enough to give her a taste of the pleasure she was reaching for. Just enough to tease her into whimpering and arching her hips higher for more.

A shudder tore through her as he rubbed at the clenched, tight muscles of her vagina. The pad of his finger rubbed in tiny circles, moved in short, easy strokes. His lips moved back to her nipples, his tongue licked and stroked, and Lilly was certain she was going to melt to the floor with the incredible pleasure racing through her and the imperative need for more.

"I can make it better, Lilly," he whispered before nipping at the sensitive tip of her breast.

"What's stopping you?" she cried out breathlessly. "Make it better. I dare you."

Let him see if she tried to stop him. God, she wanted more so damned bad she was on the verge of begging for it.

"You dare me, do you?" A quick, heated lick of her nipple had her jerking in reflexive pleasure.

"Double-dare you," she gasped.

His finger moved, retreated, only to return thicker, stronger, stretching the sensitive portal of her pussy as her neck arched and a low, ragged cry tore from her lips.

A fiery aching pleasure centered in the very core of her, convulsing through her womb as she almost, almost reached that peak she was searching for.

She was so close. Right there on the verge.

"Mr. Caine, we have company." A harsh, rough voice spoke from the other room. It sounded as though it came from a wild creature, one whose vocal ability was still more animal than man.

Travis jerked against her, his hard body suddenly tense and prepared for battle rather than focused entirely on her.

"Who is it, Nik?" he snarled.

"I do believe it's the girl's uncle," the "Nik" in question answered. His voice, though lower, was no less rough. "He's demanding to speak with you."

Demanding. Yes, that sounded like her uncle, but he'd picked a hell of a time to demand anything.

Staring back at Travis, her body aching in regret, she watched, felt the complete distance he placed between them.

"Would you like to freshen up before facing him?" he asked, his hand gesturing toward a guest bathroom. "Make yourself at home."

He fixed his pants, tucked in his shirt. Within seconds the only outward sign of passion was the slight flush to his cheeks and the glitter of green in his brown eyes.

Lilly stepped back. She wanted to know why her

uncle was there, but she had a feeling she would learn much more if they both believed she was occupied.

Lilly knew the fine art of pretending to give what was wanted. It was one of the first lessons her mother had taught her.

She had excelled.

CHAPTER 4

TRAVIS STEPPED INTO the reception room. The room was off a small foyer at the wide front door, marble-floored, the furniture less than comfortable but sleekly modern. Nik had had the butler light the fire, which glowed with cozy warmth in the huge fireplace. It did little to warm the cold appearance of the room though.

"Mr. Harrington." Travis stepped into the room casually, displaying the lazy, almost insolent grace he had brought to the persona he had been given.

He didn't extend his hand; an insult, he knew, to a man considered near royalty in England. Desmond Harrington was a lord of the realm as well as a member of the House of Lords now that he had acquired the Harrington title. He was a powerful, dignified figure, despite the fact that he looked more like an American thug.

His red hair was cut close to his scalp. His mustache grew long down the side of his lips and beneath his chin to meet a sparse beard in a wide goatee. The rest of the beard was trimmed closer to the face and gave him a scruffy appearance, while the minute lines on his forehead and at the corners of his eyes, along with the hollowed appearance of his cheeks, spoke of a rough-hewn determination.

Blue eyes watched Travis with a hint of anger, his lower lip tight with disapproval as he moved to the couch across from the chair Travis had taken.

Behind him was his bodyguard, and Travis almost laughed when the he recognized the man. Amazing that a man suspected of terrorist ties and international loan-sharking would have a bodyguard known better for his sense of fair play and honor than he was for his brutality.

"Mr. Caine." Desmond hitched his slacks with an angry jerk of his hands before taking his seat with regal arrogance. "I won't take up much of your time. Produce my niece and I'll leave."

Travis arched his brow as he sensed Nik moving in closer behind him.

The butler, Henry, balding, under six feet, but more than capable of providing any backup they needed, entered the room and went over to the bar.

"Would you gentlemen like a drink?" Travis asked Desmond as the other man glared at him.

"My niece, if you don't mind." The precise English accent was clipped and demanding.

"She's in the powder room." Travis shrugged. "You know how long such things can take. I suggest you relax for a bit and we can chat."

"I have nothing to chat about with the likes of you." Self-importantly, he lifted his rather heavy nose in the air as though he smelled something offensive.

Travis chuckled. "Ah, I have to say you're quite wrong

there," he retorted. "We have quite a bit to discuss. I want my Lilly back."

It was kind of funny to be "playing" Lilly's lover when he actually was her lover. Except there was nothing the least bit humorous about the situation.

"Lilly Belle no longer exists," Desmond hissed as he nearly came out of his chair, his face flushing brick red in anger. "She is Lady Victoria Lillian Harrington. Period. She is related to royalty and her station does not allow her to be your toy any longer."

Travis's brow arched. "That's Lilly's choice to make, not yours."

"She no longer remembers you. She will never remember those years she has lost. The doctors are certain of that. Leave her be, man. Allow her the life she was born to live," her uncle demanded.

"The life she ran from?" Travis asked as he leaned forward. "She was nearly killed living your life, as I remember it. Lilly left voluntarily. She didn't return with the same mind-set. She's back, not because she wanted to be, but because once again someone tried to kill her and she forgot she was running. So don't presume to preach to me about the life that she should be living, or the reputation she should be cultivating."

"Victoria belongs with her family," Desmond snapped. "No matter how you twist the truth, you are nothing but a danger to her."

Travis laughed. "She created the danger in her life as I'm certain your investigator told you. Do you think her enemies aren't well aware that she's now Lady Victoria Lillian Harrington? Do you honestly believe her past isn't going to return to bite her on the ass?"

He was the concerned past lover. He was the man that knew her secrets better than any other. He was the man her family was going to have to accept whether they wanted to or not.

"Leave it alone," Desmond fired back. "I can take care of any repercussions if you'll walk the hell away."

"And what repercussions would that be, Uncle Desmond?" Lilly stepped into the room.

Travis knew the creature Lilly Belle was. Silent, stealthy, but too damned curious. She was known for her inability to keep her nose out of danger. Even within the Ops her reputation was fairly solid in that regard.

She stepped into the room, obviously surprising her uncle with her clothing, as well as her demeanor.

Desmond Harrington rose to his feet, shoved his hands in the pockets of his slacks.

"I have the limo outside," he stated, his tone grating. "We need to leave, Lilly."

A smooth, negligent shrug of her shoulders was the first indication Travis saw of the agent he once knew. Lilly pursed her lips thoughtfully as she propped her hands on her hips and surveyed the room silently for long moments.

"You said you didn't know anything about where I've been or what I've been doing for the past six years," she told her uncle. "You lied to me."

A dark frown creased Desmond's brow. "At the time, I had no idea," he bit out, his tone icily angry now. "If you recall, I informed you I would hire investigators to pursue the subject. Their report came in weeks ago."

"And I wasn't told?" She leaned a shapely hip against the back of the couch Travis sat in. A move that Desmond clearly understood. Lilly Belle was in the room right now.

"Could we discuss this at home?" Desmond demanded. "With your mother present, if you don't mind, rather than with this gentleman." He made the last word sound like a curse.

"Funny, Uncle Desmond," she mused then. "Your investigators know so much now, but they didn't find me in the six years I was missing?"

His expression became pinched. "We believed there was no way you could have survived that explosion," he answered. "You were declared dead when no evidence of your whereabouts could be found."

"And now my whereabouts are known," she drawled, her tone cold.

"Once we had your new . . . ," he looked uncomfortable, "identity was rather easy."

Travis wanted to shoot the bastard.

He rose slowly to his feet and moved to the bar. All the while he kept his gaze on Lilly's face through the large mirror on the other side of the room.

"This gentleman, as you call him, seems to know more about me than you or Mother," she informed him, her tone calm and quiet as she moved from the couch.

That wasn't a good sign. A nice calm tone from Lilly Belle was usually something to be wary of.

Desmond grimaced. "And I know more about him than he can imagine. He's not the sort of person you want in your life, Lilly."

"I think I've always been able to make that decision on my own, Uncle Desmond," she reminded him, her smile tight now.

Damn, good ole Uncle Desmond was really starting to piss her off now. And he seemed to realize that. Travis was almost amused.

Travis watched as the other man took careful control of himself and attempted to repair the damage.

"I regret I haven't given you the information I received," he stated, and there seemed to be sincere regret in his tone. "The psychologist you were seeing in the hospital suggested it might be best that you remember certain things on your own. In the interests of your health, we elected to wait." He cast Travis and Nik a harsh glare. "Victoria, please . . ."

"Lilly," she informed him, the quick, sharp tone of her voice drawing a reaction from her, as well as surprise from Desmond. "Please, call me Lilly."

Travis cast the other man a tight smile of victory. She was Lilly Belle, Lady Victoria Harrington be damned.

"Lilly." Desmond obviously didn't approve of the name. "Please, dear. Let's return to the house, and we'll discuss this. The limo is waiting outside."

"I brought the bike. I'll follow you back."

Desmond frowned, obviously caught off guard. "What bike?"

"My motorcycle," she stated, watching him carefully now. Travis could feel the tension radiating from her now.

Desmond shook his head. "You have no such thing."

"Really, I do." She strode across the room. "I'll meet you at home." Pausing at the door, she turned back to Travis. "I'll be in touch."

"I'm certain I'll enjoy the experience," he taunted her, to remind her of the few stolen moments they'd had in the kitchen.

Amusement gleamed in her green eyes before she pushed through the kitchen door and, he knew, strode to the garage.

"Henry, make certain the garage door is open for her," he ordered the butler as he hovered silently on the other side of the room. "And make certain Miss Harrington has access to the house whenever she wishes."

"Very good, sir." Henry nodded stiffly and followed her.

Travis turned back to Desmond. He was watching the door with a sense of bemusement, as though the woman that had stepped through it were a stranger rather than the niece he had once been rumored to love.

"She's not the woman you lost six years ago," Travis reminded him quietly. "Try to turn her into that woman and you'll make an enemy of her."

Her uncle turned back to him slowly. "If I allow you to have your way, she'll remain one step above a criminal," he said hollowly. "Or slip those final inches and be lost to us forever."

"Lord Harrington, I didn't return to destroy Lilly's life, I returned to save it," Travis informed him.

Desmond grunted rudely. "Your past actions do not speak of your desire to save her. Training in demolitions and explosives. Military and martial arts training in Asia for eighteen months while conducting so-called ventures into pirate-held territories. And that doesn't count the dozens of near arrests, near fatal crashes, and God only knows how much weapons fire she's faced while she's played your whore." By the time he finished his face was bloodred, his blue eyes snapping with rage, and his accent more clipped than usual.

Travis tilted his head and watched curiously. It had been a while since he'd seen such a blue-blooded tantrum.

"Perhaps I should remind of you the reason why she was learning how to fight, how to kill, and how to protect herself," Travis stated calmly when the other man had finished. "Because you and your polite, well-heeled English society, your blue-blooded aristocracy, allowed her to nearly be murdered. You accepted her death, gave her a nice tear-filled burial, and went about your lives without once questioning the results you were given, despite the inconsistencies. Get your head out of your ass, Desmond. She's a big girl, she's been a big girl for a long time, and she's damned sure more woman than your prissy little English boys can handle. You can accept it, and help me protect her, or you can continue to stand in my way and bury her for real next time." Travis turned on his heel and headed into the living area of the house. "Let me know what you decide. Before it's too late."

He didn't turn back to the other man as he delivered his parting shot. Nik opened the door that led into the short hallway and then into the house that was as pristine, just as fucking modern and icy cold, as the reception room.

As cold as Travis's fucking life had become.

Lilly parked her cycle at the curved cement and stone steps that led up to the mansion her family had taken for the spring and summer months. She had beat her uncle home. No surprise there.

The low heels of her boots were silent as she climbed the stairs, and the lack of sound seemed odd. Shoes made noise. Even sneakers made a slight noise when walking. But hers didn't, and it wasn't the shoes. It was her.

It was the way she walked, the way she moved. She could move silently, or if she thought about it, as she made herself do now, she could allow the slight click of the heels.

Had Travis trained her how to walk with such stealth as well?

The door opened, and the butler stood aside as Lilly stepped into the warm, golden wood tones of the entryway.

Shedding her leather jacket, she handed it to the butler, then lifted her head as her mother walked into the foyer. She carried some papers she had been reviewing, probably her latest financial statements. Her mother had come into her first marriage independently wealthy and she was amazingly adroit at managing her own finances.

Lady Angelica Harrington. She was also a distant cousin as well as a confidante and friend to the Queen. She moved in circles so influential it boggled the mind. Her social life was her career—the parties, teas, luncheons, and charity events.

Her son, Lilly's brother, Jared James Harrington, was a solicitor with a law firm that the Queen often relied upon. He had been introduced to his wife by the Queen and had married with her blessing. He had become just as cold and unemotional as her mother sometimes seemed to be.

"Oh my God! What on earth are you wearing?" Lady

Harrington's tone wasn't scandalized, it was purely horrified.

"Leather," Lilly answered gently, wishing she could find a way to take that fear from her mother's eyes. "Did you think that because you didn't inform me about my past, it wouldn't come back to haunt you? Or me?"

She pulled her gloves from her hands and slapped them on the shiny, dark cherry bureau that sat in the foyer as she held her mother's gaze.

Angelica lifted her hand slowly to her throat, her pale blue gaze flickering with indecision as she watched her daughter now. She wasn't quite certain how to handle this version of Lilly.

Her poor mother, Lilly thought. She likely had dreamed of having her daughter back, but Lilly doubted she had imagined the woman who had returned. Even Lilly didn't know the woman who had returned.

Lilly pushed her fingers through her hair, feeling the long strands drifting through her fingers and over her shoulders as a familiar wildness rose inside her. She knew this feeling, she had known it for a long time. The same feeling she had fought before her supposed death six years before.

"Who am I?" She stared back at her mother, suddenly fearful, almost terrified that despite the urge to solve the mystery of those missing years, perhaps she really didn't want to know.

"My daughter," Angelica whispered, her voice filled with sorrow. "The daughter I never want to lose again."

Lilly wanted to hit something. With her fist. Her fingers curled with the need to ram it into a wall, a door, a bed, a punching bag . . . A memory flashed in her mind.

A sweat-stained punching bag swinging before her, her fists pounding into it, her heart racing, perspiration pouring down her body . . .

Just as quickly, it was gone. The second before the memory was able to solidify, it was gone.

"Your daughter changed," she rasped. "What did she change into?"

Who was she? Where had she been? Why had she run?

"Lilly." Her mother's hand dropped from her throat as she stepped closer, the silk of her dress floating gently around her knees as the faintest hint of cigarette smoke wafted to Lilly's senses.

She blinked. She saw her mother through a sniper's scope. She was wearing her mink coat. Cigarette smoke drifted in a cold breeze. Lilly blinked again and it was gone.

"Lilly?" Angelica reached out for her, her cool, graceful fingers touching Lilly's arm gently as she attempted to draw her closer. "I want you to enjoy being with the family again. Those years you were gone." Angelica blinked back tears that filled her eyes as Lilly stared down at her. "You were alive, yet you didn't allow us to know it. You changed your pretty face." Her mother reached up and touched her face. "Even your eye color is different. You changed everything, as though your family no longer mattered."

And those changes had had their consequences. Her brother had walked out of the hospital when he came with her mother and uncle to see the woman the doctors were claiming was Lady Victoria Lillian Harrington. Jared had sworn his sister would never deny her family to such an extent.

Why had she done it? Changed so much of herself?

"There are no answers." Her mother's voice cracked with emotion. "Desmond and I have tried to find the answers. All we can find is a woman that lived as though she wanted to die. As though she had lost everything precious to her. And yet we were right here." A tear slipped down Angelica's cheek then. "Was I so wrong to keep that from you? Was I wrong to hope you never remembered that you were trying to run away from us?"

"That wasn't it!" The words, the emotions, flew from her lips before she thought, before she could understand why.

There was a memory there, for just a second. For just a fragile moment clarity had almost overtaken her, only to disappear once again.

"Then what was it?" her mother cried out desperately. "Tell me, Lilly, why can't I call you Victoria as I once did? Why do you wear leather clothes and boots that make you look like the tramp? Why the changes to your appearance and why the changes to yourself if you weren't trying to deny the very people who loved you?" Her face twisted. "I nearly died when I thought I was burying my only daughter. Instead you were out raising hell and throwing away everything your father and I tried to provide for you. You left your family, *Victoria,* for a life that bordered on the criminal and a lifestyle that was little better than that of a terrorist."

Lilly stood still and silent, watching the emotions that tore through her mother as she felt something shut down inside her. The woman her mother was talking about wasn't her. Something didn't sound right, it didn't feel right. Something was wrong with the scenario her mother was laying out.

She hadn't been a terrorist. She hadn't been a criminal.

She looked down at the clothes she wore and felt a shudder go through her.

"I wouldn't have turned my back on you," she whispered as a tear slid down her cheek. "Not like that. I don't know what happened. I don't know who I am or what I was doing, but I do know my family was everything to me."

Sure, her mother was difficult—to say the least. And yes, Lilly had often wanted to run away from all the expectations and rules piled on top of her, but she had never imagined turning her back on her family, pretending to be dead, going through reconstructive surgery, and taking up a life of crime—or something close to it—just to escape it.

She had followed in her father's footsteps as an informant for MI5. She had worked diligently to uncover evidence the agency needed to identify terrorists, terrorist sympathizers, and other criminal elements. And she had done it, ultimately, to protect the ones she loved.

So what had happened? Why had she turned her back on all of that?

Just then the door opened, and Lilly swung around to meet the furious expression of her uncle. No, her stepfather. God, why had her mother married Desmond Harrington, her father's half-brother and business partner? Had she missed her husband so much that she had married his brother to replace him?

"Victoria." He stopped as his bodyguard came in be-hind him and closed the door. "At least you made it home."

Anger ripped through her, and she had no idea why. She loved her uncle. He had been an integral part of her life from her birth to her death.

"Of course I made it home." She had to fight back the conflicting emotions she didn't know what to do with. "It seems I'm a rather good rider."

He wiped his hand over his face as he shook his head, obviously weary and attempting to hold on to his temper. Desmond Harrington was known for his tem-per, courtesy of his red hair, but he was also known for his compassion and logic.

"A rather good rider," he muttered as he rubbed at his forehead before lifting his head and staring past Lilly to her mother. "It seems, my dear, that this hardheaded child has found a new hobby."

He pulled his jacket off, handed it to the bodyguard, Isaac, then strode through the foyer to the living room.

"It's obviously not a new hobby," she stated as she fol-lowed him and her mother, only to pause just inside the door and watch as he strode to the bar. "A Crown on ice would be lovely," she suggested as he lifted a decanter of liquor.

Desmond paused before pouring the desired drink as well as a snifter of brandy for her mother.

"Crown and ice." Her mother sounded furious now. "That is not a proper young lady's drink, Victoria."

"I asked you to call me Lilly, Mother." Lilly stepped into the room and accepted the drink from Desmond before striding to the sofa and lounging back. She smothered a sigh of exhaustion. Lifting the drink to her lips Lilly sipped the smooth liquor, nearly closing her eyes at the pleasurable burn that hit her stomach.

She watched as Desmond handed her mother her drink then took his seat beside her on the couch. Strange, she had never seen her mother sit with her father like that, close, intimate. They had rarely sat on a couch, they had each had their own chairs instead. But the distance she had always sensed between her parents was present here as well.

"We need to discuss tonight," Desmond told her firmly after taking a long sip of his drink, as though needing fortification.

"What is there to discuss?" Lilly asked him. "I met a friend for drinks. I'm of age, I have no curfew. What we do need to discuss is what the hell you were doing following me at this hour of the night."

"What did you do?" Her mother almost whispered the words, as though terrified of the answer.

"I found her with Travis Caine," Desmond informed her. "He has a house here in Hagerstown as well. Your daughter somehow acquired a rather racy motorbike and she broke several speeding laws to meet him at a bar, and then followed him to his house."

"Caine?" Wide-eyed, Angelica turned to Desmond. "My God." She turned back to Lilly. "He's a suspected terrorist, a man known to associate, if not partner with criminals! Victoria . . ."

"Lilly." Determination surged inside her. She hadn't been Victoria for six years. She was Lilly.

"Why are you doing this? Do you want to be taken from us again?" Her mother ignored the reminder. "You'll be arrested for sure!"

"I rather doubt there's a warrant out for my or Travis's arrest," Lilly objected.

"There's a warrant for your arrest in China, should you ever reenter their sovereign borders again, for theft of a government artifact, which they can't prove to America. There's a warrant for your and Caine's arrest in Iran for the suspected death of a militant who was related to the current ruler. There's also a warrant to bring you in for questioning in Spain for the death of a Spanish militant suspected of being part of a radical extremist group protesting against the government."

Had she killed?

She had. Lilly felt that knowledge bleeding through her, bloodred and stained with guilt.

Had she killed in cold blood? She couldn't imagine that. She had a healthy respect for life, more for others' than for her own. At least, that was the thought that flitted through her head.

How would she know these things? And why was she suddenly so frightened at the thought of her mother or her uncle knowing the full truth about her?

"From what I'm hearing, if I did kill, then it was no one that didn't deserve it," she informed them both with an air of unconcern.

She was aware that she would have never made such a statement six years ago.

"Victoria . . ." Horror rippled through her mother's voice.

"Mother." Lilly shook her head as she leaned forward. "I don't know what happened to me. I don't know who I was, or what I did. But I do know I wasn't a criminal."

"I have the report on you, Victoria," her uncle said.

"The governments may not have proof, but I have enough evidence to substantiate, at the very least, a strong suspicion that you did kill."

There was something in his gaze then, some thread of compassion, perhaps? Understanding? What was she seeing there, and why did it bother her so much to see it?

Lilly wanted nothing more than to run now. To escape the judgment and the disapproval she could feel coming from the mother.

She didn't know if she could live much longer without somehow figuring out who or what she had been and why she had killed.

"I want this report you have on me." She rose to her feet and stared at her mother and uncle. "Then, I want to know how the two of you ended up married, and why the hell my father's murderer was never found."

That was the source of her anger. Her father was dead, murdered, and his killer had never been caught. From what she gathered since she had been back, the search for his killer had been less than enthusiastic.

With that last warning she strode from the living room, ignoring her mother calling out to her, and her uncle's almost silent curse.

She needed answers. She needed to know what had happened and why. And then she needed to figure out just why the hell Travis Caine felt more like a lover than a trainer, more like a friend than an enemy.

Travis sat in the underground room Wild Card had been assigned as the Harrington's driver and listened to the confrontation as it played out in the Harrington living room.

Wild Card, a.k.a. Noah Blake, sat at the small table across from him, earbud attached to his ear, listening as well.

Travis watched the small, portable monitor as Lilly stalked from the room.

"Have the file sent up to her." Lilly's mother rose jerkily from the couch, her expression and her tone icily furious.

"Angelica, she doesn't need the file yet." Desmond sat forward, his expression concerned now. "She's barely healed physically. The shock could be detrimental."

"And what of the shock to the family?" She turned back, her pale face furious. "She's determined to bring this family down to the same level she's existed at for the past six years. Let her see the damage she's risking by continuing along this path."

Travis's lips thinned at the judgment in Lilly's mother's voice.

Desmond sighed wearily. "She's been through a lot, Angelica."

"And you think I don't realize this?" Angelica's voice roughened. "My God, Desmond, the thought of that report destroys my soul. Why? Why did she allow us to believe she was dead? Why live the life she lived rather than returning to us?"

"That's a question only Lilly can answer." Desmond rose to his feet. "And the doctors fear it's a question she will never be able to answer."

He glanced back at Angelica as he made his way back to the bar.

"She was always so damned stubborn," Angelica stated, tears filling her eyes. "I tried to tell Harold that if she were not dealt with properly when she was a teen-ager, then she would only harm herself."

Desmond seemed to stiffen before turning back to her.

"The clinic was not the answer, my dear," Desmond sighed.

"You are as ineffectual where she is concerned as Harold was," she snapped.

Desmond's voice hardened. "This is not an argument I will have with you tonight."

"You never wish to discuss it," Angelica said. "It's as though you want nothing more than to bury your head in the sand and pretend this situation does not exist."

Desmond stared back at her coolly. "I can think of nothing better than burying the entire matter for good."

With that he tossed back his drink, slapped the glass on a table, and stalked from the room.

A throttled, furious scream erupted from Lilly's mother's throat as she flung her glass at the door and watched it burst into fragments.

A tear slipped down Angelica's cheek as Travis turned from the scene and leveled a look at Noah. A soundless whistle pursed his lips as Angelica left the room, slamming the door behind her.

Travis pulled the earbud from his ear and dropped it to the table as Noah activated the cameras throughout the house, tracking Angelica's movements.

She stalked to her bedroom; minutes later, a manser-vant knocked. Angelica appeared at the door, handed a thick file to the servant, and pointed to Lilly's suite.

"Hell of a thing for a woman to have to face at four in the morning," Noah stated quietly.

"At any time," Travis growled.

He hated that damned report. Hell, he had never agreed with the cover those girls had been given. They were called security "escorts." Military trained, exceptionally lovely, and dangerous as hell. They were "hired out" to men who required beauty and brains in a deadly package.

They were rented to legitimate businessmen as well as criminal bosses and cartel leaders. Sexual services were not part of the package, but few of the men who paid for their services admitted that. They thought they were hiring discretion and protection. They had no idea they had hired highly trained operatives who reported back to an agency created for secrecy and efficiency.

To the world, though, the girls Santos Bahre and Rhiannon McConnelly handled were no more than well-armed whores.

And that's what Lilly would read in that file.

Would she believe it?

"Everyone is now in their respective rooms," Noah reported as he continued to scan the house. "Nik is slipping through the garden now."

Travis stood with a quick nod and moved to the single bed where he'd placed his bag earlier.

Noah eased the door open, stepped into the hall, and waited, while Travis quickly packed the gear needed into the pockets of his mission pants.

As he pushed a small tool pack into the pocket at the knee of his pants, Nik stepped into the room ahead of Noah.

The door closed silently as Noah stepped back inside. Nik carried a small backpack, filled, Travis knew, with the electronics needed to finish bugging the house for sound.

He handed the bag off to Noah and moved to the table where the portable monitors waited.

Travis slipped out of the room with Noah, moving silently through the house to the office both Desmond and Angelica Harrington worked from.

They had yet to get camera or audio in the room. Each time they had attempted it, Harrington or his bodyguard, usually both, had been too close, if not in the room itself.

This time, the office was empty.

Moving to the door, he attached the security device to the lock, activated it, and waited as the alarm was bypassed.

When the green light blinked, he turned the doorknob and they slipped in.

He reattached the device on the other side, reactivated the alarm, and then he and Noah went to work. Noah began installing video and audio while Travis moved to the desk.

There was no time to check the computer, that would come later. Picking the lock to the file drawer at the side of the desk, Travis began searching files and papers instead.

The drawer held nothing of interest. The desk was scrupulously neat. Working silently, Travis searched the room. There were business logs, files, contracts, all as boring as hell. Rifling through them, Travis was ready to move on when he glimpsed a thick narrow envelope tucked into a file regarding real estate in the D.C. area.

Pulling the envelope free, he opened it quickly and pulled out several pictures and a three-page report dated a little more than a year before. The report wasn't signed. It was handwritten. The last line held an account number.

Travis pulled a small digital camera from his pants and quickly snapped pictures of each page as well as the pictures.

Pictures of Lilly.

Each one had been taken in a different location for a different assignment. If he wasn't mistaken, part of the report also held the name of the plastic surgeon who had supposedly changed Lilly's face.

The same doctor who had been killed the day before Lilly had taken a bullet to the side of her head.

Desmond Harrington had known Lilly was alive long before he had been contacted by the hospital. Renewing his search through the files, Travis found two more similar envelopes, recorded the contents, and quickly replaced them.

It was nearly dawn before he and Noah finished. They were moving for the door when the sound of the alarm being deactivated had them racing for whatever cover they could find.

Noah headed for a heavily curtained windowseat while Travis ducked into the closet to the side of the desk.

Isaac Macauley stepped into the room silently, closing and locking the door behind him before moving to the desk.

Through the cracks in the folding doors, Travis

watched as the bodyguard opened a drawer, pulled a device free of the desk, and opened it.

Well, now, there was a problem. That particular device was extremely difficult to come by and could block even Noah's little electronic bugs.

Activating the device, Isaac pulled a satellite phone from inside his jacket pocket and keyed in a number. An international number if the amount of keys he hit was any indication.

"Harrington gave her the file," Macauley stated, his voice low. "There was no chance to delay it."

Macauley waited for whatever response came.

"Not as far as I can tell," he answered moments later. "She appears less than stable now that Caine has shown up."

Travis's brows lifted. He thought Lilly was very stable.

"I've advised Harrington to deal with the mistake," he reported after another silence. "He seems a bit squeamish at the idea, though."

Strange, Macauley's reputation was impeccable. This didn't sound like an innocent conversation, though.

"I'll take care of it," Macauley stated. "I'll let you know when they arrive."

The call disconnected.

Macauley stood still and silent for long moments afterward before replacing his phone and deactivating the blocking device he had used.

Replacing it in the desk, he turned and left the room, reactivating the security behind him.

Travis moved from the closet as Noah met him at the desk.

"Let me check this," Noah hissed as he pulled the device free again. "This bastard will screw with my electronics."

"Why here rather than his room?" Travis mused, wondering why Macauley didn't have the device in a place he wouldn't be caught using it.

"Security," Noah stated. "Harrington obviously uses it. If it were found in his room, he'd have to explain it. Besides, these puppies are damned hard to acquire."

Noah attached it to another device he had with him.

"Can you bypass it?" Travis asked.

"Maybe," Noah answered. "I'll try, but it sounds to me like we're not going to have a lot of time here."

"Then we better hurry," Travis growled. "The next time, Lilly's luck just might run out."

And that he couldn't allow to happen.

Travis simply couldn't imagine his life without Lilly, which made her a very dangerous weakness.

A weakness he knew he could ill-afford.

"Got it." Noah quickly replaced the device, then stored his own in a pocket of his pants. "Let's roll."

They left quickly and made their way back to Noah's room. Travis left the house just as dawn began to brighten the sky and he couldn't help but stare up into Lilly's window.

The lights were on and he had no doubt she was reading the report Harrington had received.

And she was alone.

There was no one to soften the shock or the blow being dealt to her. He wasn't there to hold her. He wasn't there to make it easier.

No matter what the doctors said, he thought, Lilly would remember everything soon, and when she did?

There would be hell to pay.

CHAPTER 5

THE NEXT MORNING Lilly lay in her bed, the hefty report given to her the night before still lying beside her, the pages scattered haphazardly across the bed.

She stared at the ceiling, dry-eyed, a frown pulling at her brow as she considered the information she had been given.

First, she had been suspected of killing her father because she had disappeared.

And second, according to the investigator—a rather reputable one—Lilly had been a high priced whore available only to certain clientele. Clientele requiring a well trained lover rather than a helpless one. And she evidently hadn't cared if the clients were legitimate businessmen, or those considered highly illegal. Criminals, suspected terrorists, or international CEOs. She had been hired out to the best of them.

Lilly had been trained in Israel, Pakistan, China, South America, and Mexico. The training she had received, secretly, through MI5, before her supposed death, paled in comparison to the eighteen-month course she had taken to become part of Santos Bahre and Rhiannon Mc-Connelly's stable.

She and the three other girls she was known to work with were considered four of the most elite whores in the world. Wow, she should be impressed with herself, she thought sarcastically. She had gone from society princess to exclusive call girl. And she hadn't stopped there. Hell, no, when she wasn't playing "eye candy" for whoever paid for her services, then she was having fun causing trouble elsewhere. It was no damned wonder someone had tried to kill her.

She had been in more than one hot spot in the world with Travis Caine, who seemed to have required her services extensively. As a matter of fact, it seemed that outside of "business" they were actual lovers as well. Lovers who caused trouble wherever they went. In more than one instance, they had started fights that had nearly gotten them killed.

It sounded like she had had a hell of a lot of fun.

Except it just didn't ring true.

There were pictures of her with Travis Caine as well as several other men. Men known for their rather subversive criminal activities. Weapon sales, drug deals, terrorist negotiations, the list went on and on. She and the three other girls were reputed to be not just highly experienced sexually, but also rather enthusiastic when it came to creating or cleaning up the messes their lovers were involved in.

The men whose identities had been included in the file seemed too familiar. Santos Bahre, Travis Caine,

Micah Sloane, John Vincent, and Nikolai Steele were the most familiar. There was something about their pictures that pricked at her missing memories.

The pictures and the locations looked familiar. The pictures themselves appeared to have been taken from security footage from hotels and restaurants. Those would have been easy enough to come by. Once the investigator had a name, and a picture of her, he could have tracked many of her movements, as well as her associations.

The pictures of the men in the file had her eyes narrowing, though.

These men she and the other three women seemed to have the most association with.

John Vincent was a "broker." Though he often brokered legitimate deals, he was also suspected to broker not so legitimate deals. Deals that often involved high-priced, top-secret stolen arms or information.

Nikolai Steele was a suspected assassin. He'd been questioned many times in regards to those activities, but there had never been enough proof to tie him to a kill. He also hired himself out occasionally as a bodyguard and was known to work often with Travis Caine and John Vincent.

Then, there was Travis. "The Facilitator," he was called. He brought together products, services, or clients. He facilitated major business deals, matching buyers, sellers, and brokers.

He was also suspected to do the same with less savory clients.

Each man had, more than once, required Lilly's or one of the other girls' services.

Somehow she couldn't see the very possessive, very

dominant Travis Caine standing idly by while Lilly slept with his bodyguard.

Then, there were the women.

Nissa Farren, Raisa McTavish, and Shea Tamallen. She couldn't rid herself of a feeling of urgency where they were concerned. There was something she should know about them. Something she was supposed to do, and she couldn't pull the memory free.

That bothered her more than the fictional information that she had been nothing more than a troublemaking whore. She knew better. She knew who she had been before she had disappeared six years ago, and she would have never elected to take money for sex, especially considering that she had been a virgin at her supposed death.

So then what was the truth?

For a while, she had entertained the thought of demanding explanations from Travis, but something told her she didn't want to do that. She felt a wariness about bringing her suspicions to anyone, as though she knew instinctively that at the moment, she couldn't trust anyone.

Rising from the bed, Lilly pulled the file together, pushed it back into the large envelope, then moved to the small safe in the wardrobe closet across the room. Locking the report safely inside, she turned and moved to the bathroom.

The large mirror beside the three-head shower reflected her image back at her, a face she still wasn't certain of, eyes that were the wrong color. Her chin was slightly more pointed than it had been, her eyes had less of a tilt than she remembered, her cheekbones were a little flatter and her nose more rounded.

Why? That question wouldn't leave her mind. Why had she gone to such extremes to hide?

And who had she been hiding from?

Or had she, as others supposedly suspected, killed her father and attempted to fake her own death?

She had loved her father. She had adored him. It wasn't possible that she had harmed him. Just as it wasn't possible that she could have been some high priced call girl with an adrenaline addiction.

Then what the bloody hell was going on?

Stepping into the large cubicle, she quickly showered as she considered her options. It was a very short list. Looked like Travis was her only choice.

Dressing quickly in a pair of cream-colored silk slacks and matching top, she pushed her feet into stylish sandals and put the articles she needed from her bureau into a tan leather purse. Slipping downstairs quickly, she headed to the narrow hall at the back of the house and into the garage.

The electric-red Jaguar rented for her use was parked in its bay, the keys hanging in the ignition.

Sliding into the driver's seat, she hit the automatic garage door opener, waited for it to slide open, then started the car and pulled out.

Her mother would go ballistic. No doubt Desmond had someone following her. The fact that he did so bothered her. There was something different about the way she felt about him now versus her feelings for him in the past.

He had been her beloved uncle. He had spoiled her all her life, but there was a distrust now that she couldn't seem to shake.

Actually, she seemed to distrust most people now.

She drove to the house Travis had taken her to the night before.

She was hurting. She felt as though her insides were being shredded by that report. As though her soul were cringing in shame.

He was the last person she should run to . . .

But she needed the sense of security she had felt in his arms the night before. She needed the mindless pleasure, a few stolen moments to forget that whatever or whoever she had been for six years, that others had seen her as a whore.

Clenching her teeth, she turned into the driveway and pulled the car to a stop. As she turned off the ignition, she wasn't surprised to see Nik as he opened the front door and stepped onto the wide stone porch.

Long white-blond hair was pulled back from his imposing features. Icy blue eyes stared at her as a small smile tipped his lips. He just didn't seem to be a man she would sleep with.

Familiarity gleamed in his eyes, though, as well as in his expression.

Tightening her fingers around her purse, she moved up the short walk to the house and stepped onto the porch.

"Is he here?" she asked, her brow arching inquisitively.

"He's been waiting for you for several hours." Nik nodded. "I'm surprised you escaped your uncle so easily, though."

Lilly shrugged at the comment. "I didn't try to escape, I merely walked out."

And strangely, no one had seemed to notice. That was odd in and of itself. Since her return, her mother had been waiting for her each morning when she came from her room. Some mornings, she'd actually brought her breakfast in bed. This morning, though, the house had seemed deserted.

"Come on in, Lilly." Nik stepped back, his large, muscular body shifting with animal-like grace as she stepped past him.

The front room he led her through was the modern, upscale room she had met Desmond in the night before. Beyond that was another living room, just as cold and uninviting. The short hall was warmer, with honey-toned wood floors and tall windows on one end. Turning into another room, Lilly was pleased to see the décor change. This was an area she hadn't seen the night before.

This room was carpeted in a rich dark honey brown, the walls were a soft pale green, the cherry furniture was polished to a warm hue with large cushiony chairs, a sofa and a couch, arranged beneath a skylight.

"Nice," she commented when Travis rose from the couch to greet her.

He was dressed in jeans and a loose white shirt. His feet were bare, his demeanor relaxed though he seemed tired. He seemed more approachable than he had the night before, and he had been very damned approachable then.

She tossed her purse on a table as she passed by it, strode across the room, and, much to her own surprise, moved to him, lifted herself against him, and sealed her lips to his.

It was like a narcotic she had to have.

Immediately his arms went around her, his head tilting, his lips slanting over hers, as sensual, sexual need began to consume her.

She could stop, she assured herself though a part of her knew better. He truly wasn't vital to her. But she didn't want to stop. She was suddenly starved for the taste of him, the touch of him. She didn't feel as though a part of her had been ripped from her very being when she was in his arms. She somehow felt complete, which made very little sense if even half the report she had read the night before was correct.

At that moment the report was the farthest thing from her mind. This wasn't a business deal. His kiss, his touch, had nothing to do with money, or selling any part of herself. It had to do with a need she didn't want to reject, didn't want to turn away from.

For four months she had seemed to exist within a void. She had been lost, too uncertain, too confused. Until Travis had dared her to come to him, she'd had no idea how to face each day.

She'd had no idea who or what she was.

The memories were still hidden, but that part of her she hadn't understood finally made sense. The part of her that ached for touch? Because she missed her lover.

The part of her that seemed restless, imprisoned? Because she sensed a freedom that didn't exist within the life she had led before six years ago.

She wasn't Lady Victoria Lillian Harrington any longer.

She wasn't the person in that investigator's report either.

She was Lilly Belle. And Lilly had waited far too long to claim the man she ached so desperately for.

As Travis's kiss consumed her, his tongue stroking across hers, his lips sealing hers, Lilly felt emotions surging inside her that she wasn't certain what to do with.

Heat and hunger held her now. As his hands moved beneath the thin sleeveless top she wore, his callused palms and fingers stroking against her flesh, she knew she might not survive the day if she didn't get more.

So much more.

She wanted to lie beneath him. She wanted to feel him pressing her into a bed, his body covering her, his possession of her burning through her sex.

Feeling the material of the silken shirt dragging over her breasts, Lilly lifted her arms, moaning as he released her lips to pull the silk over her head.

It was tossed aside negligently as her fingers attacked the buttons of his shirt, quickly pushing it over his powerful shoulders as her lips went to his neck, his upper chest.

She could feel the muscles beneath her lips flexing as pleasure surged through his body. His hands were just as desperate as hers as they stroked over her back, then allowed one hard palm to cup her breast through the lace of her bra.

The pleasure of it drew her tight. She lifted closer to him, pushing her breast more firmly into his hand as his fingers began to pluck at the tight peak of her nipple.

"Travis." She whispered his name imploringly as his lips moved to her neck, spreading stinging kisses along her flesh as he suddenly lifted her.

A second later she found herself on her back on the

couch. The cool material of the cushions stroked against her shoulder blades as he came over her, his thigh pushing tight and hard between hers until it was wedged firmly against her pussy.

Her clit swelled and throbbed with impatience. Her juices dampened the swollen folds and the silk of her panties, the friction causing her to grind her sex against the hard muscle of his thigh.

This was what she needed.

Her neck arched as his lips moved to her breasts, his fingers pushing the material of her bra to the side until they encased the swollen mounds and pushed them closer together.

Tight hard nipples begged for his touch, his kiss. They ached for the stroke of his tongue and the suckling pressure of his hot mouth.

She had told herself on the drive over that she was coming here for answers, but that wasn't all she needed from him.

This was what had haunted her through the long, lonely nights for the past months. This hunger, this need for the touch of one man.

"Damn you," he growled, pressing closer to her, the hard length of his cock, separated by their clothing, pressing into her lower stomach as one hand gripped her hip and urged her closer.

His lips were at her breast, stroking over a nipple, heating it with the slight velvety rasp of his lips as Lilly shuddered beneath him. The pleasure was like a stroke of electric heat along her nerve endings as it raced to her clit to flare with vibrant sensation.

"Damn me?" she groaned back at him, her fingers

burrowing into his hair. "You tortured me all night. This was all I could think about."

Well, the majority of it anyway. There was that pesky little detail that she was a suspected call girl, but that had only taken her imagination into other avenues. Avenues that had led directly to Travis's arms.

"That wasn't torture," he breathed against her nipple. "This is torture." His lips opened over her nipple, sucked it inside and sent her pulse racing.

His tongue was like a lash of pure sensation, licking, stroking, causing her body to arch as she fought to get closer to the incredible agony of pleasure.

It wasn't supposed to be like this, she was sure. She had never heard her friends describe sex in a manner that could have warned her it could be this damned good.

How had she forgotten this? How had she lived without it for the past few months?

She couldn't live without it again. She needed him. She ached for him. It was like a ravening beast inside her, a hunger she couldn't deny any longer.

"So good," she whispered, a low wail of unsated desire echoing through her voice as her clit began to throb in hard demand.

Her juices spilled from her pussy, dampening her panties beneath her slacks, causing her to rub herself tighter, harder, against the muscular thigh pressed against it.

His tongue rolled around the extended tip of her breast, his teeth raked against it, sending an incredible storm of sensation racing through her bloodstream.

One hand cupped the swollen curve of the breast he was suckling while the other smoothed down her side, to her hip, then her stomach. Deft fingers released the hidden button to her slacks, then rasped the zipper down slowly.

She could almost feel the heat of his fingers moving closer to the needy flesh of her pussy.

His body shifted, the hard pressure of his thigh easing as his fingers slipped past the elastic band of her panties. The callused tips rasped the soft curls between her thighs, then with exquisite care parted the heated, wet curves that ached for his touch.

"Oh yes," she breathed out roughly, her hips arching. "I want your fingers, Travis. Please . . ." Her head ground into the cushions of the couch beneath her. "Please, fuck me with your fingers."

A hard groan tore from his lips. His fingers delved into the slit of her pussy, then two pressed together and thrust firmly into the clenched, tightened opening.

Travis was dying of lust. The feel of her pussy, so hot and wet, gripping the tips of his fingers, was almost more than his dick could bear. He wanted inside her, then and now. He wanted to tear the clothes from her body, slide between her thighs, and fuck her until they were both screaming in ecstasy.

Instead, he was feeling her snug sex as it clenched around his fingers and her juices flowing to meet the shallow thrust.

Twisting his wrist, Travis began burrowing deeper, stretching the tender portal open, amazed at the near-virgin snugness as the delicate tissue and muscle clenched tight around his fingers. How much better would it be when he finally managed to get his cock inside her?

Pushing in deeper, Travis forced himself to release

the captive bud of her nipple to draw in a hard, deep breath. Then, he simply watched her face come alive as he began to fill her pussy with his fingers.

Stroking inside her with tight, forceful thrusts, Travis found himself entranced by the emotions washing over her expression. She had always kept herself in such tight control in the past that it was often impossible to know what she was feeling, if she was hurt, angry, or happy.

There was no mistaking the pleasure on her face now. Her neck arched with it, her eyes were slitted, staring back at him in pleasured agony as he fucked the sweet portal of her pussy with two fingers while raking around the delicate bud of her clit with his thumb.

She was more responsive now than she had been so many months ago when he took her virginity. She was arching beneath his touch, driving his fingers deeper inside her, her hips flexing, grinding into each thrust he made inside her.

The snug depths of her sex milked his fingers as he stroked inside her, rippled around them. Her juices flowed like sweet, hot honey, slickening his fingers with each thrust.

Taking her like this was agony and ecstasy. He could watch her face, watch the pleasure that darkened her eyes and tightened her expression. But his cock was raging, demanding, throbbing inside his jeans with a voracious desire nearly impossible to control.

He had so very little time with her this afternoon. The first test of her memories that the Elite Ops was demanding would begin here, today. They knew she would end up back here once she read the report Desmond

Harrington had been given by the investigative firm he had hired. She was being watched. The second she had left her home and driven toward his house, the plan had been put into effect.

What he hadn't expected was to have her walk into his arms and take what had been on his own mind since the night before. The passion burned brighter between them now than it ever had. It had always simmered, burned, but now it flamed with a white-hot heat he couldn't avoid. As though Lilly had decided for herself what she wanted, and how she was going to take it. She was a woman tired of waiting, whether consciously or unconsciously, and a part of him realized he had been dying for her to reach out and take it. Unfortunately, now that she had, he didn't have the time he needed to revel in it.

"Damn." The groan was ripped from his throat as he pulled back from her, sliding his fingers slowly, so slowly, from the incredibly hot depths of her pussy.

His cock throbbed in objection, his balls were drawn agonizingly tight beneath the shaft of his erection.

"Travis." Silken hands gripped his shoulders, sharp little nails pricked against his flesh. "What the hell is your problem?"

It was almost laughable. He wanted nothing more than to fuck her silly, but he was damned if he'd do it in front of an audience. And unless he missed his guess, they'd be there any second—

"Travis, you have company." Nik knocked on the door, the sound causing her to flinch as Travis shot a murderous look toward the entrance.

Hell, this was just what he needed right now. His woman lying hot, silky wet, and willing beneath him and company on the other side of the door.

Grimacing, Travis pushed himself to his feet and stared down at her as she hurriedly fixed her clothes. Her face was flushed, breasts heaving; the hard points of her nipples were easy to detect beneath the thin silk blouse she wore.

Her soft lips were swollen, her hair mussed around her face. She was so damned pretty he had to clench his back teeth to keep from going back to her.

"Remind me to check your schedule next time before I decide to visit you," she snapped, her voice low. She looked presentable again. "You have too much damned company at inappropriate times."

He grunted at that, ran his hand around the back of his neck, then strode to the door and jerked it open.

"Travis." Santos Bahre, co-commander of Elite Two, stood on the other side, along with his partner, Rhiannon McConnelly.

Santos was six-three, had dark hair brushed back from his face, a neatly trimmed beard and mustache, and he wore a gray silk suit and white shirt, paired with expensive leather shoes. He was every inch the suave, debonair Irish pimp he portrayed.

Beside him stood his counterpart and co-commander, Rhiannon McConnelly. The madam to his high-class pimp. The cover they had created was perfectly designed to allow the female agents they oversaw to work closely with the covert agents sent in on specialty assignments.

"Santos, Rhiannon." Travis stepped back, wishing

there were some way to warn Lilly, to guide her through this.

If she remembered her commanders at this point, then they were fucked. The risk to the Elite Ops would be too high to allow her to stay in the game.

"You have company." Smoothly cultured, Rhiannon's voice was friendly and warm as she entered the room, her gaze going to Lilly.

They knew she had seen the file. They knew Lilly was aware of the report the investigator had compiled.

Travis turned in time to watch her face pale, her green eyes darken, widen, as she stepped back into the room.

"I'm leaving now." Her voice trembled as she cast him a look filled with betrayal. "I won't be back."

Good. Lilly thought she was coming face to face with her pimp and her madam, not her commanders. And she was searching for a way to leave, a way out of the room other than the one they blocked.

"Does she think we're here to force her back, Travis?" Rhiannon asked gently, her smile one of compassion and sympathy as she stared at Lilly. "What have you been telling this child about us anyway?"

"Child?" Santos murmured, the smooth hint of a brogue entering his voice. "You're only a few years older than she, Rhia love."

Lilly backed up further, her fingers moving restlessly at her thigh as though for the weapon she once wore there.

Instinct or memory? Travis wondered.

"I haven't mentioned you, Rhia," Travis assured her quietly as he watched Lilly, watched the pain and the denial that filled her face, her eyes.

He knew parts of her. Over the years, he had learned things he hadn't realized he'd known about her. One thing he'd learned was that Lilly had pride. Enough pride that it had gotten her into trouble more than once.

She couldn't see herself as a call girl, no matter how highly paid, no matter how exclusive or security-trained.

"He didn't have to mention you," Lilly spat out furiously. "My uncle has a full file on you."

"Then he must have one on you as well." Rhia stepped further into the room as she laid the red purse she carried on a side table.

The purse matched the red high heels she wore with well-creased silk slacks and a light cotton blouse. The shoulder-length dark red hair was brushed back from her face, her bangs skimming her brows.

She was classy and stylish. Pretty much exactly what Travis would have imagined a successful madam looked like.

"I'm leaving." She moved around Rhia carefully as she stared at the doorway Santos and Travis still stood in front of.

"They just wanted to see you, Lilly," Travis told her quietly. "You've worked with Santos and Rhiannon for over five years now. You're friends as well as associates."

"So Desmond's file says," she retorted sarcastically, as Travis sighed and stepped back from the door.

"Running won't help, Lilly," he told her softly, though he hoped she could read the message in his eyes to do just that. To run. To get the hell out of there before her past rose up and bit them both in the ass.

"I'm not running," she informed him sharply, fear

and anger showing in her eyes now. "And I'm not frightened. I'm simply refusing to be a part of this."

She edged around the room, watching them all carefully, her fingers still searching instinctively at her thigh for that weapon. He was damned glad she didn't have it; he had a feeling she would have shot them all.

"Lilly, you're running," Rhia said softly, her gaze never losing that innate compassion as she watched the woman she had helped train for so many years. "Surely you remember something about us."

"There's nothing to remember," Lilly snarled. "There are only the lies you had some investigator make up. What do you think you can do? Do you think you can blackmail me or my family?" Her nose lifted with aristocratic pride. "Trust me, lady, no one would ever believe Lady Victoria Harrington was little more than a whore. You're wasting your time."

"I believe I'm insulted," Santos drawled as she moved past him, watching him warily. "My girls have never been called such a thing."

The glare Lilly shot him should have withered him. Instead, with steady Irish charm Santos tossed her a wicked grin before extending his hand to the door. "We wanted only to say hello, my dear, and to let you know if you need us, we're here."

"I rather doubt I'll need you." The look she shot Travis assured him she wouldn't be needing him either.

She had passed the test. She knew who they were only through the report her uncle had given her. She hadn't recognized them, she hadn't remembered her past.

She slipped from the room. The sound of her heels

clicking on the marble floor could be heard just before the front door slammed closed.

Travis turned to Rhiannon, his brow arching.

Rhiannon stared back at him, her brilliant green eyes eerie, too aware, too knowing.

"She's hiding something, Travis." Her gaze hardened. "Find out what."

CHAPTER 6

LILLY STEPPED BACK into the house, smiling at the butler as he opened the door for her. The brightly lit marble foyer was warm and welcoming, but there was a core of ice forming inside her that she couldn't seem to dispel.

Moving quickly through the foyer, she pushed through the doors to the library, intending to confront Desmond with the information he had given her the night before. She hadn't expected him to have company.

"Victoria." Desmond came to his feet, a worried smile on his face. Lilly smiled when she saw who was behind him.

"Jordan," She said, coming forward and hugging him.

Jordan returned the hug. "I wanted to stop in to see you while I was in town. It's a miracle that you've returned."

"So my family tells me." She stepped back and restrained the need to rub at the chill in her arms.

"Your uncle mentioned you may have a bit of a past that could cause you some problems," Jordan stated, as

Desmond went over to the bar. "I wondered if I could be of help."

"Did he now?" She glanced at her uncle, noting the heavy breath he took as he lifted a bottle of wine from the bar. She was within seconds of asking for something stronger, only to quell the urge as she noticed Jordan's gaze sharpening on her.

"Don't be embarrassed," Jordan urged her. "Grief does amazing things to a young mind. Desmond is fairly certain you must have walked in on something that night, perhaps even saw your father's murder. He's concerned that you could be targeted because of that, or because of the information the investigator uncovered."

Lilly took a seat in the chair beside her, watching as the two men settled back into their seats before speaking.

"What, then, is the general consensus?" she asked. "Did I become a whore because I was grieving, or running from criminals or my own guilt?"

"Dammit, Victoria, no one believes you killed your father," Desmond bit out. "Quite to the contrary, I believe you were hiding, perhaps even frightened of endangering your mother."

Lilly sipped at her wine. "I've asked you before, Uncle, to call me Lilly."

Desmond grimaced but said nothing.

"The fact remains that no one would believe such a tale," Jordan stated quietly.

Do you want to live, Lady Victoria, or die forever? Jordan's voice. Jordan's face. Younger, less savage. The memory flashed through her head, sticking to her mind, and almost had her shaking her head as she tried to dispel it.

Memory or insanity?

"It's much easier to believe I was a whore, then?" she asked, her brow arching curiously.

Jordan's head lowered as her uncle looked away.

"Gentlemen, I have things to do today." Lilly got to her feet. She was finished with the conversation. "If you will excuse me, I believe I'll take care of those things."

She turned and swept from the library, ignoring her uncle's protest as she pushed the doors open and headed for the stairwell.

What did she have to do today except read that damned file again? That and try to understand why Travis hadn't warned her of the "company" arriving earlier.

Who could she trust? She had wanted to trust Travis so badly she ached with the need.

No one, her mind screamed. There was no one she could trust, and that was terrifying. She felt as though there was no place to turn, and no place to find answers.

"Lilly." Her mother stepped from the living room as Lilly was turning to the foyer and headed for the stairs. "Could we talk for a moment?"

Lilly pushed her fingers through her hair and fought to restrain the impatience roiling through her. "Is my room all right, Mother?"

The living room seemed too open, with too many potential ears listening.

"Of course, dear."

Lilly could see the nervousness in her mother's face, the hint of sorrow and pain that shadowed her eyes. She hated hurting her mother, but there was a part of herself that she couldn't help but hold back. There were too many secrets that she sensed she had to hold in.

Entering her bedroom, she turned and waited for her mother to enter. Immediately Angelica moved to the bedroom window, opened it, then pulled a pack of cigarettes and a lighter from the pocket of her slacks.

"Mother, you know you shouldn't smoke," she said, sighing.

"My one guilty pleasure," she said as she lifted the slender cylinder to her lips and closed her eyes in pleasure.

Lilly waited until she finished, knowing it would take only moments. When Angelica finished she moved to the bathroom, flushed the butt, washed her hands, then returned.

"Your brother called this morning." She smiled sadly. "He and the children are going to Hawaii this summer."

They usually joined the family in Maryland.

"He doesn't want to see me," Lilly guessed.

"So many changes." Angelica sighed as she sat on the edge of the bed. "Jared has never dealt well with change. He brooded for months when we thought you were dead. He can't believe it's you now, because the changes are so drastic, and there's no explanation for them."

Her mother stared at her as though she should have answers.

"I'm sorry, Mother." Lilly sat in the chair next to her bed and watched her mother as she ruffled her fingers through her perfectly streaked dark blond and brown hair.

"You read the report your uncle gave you, then?" she asked. "Did nothing trigger a memory, Lilly? Nothing at all?" She was so hopeful, so desperate, that Lilly wanted nothing more than to confide in her.

"Nothing," she whispered. "I'm sorry, Mother."

Angelica's hands twisted restlessly in her lap as she stared down at them for long moments.

"You've changed so drastically," she said softly as her head lifted, her pale blue eyes reflecting a glimmer of pain and tears that tore at Lilly's heart. "Sometimes, Lilly, it's as though I don't even know you."

Lilly swallowed tightly and forced back her own tears. "I'm still me. I don't know what happened, or why I changed so severely, but I'm still me. I remember shopping with you, crying with you, my coming-out ball and my first date. You cried each time." A tear slipped free. "Just because my face changed doesn't mean I'm not still your daughter."

A soft sob tore from her mother's lips then. She moved jerkily from the bed and in the next second Lilly found herself in her arms. Arms that had sheltered her, that had helped protect her.

In that moment, she closed her eyes and wanted to cry herself. She wanted her father. When she had cried, they had both held her; the warmth and acceptance of their embrace had always been all she needed to hold her world together.

Now, her world was torn apart, confusion and fear tore at her, had her holding tighter to her mother and fighting the need to confide all those fears in her. She wanted the easy, carefree relationship they had once had. She wanted the involved, complicated relationship she'd had with her father. She'd been his confidante and his partner, she had been her mother's friend, her brother's baby sister. Once upon a time, she'd had a full, happy life.

And she had no idea what had happened to it.

"You can talk to me, Lilly," her mother whispered tearfully as she drew back, her soft fingers easing the tears from Lilly's cheeks. "I'll always be here for you. I've always been here for you."

So why hadn't she let her mother know she was alive? God, what had happened to her?

"I know that, Mother." She had to fight back the need to confide, to tell her of the pieces of memories she had, to plead for her help in figuring them out.

Yet she couldn't. She couldn't allow herself to do it.

"Promise, if you need to talk, you will come to me, baby," her mother begged, another tear slipping down her pale cheek. "Please don't hide from me any longer. You're breaking my heart."

"I promise, Mother," she lied.

Lilly knew she couldn't go to her mother with whatever her past entailed. But until she knew what it entailed herself, then she wasn't even certain how dangerous she was to her.

And there was simply no one left to run to.

But Black Jack.

She almost froze in her mother's embrace.

Pulling back, she breathed in heavily. "I need to rest for a while, Mother. Perhaps a nap would help this headache that's brewing at the moment."

She rubbed her temples as though there were truly a headache coming on.

"Of course." Her mother kissed her cheek gently. "Rest, darling. I'll have the maid call you for dinner."

Lilly watched as she left the room, her heart thundering, her mind churning. Black Jack. She could trust

Black Jack, she thought desperately. The urge to do just that was building in her mind, beating at it.

Who was Black Jack?

Travis.

She could see him in her mind's eye, as he stood with Santos Bahre and Rhiannon McConnelly hours before in his home, a frown on his dark face. Green-flecked brown and gold eyes had been filled with concern, and a warning.

That was it.

She rubbed at the back of her neck, frowning now as she let those moments roll through her memories again. In Travis's eyes there had been a warning. But why? What had he been warning her of?

Santos Bahre and Rhiannon McConnelly. They were partners, according to the file she had, in a very profitable business. That business included providing women to a very select clientele. According to the investigator, the rates for the female companionship rose in relation to the level of danger the companion would face.

Had she been a whore or a very good mercenary? What the fuck was going on?

A part of her was screaming that she should run to Travis, that she should talk to him, confide in him.

Black Jack. It was a code name.

She fought to still the rapid beating of her heart, the fear that raced through her like a locomotive tearing out of control. She felt her breathing constrict, felt the warning flashing in her mind that she couldn't trust Travis any more than she could trust Santos Bahre, Rhiannon McConnelly, or Jordan Malone.

And yet another part of her was demanding that she do just that. That she trust him, possibly with her life.

I'll be here for you, Lilly. His voice whispered through her mind, seductive, alluring. But what she sensed about that voice was anything but seductive and alluring.

As she fought to pull those memories free, a sharp ache sliced through her temples as though in retaliation.

Dropping her head, Lilly pressed her fingers to the sides of her head and fought to breathe through the pain.

The headaches had been common the first month after she had been shot. The memories she had lost had seemed to be closer at that time as well.

Turning, she stared into the mirror and gazed into the same unfamiliar face—which was at the same time familiar.

Reaching up she touched the arch of her brow, the slender line of her nose, the curve of her lips.

She was becoming more accustomed to this new face, as though a part of her was finally accepting the changes.

Wild, her father had always called her. A woman poised on the edge of danger. And she had always laughed at him.

Going to the closet, she opened the door, stepped inside, and moved to the back. There, she had hidden a smaller suitcase inside a larger suitcase. She had found the small suitcase in the storage shed where she'd kept the motorcycle.

There was cash, bank records and checks, an alternate ID and credit cards, as well as a lethal Glock and a dozen clips of ammo. She had been prepared for trouble. A call girl wouldn't have done something like that; only an agent or a criminal covered their ass in such a way.

She tucked all but the weapon and the cash in a compartment of her suitcase. The weapon, clips, and cash she kept in the small leather bag and moved back to her bedroom to pull one of the outfits she had found in the storage shed from the back of the bureau.

She would keep herself busy during the day today. Lunch with her mother and her mother's friends. A meeting later to discuss the charity ball her mother co-hosted each summer.

But night was coming. Lilly could feel the restlessness surging inside her as well as a need to learn more about herself.

Hagerstown was familiar to her, as well as the surrounding area. There were pieces of herself here, she could feel it. She had planted parts of herself here, close to the area her family called home for several months out of the year.

Lilly needed to find those parts of herself. She had to find them, before the confusion and the need drove her insane.

It was midnight, Lilly's time of night. Travis waited on the street down from the gated property Lilly and her family were staying at, one leg folded over the breast of the bike, his elbow resting on his knee.

She was the restless type. The information she had received the night before as well as the confrontation with Santos and Rhiannon would push the buttons inside her that would send her searching.

Rhiannon predicted Lilly would hide for a while, that as a former agent she would sense that she shouldn't venture out quite yet. Travis knew better. He had trained

Lilly. He had forced her to have patience during the months she had undergone the psychiatric evaluations. He'd taught her how to deceive her commanders, how to hide her true self. He was an agent, he knew the dangers inherent in the type of work they were doing.

He trusted Jordan. His own commander had proven himself. He couldn't say the same for Santos and Rhiannon. They had created a cover for their agents that had never sat well with Travis or his sense of decency. Their girls were delicate, beautiful, better hidden than displayed. But they had placed them in the eye of danger in order to shield the agents they were often paired with.

They were a commodity to their commanders, nothing more.

Rubbing at the short growth of beard at his chin, Travis considered the best course of action in the coming game.

Travis knew Lilly knew more than she was letting on.

He also knew that she would realize that he wouldn't betray her, despite the appearance that he had done so with Santos and Rhiannon.

She had been shocked, furious, but he had also seen fear in her eyes. The fear that the investigator's report was true. A fear that somehow she had been the person described in that report.

It wouldn't take her long to piece the information together now, and Santos and Rhiannon knew that. And that made Travis wonder what the fuck they were up to.

The sound of gates easing open had his head turning. There, emerging between the slowly opening gates, was the gleaming black front fender of Lilly's powerful Ninja.

He pulled the helmet from the back of his own machine, eased it on, and strapped it beneath his chin before activating the Bluetooth communication set within it.

It was connected to Lilly's, a precaution they had begun using several years ago to ensure security when they met. He watched as she parked the bike, eased the gates closed, then ran back to the machine to straddle it.

She pulled the wicked black helmet over her head, tucked her hair inside, and secured it.

Travis chose that moment to strike.

"Are you ready to ride, Lilly?"

She froze. Across the distance Travis could sense her searching, finding, staring back at him.

"What do you want?" Wariness filled her voice.

"You," he answered her. "Are you following me or do I follow you?"

She didn't answer. The powerful engine kicked in. Travis followed suit and started his own bike with a flick of his wrist.

He was ready when she moved. She shot ahead of him like a rocket, a black shadow burning down the road, her lithe body lying over the breast of the bike, shifting and flexing with innate grace.

"It looks as though I'm following you then," he commented through the link.

"If you can." There was a chill to her voice that had a hint of concern brewing inside him.

"Easy, Lilly." He kept his voice casual, soothing. "I'm not a threat to you."

How many years had he worked to gain her trust? Definitely the entire time Elite One had been training her team. A full year. And during that time he had laid the foundation that he'd only built upon in the years after that.

"No, you're not a threat to me," she agreed. "And I won't let you become one."

She sped up as she took the exit to I-81. Traffic was moving quickly, but Lilly was moving faster. Travis stayed close behind her, his attention on their speed, their location, and the display in his helmet that would tag any law enforcement vehicles that could catch sight of them.

"Lilly, we're coming up on radar," Travis warned her as his display indicated the speed check ahead.

She eased back as they passed the first state police cruiser on the other side. Once he was clear, she shot back into high speed and continued to try to shake Travis.

"It's been nice riding with you, Lilly," he told her five minutes later as she hit 71 and began to head toward the state line. "I'd hoped we could talk."

There was silence for long minutes.

"I have a cabin." Her voice was low now, confused, breaking his heart with just a hint of tears. "I have a cabin, Travis," she repeated.

She didn't sound broken, she didn't sound scared. She sounded lost, and that was harder to hear than the former.

"Slow down, Lilly, if you want me to follow you."

Instinct was all well and good, but she didn't have knowledge, not yet. Without knowledge of the powerful machine she was riding, instinct might not be enough to keep her alive.

Ahead, she slowed until he caught up with her. Pulling in beside her, he glanced over to see nothing but the black shadowed visor pulled over her face.

He heard her breathing hitch, though, and he sensed her tears.

Lilly wasn't a crier, he'd learned that. She would lift that stubborn little chin and hold back the tears if it meant death. She had a backbone of steel and a sheer iron-strong core of determination that had had him clenching his teeth in frustration more than once.

Following her along the highway, he crossed the state line out of Maryland into Pennsylvania with her, staying silent as they made their way toward the West Virginia line.

Their absence would be noted, but he'd been ordered to figure out what she was hiding. That was his mission and that was where he would lay the blame for his disappearance. He just hoped she'd been smart enough to cover her ass with her family.

No doubt she had. No one had ever accused Lilly of being stupid.

Her voice was hollow in the link. "I know where I am. I know where to turn. What to watch for. I know I've been here before, but I don't remember why or when."

"Who am I, Travis?" she asked him then.

"A partner," he said softly, his gaze trained on the road as they took an empty exit and hit a narrow two-lane road.

The paved road soon turned into an unfinished lane, then gravel. They had to reduce their speed drastically, until they were creeping beneath the heavy branches of the sheltering trees that surrounded the lane.

Travis almost missed the turnoff to the cabin. He may well have missed it if he wasn't following Lilly.

They parked the bikes beneath a small garage at the

side. Swinging from the seat, he watched curiously as Lilly headed toward the entrance of the parking bay, reached up and pulled down the garage door before securing it to the ground.

She didn't speak, just turned and pushed open the heavy entrance door before stepping inside.

Lilly stared around the single-room cabin. A small gas stove, which explained the gas tank in the rough garage outside. A woodstove, a table pushed against the wall and two chairs, a large bed on the other wall, and a bathroom beyond.

It was a safe house, nothing more. It wasn't a home. It was a place to retreat and hide.

She turned to Travis, staring at him silently as he removed his helmet and set it on the small table by the door.

"Nice." He looked around before his gaze came back to her. "Have you ever stayed in the winter?"

Had she?

She lifted her shoulders in a heavy shrug. "I don't remember."

She was staring around her, knowing where everything was hidden. Cash, ammo, weapons, and clothes. IDs, phone numbers, a laptop, and disconnected satellite and cell phones.

There were canned goods in a tiny, narrow cupboard by the stove. There was a fresh underground spring that fed water into a well. There was hot water, clean towels, fresh water, and a measure of safety because no one had known about it but her. And now Travis.

She pulled the helmet from her head and stared around curiously. Who was the woman who had needed this refuge?

She turned to Travis. "A high-priced call girl wouldn't have a safe house, would she?"

She watched, her heart heavy, as he turned away and stared around once again.

"You're not going to tell me anything, are you? Can you tell me this? Why are you here? What hound do you have in this hunt, Travis?"

She watched his lips quirk. "It's been a long time since I've heard that phrase."

Her father had often used it.

"That doesn't answer my question," she told him.

He shook his head before staring back at her, his golden eyes dark now, concerned. "I can't answer your question."

"Who can, then?" she asked. "Somehow, I don't think my former employers can."

He snorted at that. "I wouldn't ask them."

She nodded slowly. "I'm in danger then."

"Someone tried to blow your head off, Lilly, what do you think?" he asked quietly. "You're in danger, there's no doubt about that. What *sort* of danger you're in is the question."

"And you can provide no answers?" she guessed.

"No," he finally said, sighing.

"It's a bloody messy situation," she bit out with a hint of the anger building inside her now. "Everyone's watching me, yet no one is willing to help me. What sort of threat do I represent, at least?" she demanded.

"The threat isn't the problem, at least not yet." He scratched at his jaw thoughtfully as he watched her.

"The assassin and the reason why he attempted to kill me is the problem then, correct?"

Travis nodded slowly. "If you remember, Lilly, if you remember anything, for both our sakes don't allow anyone but me to know it."

"Why you?" Lilly moved across the small room to the cabinets over the stove and pulled free a bottle of her favorite whisky.

Turning, she lifted the bottle to him in invitation. At his nod Lilly took two glasses from the cabinet, rinsed them, then poured the drinks.

"You didn't answer me," she reminded him as she handed him a glass. "Why should I trust only you?"

Travis stared back at her, seeing Lilly rather than Lady Victoria as she stared at him, her green eyes flat and hard.

"Because if you think about it, if you remember or suspect anything about the past six years, then you know there wasn't a chance in hell that I was the one to betray you."

She sipped at the whisky, her gaze never leaving his for long moments as she considered his answer.

"You suspect whoever killed Father and attempted to kill me six years ago managed to find me?"

"It makes sense to me." Travis shrugged his jacket off and tossed it to a nearby chair. "The day before you were shot, the doctor who supposedly did your plastic surgery was killed in a fire that destroyed his office and all his records. Somehow, someone has learned too much information about you, Lilly."

Picking up his drink, Travis watched as Lilly leaned against the counter, sipped her drink, and stared at him thoughtfully for long moments.

"Supposedly," she finally murmured. "Does that mean he didn't actually do the surgery?"

He inclined his head in agreement. "Certain steps were taken to ensure your identity was well hidden."

"That's a lot of trouble to go to for a high-priced escort," she drawled sarcastically.

Travis merely quirked his lips in amusement. She knew as well as he did that she had never sold her body.

She had shared her body with him, though. She had given him her innocence and formed a bond between them that he still didn't completely understand.

Finally, when he said nothing more, Lilly shook her head before finishing her drink with a small grimace.

"Then I need to find my father's killer to find my own," she stated. "I imagine that killer is also the person behind the embezzling Father was investigating six years ago?"

Travis nodded. "That's what I think. I suspect the killer has been tracking you for the past six years."

Lilly's quick little exhalation, a mocking sound, had Travis almost grinning. That sound normally indicated a flare of irritation.

"Father drove himself crazy searching for the person responsible for the embezzling." She pushed away from the counter and paced across the room, a thoughtful frown marring her brow. "And I have no doubt MI5 has continued the search."

"No doubt." Travis's gaze focused on her ass beneath the snug leather pants as she paced. The sight of it was enough to steal a man's breath.

"If Mother suspects I'm investigating what happened

six years ago, then she'll have me hospitalized for sure."
She shook her head, the silken strands of dark hair rippling against her shoulders, tempting his fingers.

"Did your father have any suspects?" Travis asked,
attempting to pull his attention back to the subject.

"Several," she admitted as she turned back to him.
"He just hadn't given me names. I was still being trained.
Certain information MI5 was hesitant for me to have.
Father followed those dictates."

"Did *you* have any suspects?" he asked.

Lilly paused at that.

"Lilly, now isn't the time to hold anything back," he
warned her.

Her arms crossed over her breasts defensively.

"There was no one person that tied into all the accounts
targeted," she answered, her expression mutinous. "My
original suspicions were way off base because of that."

"And they were?" Travis pressed.

"My uncle, Desmond, and my brother. Other than
my father, they had access to the Harrington funds that
were targeted but not to the other targeted accounts."

"Your brother Jared works for a very exclusive law
firm," he pointed out. "The clients targeted were also
represented by that firm."

Jared Harrington as well as his uncle Desmond were
still suspects as far as the Elite Ops were concerned.

"Yes, but not all of them. At least three other families who had no such connections were targeted as
well," Lilly said. "Besides, Jared wouldn't have done
such a thing. He especially would have never killed
Father."

"Yet you suspected him of embezzling," he pointed

out. "He and your father argued often about the business as well as about the title."

"Jared wouldn't kill Father . . ."

"You're defending a man who essentially disowned you." Anger surged through Travis at her defense of the other man. "Perhaps he wants you dead, Lilly. With you out of the way, he doesn't have to share the Harrington inheritance."

"Stop." He could see the pain glittering in her eyes now. "Jared wouldn't do it. I know he didn't because Father and I eliminated him and Uncle Desmond as suspects."

Travis's lips thinned. As far as he was concerned, Jared and Desmond Harrington were still at the top of the list.

"Stop!" She lifted her hand as his lips parted to argue further. "I'm certain I can easily prove Jared isn't involved. But to prove it, I'll first have to gain access to the family financial vault. It should be easy enough. I know Desmond and Jared share the online financial vault. I'll see what I can find."

But that didn't mean it wouldn't hurt to do so. Travis moved to her, the need to comfort her, to ease the confusion and pain glittering in her eyes, was overwhelming.

"Lilly." He drew her against him, his hands caressing her slender hips. "We eliminate Desmond and Jared and then go on from there. But make sure they have no contacts with anyone listed in that investigator's report on the past six years of your life."

His money was still on Desmond, but Jared was in the running.

"Check files and financial reports Desmond brought with him." He wanted her to find the information Desmond had in the office. "Go through the online vault. Get the account numbers and I can go from there. We'll do this together, love."

He reached up, his thumb caressing her trembling lower lip. "You know how to do this."

"Because you trained me?" Breathy, filled with sensual awareness now, the sound of her voice stroked over his senses.

"I trained you," he agreed.

"You protected me." She licked at his thumb, tempting him.

"I'll always try to protect you." His head lowered.

He needed a taste of her. A touch. For just a moment he needed to fill his senses with her.

Though he knew a moment would never be enough.

CHAPTER 7

IT WAS ALMOST A DREAM.

Lilly stepped into Travis's arms, felt them come around her, felt his lips slant across hers and the world around her go up in flames.

She couldn't have this man, and she knew it, but she knew she already belonged to him. She had somehow always belonged to him.

Lifting herself to his kiss, Lilly let her hands grip his hair, pulling at the coarse strands to deepen the kiss as she felt a raging hunger begin to burn inside her.

That wildness she remembered fighting all her life took control, she became a woman who instinctively knew what she needed and who she needed it from.

Never had arousal taken her like this.

Pulling her head back, she stared up at him, her breathing heavy, rough. "You were my first, weren't you?" She knew it, sensed it.

"I was your only," he growled, possessiveness raging in his tone and fulfilling some need she hadn't known existed within her. A knowledge, that final certainty, that she hadn't been the woman her uncle's report al-leged.

His head lowered again before she could voice any further questions, his lips took hers again, his tongue pushing past her lips, stroking over hers and locking her in a battle of desire that she knew she had no hope of winning. A battle she didn't want to win. It was a tri-umph she wanted to share.

She was only his woman. She had shared herself with no other man, just as she had known instinctively, but the woman inside had needed more proof. She had needed the verification that only one man could give her.

Black Jack.

Her hands fell from his hair to his shoulders, then the front of his T-shirt. Pulling, tugging, she dragged at the material until it came free of his jeans.

He shrugged his jacket away, allowing the cool leather to fall to the floor before his hands returned to push her denim jacket from her shoulders.

She wasn't moving her arms. She wanted that shirt off his back. She wanted to feel his flesh, naked and hot, against her palms.

He tore off the t-shirt then returned to her jacket, forcing her arms down and pulling the denim over it to reveal the sleeveless camishirt she had on underneath.

The slender straps cleared her head as he jerked the material from her waist, up, baring her breasts, and tossed the top aside. He filled his palms with the swol-len curves, his thumbs raking over the hard tips of her nipples and sending fingers of raw sensation to attack her womb, to heat her clit.

Lilly arched into the touch, a gasp passing her lips as

her back met the wall, and her palm flattened against the bare skin of his chest.

Curling her fingers, Lilly raked them down his chest, just enough to feel the flex of muscles beneath, to relish the heat and hardness of his corded body.

Her fingers rasped to the band of his jeans where she found the snap and zipper of his pants and quickly released them.

She couldn't touch him enough. She couldn't get enough of his kiss. She wanted to feel all of him against her at once. She wanted all the pleasure at once. She wanted to feel alive, something she hadn't felt for six months.

Alive. Living. A woman that had no part of her missing.

In Travis's arms, there was only the woman, there was no past, no danger, and there was nothing to fear.

"God help me, I missed you," he groaned as his lips tore from hers and moved to her jaw, her neck. "Missed seeing you, touching you."

A moan echoed from her chest as her heart tightened in a realization that she had missed him as well; even though she hadn't remembered him, she had missed him, achingly.

He was making up for whatever time they had lost though. His hands cupped her breasts, lifted them. His head descended, his tongue licking over the tight thrust of her nipples as shards of sensation began to tear over her nerve endings.

It was incredible. It was the fantasy that followed her when she slept, the one she awakened from, her body dampened with sweat.

This was Travis, and denying him wasn't something she could allow herself to do. Not this pleasure. Not this incredible, blinding heat.

Her fingers stroked into his jeans and found bare flesh. No tighty-whiteys, no boxers, just the hard, thick thrust of his cock pushing into her hand. The wide crest was hot to her touch, slightly damp. The heat of it sent a rush of pleasure flexing through her pussy as she felt his hand smooth from her breast, down her stomach.

His fingers worked her jeans loose as her hands stroked and memorized the iron-hard width and length of his cock. The more she touched him, the more she wanted.

Looking down, Lilly lost her breath as she watched his cheeks draw in, watched him suckle at the hard tip of her nipple. His eyes were slitted, staring up at her, the spark of green in the golden brown more intense now, glittering in his dark face.

Her knees were getting weak. Standing wasn't as easy as it had been when she first walked into the cabin, or when she had first seen him in Hagerstown. It made her wonder what she had felt when she had first met him, six years before.

Just when she doubted she could remain upright, his head lifted. He licked her nipple, first one, then the other. His expression was tight with hunger, with sensual pleasure, as he stared up at her, need glowing in his eyes.

Then he straightened to his full height, lifted her in his arms, and strode to the large bed with its old-fashioned quilt and large fluffy pillows.

Her head fell back on the pillow as Travis's hand moved beneath her back and cupped her shoulders, pressing her breasts firmly into the heat and hardness of his chest as his lips moved over her neck and breasts in heated, nipping kisses.

Arching beneath him, Lilly felt her blood boiling as pleasure heated her flesh and left her trembling. Within seconds he was moving down her body, removing her boots, his own. He shed his jeans, then smoothed hers down her legs, leaving her dressed in nothing but the contour-hugging soft cotton panties she wore beneath the jeans.

Standing at the bottom of the bed, he let her look her fill. He stood before her as her gaze roamed his hard body and paused at the jutting length of his cock.

Before he could come down to her, Lilly was on her knees. She saw the surprise in his face, though how he could truly be surprised she couldn't explain. Surely he felt the wildness rising inside her, the hunger burning deep and hot?

Travis watched as she came to her knees like a sensual, sexual little cat. Her back arched, her head lifted as she crawled to him, her green eyes narrowed as she licked her swollen, sexy lips.

She was the most exquisite sight he had ever seen. The sexiest thing he had ever known.

His breath caught as she came level with his dick, her tongue peeking out, stroking over the flared head with a hot, luscious lick.

"Fuck!" One hand buried itself in her hair as the other caught the base of his hard erection.

He saw it in her now, felt it in her. She was as wild as the wind, the sexy, sensual creature he had known existed inside her.

Holding her firmly, he restrained that fire, controlled it, and watched it burn brighter inside her as her lips opened over the thick crest and took it into the burning heat of her mouth.

Clenching his teeth, Travis only barely held back the groan of complete ecstasy as the inexperienced wonder on her face held him entranced.

Innocent though she might be, she knew how to drive him crazy. Her tongue stroked around the too-sensitive head as she sucked at his cock hungrily. The heated licks were a hot counterpoint to the firm sucks, to the warm moisture he was delving into as she took as much of his dick as she could into the wet, velvet interior of her mouth.

"Hell yes." He couldn't hold back the growl, the hoarse rasp of complete pleasure that tore from his chest. "Damn you, Lilly. Your mouth is like pure pleasure."

It was more than pleasure. There were no words that he could find for the exquisite sensations racing from his cock, to his balls, and up his spine. It was like being immersed in pure sensation, pure ecstasy. Undiluted with worry, danger, or upcoming missions. It was a pleasure that built upon itself, that intensified and filled him with a driving need for nothing but the pure heat of her body.

His thighs strained with the effort it took to hold back. He could feel perspiration building at his temple, on his shoulders. Heat surrounded him, burned through him. The effort it took to hold back, to allow her the time she needed . . .

"Fuck yes!" Her head lifted from his cock, slid down the shaft to the tight sac below where her tongue licked and stroked, played and wreaked havoc on his control.

Damn, she was making him crazy. Rapid-fire pulses of sensation raced through his dick, tightened through his balls, and tore across his nerve endings as he fought to enjoy it for a few more seconds.

Just another lick. Just another kiss of those satiny lips. Both his hands went to her head, his fingers threading through her hair. Short, agonizing strokes of his cock past her lips tested that final limit of his control as he fucked her sweet mouth, slow and easy.

He was on the edge. Holding back his release was nearly impossible but he had no intention of allowing it to end here. When he came, he had every intention of coming deep and hard inside her tight little pussy rather than the suckling heat of her seductive little mouth.

Ignoring her startled mewl of protest, he forced himself to remove his cock from the ecstatic grip she had on it.

"Not yet, minx," he growled, as she gripped his thighs and attempted to pull the hardened flesh back to her honeyed lips.

Gripping her shoulders, he tried to ease her back onto the bed. That wicked feminine smile that drove him insane crossed her lips. She resisted him, refusing to ease back.

Travis's eyes narrowed.

"I'm going to taste that sweet pussy before this goes any further," he informed her, his tone rougher than he intended. "I'm going to fuck you with my tongue, suck that hard little clit, and feel you unraveling to my mouth before I fuck you."

Her gaze glittered, the green flaming as her face flushed with heightened arousal.

"Sounds like a rather tall order." Still on her knees, still so tempting, so seductive and demanding, she blew his fucking mind.

"Sounds like a plan to me." Before she could evade him he had her on her back, struggling halfheartedly against him, a light, arousal-filled laugh leaving her lips as he forced his way between her thighs.

Before she could push him back, before she could distract him, he wedged her thighs farther apart, then laid his lips and tongue to the sweetest honeyed flesh he had ever known.

Her juices were slick and hot, like the finest syrup, glazing his lips and tongue as he bestowed kiss after kiss to the intimate folds. He sucked her clit into his mouth, tasted, laved it with his tongue, and lost himself in the intoxicating taste and heat of her.

Lilly stared at the ceiling, dazed, submerged in sensations that washed over her with the force of a tidal wave. Spreading her thighs wider, she tangled her fingers in his hair and lifted her head, watched and became mesmerized by the complete sexual absorption on his face.

This was paradise. It was pure ecstasy. His tongue licked around her clit, flicked the tender bud, causing her to jerk with an excess of sensations.

"Travis." The little cry came unbidden from her lips as pleasure raced through her system. It wasn't confined to the area he was kissing so intimately. The pleasure tore across her nerve endings and invaded every cell of her body.

Perspiration sheened his flesh as well as hers, as her juices glazed his lips.

He parted the swollen folds with his fingers, and his tongue licked, laved, loved. It circled the clenched opening to her pussy, flicked inside only to retreat as her hips jerked closer in a silent plea for more. Always more. She could never get enough.

She arched beneath him, her hips lifting to his lips, watching as slowly, so slowly, he licked to the aching center of her pussy, then, slow and easy, pushed his tongue inside her.

A long desperate wail left her lips. Her fingers tightened in his hair, trying to force him closer as she felt his tongue inside her taking quick shallow licks that stroked and caressed nerve endings she hadn't been aware she possessed.

It was incredible.

Heat surged inside her, built around her. White-hot, blinding pleasure exploded inside her with a force that had her arching tight and hard to his lips, her pussy flexing around his tongue as she cried out his name, held on to him, relinquished control and gave herself to him.

She was still flying. Ecstasy still held her in its grip when she felt him move between her thighs and thrust inside her with a fierce, hard stroke.

The forceful, immediate stretching of tender muscles, the pleasure-pain that tore through her, brought her higher. Shock widened her eyes, rapture tightened her body, as he pulled back and began working inside the tight grip of her climaxing pussy with powerful strokes that pushed her deeper into ecstasy, flung her into a white-hot center of pure pulsing sensation that refused to release her.

Travis was dying. Sweat dripped down his face as he buried his cock inside her to the hilt on the fourth stroke. The orgasm that held her in its grip tightened her pussy to a near-painful snugness that had his release threatening to explode out of his control.

Pushing inside her again, he stilled, grimaced, and fought not to come. Hell, he was going to come. His balls were so tight they were painful, the sensitivity in his cock was near agonizing. He wanted to fuck her forever but he knew if he didn't come soon he was going to die of a stroke.

Her pussy rippled around him, the ultratight muscles clenched and gripping, milking him with ever-increasing little tremors that stole his mind.

He was lost in a world of such sensual pleasure that nothing mattered but the moment and the woman. He was bound to her, more than just physically, more than just his cock buried inside the tightest, sweetest pussy he had ever known. He was bound to her soul, and he knew there was no way to escape.

Flexing his hips, he moved, dragging the fiercely throbbing length of his shaft back before thrusting inside her. Slowly. He couldn't go faster, not yet. One wrong move and he was gone. He'd never manage to feel her pulsing around his cock in release again, he'd spill into her without thought.

Without thought.

He shook his head. He fought to pull free of her.

Condom.

There was a condom in his bag. Across the room. Clear across the room.

"Lilly." He groaned her name as her legs wrapped around his hips and held on tight. "Baby. No condom. I forgot. Fuck."

She shook her head as he tried to pull back again.

Her eyes opened, deep green eyes filled with mystery, with promise.

"Fuck me, Travis. Harder. Oh God, I'm so close . . ." Her hips churned beneath him. "I'm so close."

And she was. He could feel her tightening beneath him again, feel her pussy heating further, her juices slick and hot as her entire body seemed to flush beneath him.

"Lilly." The protest was halfhearted at best.

Never had he had taken a woman without protection. Never had he filled a woman with his come, even the wife that had betrayed him. He had never given that much of himself.

Lilly already held all of him.

Throwing his head back, he gritted his teeth and let go the last measure of control he had held on to. Fucking her with desperate driving strokes, he felt his release building, heating, threatening . . .

Lilly exploded beneath him. A long, low wail of completion filled the cabin as he powered into her again, again, driving her through another orgasm as fierce, as deep, as the first.

Her pussy flexed around his shaft, stroked it tighter, gripped him, milked him, sucked his release from him with such a violence that he knew he had lost himself inside her forever.

Burying in deep, hard, he gave in to the fierce, white-hot spurts of semen as it began to jet inside her. The more he gave her the more her pussy tried to milk from him. It rippled and gripped, stroked and sucked at his cock until he was shaking, shuddering, certain he would never survive.

When it finally began to ease, as the strength seeped from their bodies and left him collapsed over her, fighting just to breathe, Travis began to wonder at exactly what point he had lost his heart to her.

With his head buried in the pillow next to hers, one hand gripping her hip, the other buried in her hair, he tried to tell himself he could control this, even though he knew he couldn't.

He felt her lips at his shoulder, her breaths shuddering through her body, then he finally felt her relax. He knew the moment exhaustion took her, eased her into sleep, and left her completely vulnerable in his arms.

He had taught her years ago to never leave herself vulnerable to a lover. A lover could be a killer. He could be the enemy in disguise. He hadn't taught her that he loved her. He hadn't taught her that he could be her greatest enemy.

But there she was, slipping into sleep, as he eased away from her and forced himself from the bed. A mumbled protest left her lips as he padded to the sink, dampened a small towel in warm water, then returned and cleaned her gently.

Spreading her thighs, he ran the warm cloth along the swollen, reddened folds of her sex, cleaning her juices and his come from the tender flesh, amazed at the complete trust she gave him as she continued to sleep.

How long had it been since she had felt safe enough
to sleep? he wondered. How long since Lilly had felt
safe, period?

After cleaning himself he moved to the bag he had
dropped at the door and pulled his weapon and a spare
clip from inside. He moved back to the bed, eased her
beneath the quilt, then slid in beside her and pulled her
into his arms after tucking the gun beneath his pillow.
She cuddled against him with an innocent trust he was
certain he should lecture her about later. After all, he
was supposed to be no more than the wolf in sheep's
clothing. The enemy posing as the lover.

Smoothing her hair back, he let his eyes close and let
himself sleep. It wasn't a deep sleep, not here, not yet.
He didn't know if there was security here, he didn't
know the area, but he knew Lilly and he knew she protected herself. For the most part.

Once they were dressed and ready to face the day,
then they would have to discuss this night, and they
would have to face the implications of what the night
had wrought.

Until then, she was sleeping in his arms, against his
heart. And for now at least, she was his totally. The Ops
didn't matter, the mission be damned. For now, he was
just a man holding his woman, and he wanted every
moment that he could steal.

CHAPTER 8

LILLY WALKED THROUGH the wide double doors of her family's home the next afternoon to face the combined disapproval of her mother and her uncle.

"Where have you been?" Her mother was smoking again. This time, she wasn't bothering to hide it. The cigarette was held between her fingers as she glared at Lilly furiously. "Do you know I was ready to call the FBI? For God's sake, Lilly."

Guilt seared her. She should have called, perhaps left a note. Travis had lectured her about that.

"I'm sorry, I needed time to think." She lifted her shoulders in an uneasy shrug as her gaze shifted to Desmond.

He was furious. His pale blue eyes glared back at her as he crossed his arms over his chest. The muscles beneath his fine cotton shirt bulged, attesting to the anger that flushed his ruddy complexion further.

"Where is your mind?" Angelica turned and stalked back into the family room, her head held high, the sharp odor of tobacco following behind her.

"I would suggest you step into the family room," Desmond bit out between clenched teeth. "Running and hiding will do you little good this time."

Lilly arched her brows. "I'm twenty-six, Uncle, not six," she informed him.

"Then perhaps you should start acting your age," he retorted as he, too, turned on his heel and followed her mother.

She really wanted to do just as he had told her not to. Run and hide. Facing her mother's wrath had never been a preferred sport as far as she was concerned.

Blowing out a hard breath, she pushed her fingers through her hair before following the two. Entering the room, she moved toward the bar first, ignoring her mother's muttered curse as she reach for the whisky.

"That is a gentleman's drink," Angelica reminded her. "It is not a drink for polite young ladies."

"I'm no longer a polite young lady," Lilly told her.

Pouring a shot, Lilly tossed it back quickly, her eyes fluttering at the pleasant burn that hit her stomach. Come to think of it, she distinctly remembered the fact that a glass of wine normally accompanied any conversation with her mother. Angelica was a dominant personality, and not always easy to get along with, even for her children.

"The least you could do is show me the respect of telling me when you will be out playing your foolish games all night," Angelica snapped behind her. "It would keep me from informing the FBI that my daughter has been kidnapped again."

"Kidnapped?" Lilly turned back to her mother. "I wasn't kidnapped the first time, Mother."

Angelica tamped out her cigarette in a nearby ash-tray before staring at her daughter disdainfully. "And how do you know? Have you remembered the past six years?"

"Why, no, I haven't," she stated clearly. "But I think I would know if I had been kidnapped, Mother."

"I rather doubt you would," Angelica told her, her voice cold and brittle.

Lilly lifted her shoulders in a shrug. "According to the investigator's report, I had quite a bit of freedom in the past six years. I can't see kidnappers allowing their kidnappee to carry a gun. And I don't remember a mention in that report of a ransom being demanded."

Lilly propped her elbows on the bar behind her and stared back at the couple.

"I'll call Dr. Ridgemore first thing in the morning," Angelica said between clenched teeth. "Clearly you need help that I cannot provide."

Ridgemore? Lilly stared back at her mother in shock. She was well aware of who and what Dr. Ridgemore was and what he did. He was co-owner and head psychiatrist at Le Fleur in France, a psychiatric hospital where her mother's cronies often sent their children for evaluations when they were considered unruly.

"Mother, that isn't a mistake you want to make," Lilly stated gently. "After all this time apart, do you truly want to make sure that I never return to this family again?"

Le Fleur was the bane of every child's existence among the social set Lilly had once been a part of. If they disobeyed their parents, they were sent to the hospital. If they became dependent on drugs, tried to marry someone their parents disapproved of, made any decision on their own, then they were shipped off.

It wasn't every family that practiced such heinous decisions, but there were more than a few. They couldn't handle their children, so obviously something was wrong with the child, not the parent. In Angelica's case, the threat and the concern were very real. When one of her family members didn't conform something *had* to be wrong with them.

"As you seem determined to get yourself killed, it seems the preferred alternative," Angelica responded furiously. "You read the report Desmond received on you, Lilly. Did you even consider the repercussions such a life could have on your family should it become known? Do you even care?"

Her mother's voice rose on each sentence, fury filling each word as her fists clenched at her side, her face flushing a delicate, rosy hue.

Once, Lilly would have been desperate to appease her mother. There had been a time when she had known nothing but fear of her mother's rages. Not because she would hit her, or even punish her, but because with it came the censorious silences, the lack of an allowance, the car keys taken, friends turned away at the door.

How childish each of those punishments seemed now. If only she had no more to worry about than lack of an allowance.

"I'm sorry, Mother, I can understand how that investigator's report could affect the family," she stated, resignation filling her.

Her mother would never let her live that report down. It would never matter what the truth eventually turned out to be; the fact that there was the slightest hint of impropriety attached to her name was enough to ensure Angelica never forgot that her daughter had been accused of such a thing. Or that that accusation could become public knowledge.

"I very much doubt you gave your family a moment's thought during the years you were away," Angelica charged. "Had you cared even a bit, then you would have at least let us know you were still alive."

Pain filled Angelica's voice then.

"Perhaps I was trying to protect you, Mother." Lilly couldn't imagine any other reason. "Have you considered that? Someone killed Father and obviously tried to kill me."

"Which only tells me you were somehow involved in his asinine little games," Angelica threw back furiously. "Were you, Lilly? Is that what nearly got you killed? Please, God, tell me your father hadn't drawn you into that paranoid probe he launched into Harrington's?"

"Mother," Lilly said wearily, not wanting to get into this with her. She had been outraged when her father suspected his own share holders of stealing from the company. The shareholders had been friends.

"Actually," Desmond breathed out roughly. "We suspect your father had developed a bit of dementia perhaps. I mean, to think that someone within Harrington's or perhaps a shareholder, was still embezzling funds from the companies. He refused to accept that whoever had stolen the money had gotten away, or that they were no longer trifling with the accounts."

Dementia?

Lilly stared back at her uncle as she fought to hold in

her shock. There was no way anyone could have believed her father had been ill.

"Father wasn't ill," she finally stated, the feeling of betrayal that filled her centering on her uncle. "Is this how you convinced Mother to marry you? By spreading such lies about Father?"

"Lilly!" Angelica gasped. "How dare you say such a thing."

Lilly shook her head as Desmond's lips thinned, his gaze narrowing on her angrily.

"Evidently, Father was dealing with much more than I knew before his death," she informed them both tightly. "How could you have believed for even a moment that Father was ill?"

Angelica stared back at her for long moments, her breasts rising and falling quickly as tension thickened further in the air.

"You have no idea what you're talking about," Angelica finally whispered. "You didn't see him as he truly was, Lilly. You saw your father, and as a child, you excuse inconsistencies."

Lilly lifted her hand to halt the coming tirade.

"I refuse to discuss this supposed illness," she snapped. "You and I both know there was nothing wrong with Father other than a family that obviously refused to believe in him. And I well understand how he felt if you were so bold as to question his sanity to his face. My God, Mother, simply because we dare to oppose you or because we create a few waves doesn't mean we're in any way mentally deficient."

"No, but when you throw away a title, wealth, and a stable home for the life you lived for six years, then there is no doubt in my mind that you were mentally unbalanced," her mother shot back loudly. "Did you read that file, Lilly? Did it even connect in that selfish little brain of yours what you did to us for six years? You deprived me of my daughter. You deprived yourself of your family. For what reason? At least give me that. Why would you do such a thing?" She was yelling by the time she finished. Her mother's voice and expression were filled with such tormented fury that Lilly had to fight the tears that filled her eyes.

"I don't know," she whispered painfully. "If I knew, Mother, then I would tell you."

But would she?

Even as the words came out of her mouth, Lilly had a feeling she wouldn't tell her mother the truth. Whatever had driven her away from her family would have had to be a threat to them as well.

"That's all well and good." Desmond's shoulders tightened as he once again crossed his arms over his chest. "That doesn't change the fact that your actions now are unacceptable, Lilly. You have gone irrevocably wild since connecting with Travis Caine again. This association must end immediately."

Lilly blinked back at him. She had the most insane urge to laugh in both their faces.

"I'm no longer sixteen, Uncle Desmond," she told him calmly. "Travis is a connection to the memories I've lost and whatever drove me from my family. Ending that association is not an action I'm willing to take at this time."

She had a feeling it wouldn't be an action she was

willing to take at any time, but wisely refrained from making mention of that fact.

"I warned you she would refuse to listen to reason," Angelica said. "Caine has somehow managed to bewitch her."

"Oh my God, Mother." Lilly did laugh this time. "Bewitch me? This isn't the Middle Ages, you know, and Travis Caine isn't some sort of wizard."

"He's a criminal is what he is," her mother argued. "An element that has always attracted you. You were forever attempting to converse with the less desirable elements that attended any party you were invited to. No matter where we went it seemed you were attracted to the shadows. I warned your father you would come to a bad end if that habit continued."

Arguing with her mother was fruitless. She and her father had often discussed her mother's inability to ever admit she was wrong, and the trials in loving one who perceived that they had no faults.

"Lilly, you're not fully healed," Desmond said softly, his expression still filled with censure as he watched her. "Until you're well enough to understand the decisions you're making . . ."

"Don't patronize me, Uncle Desmond," she warned him then. "I'm not a child, nor am I a simpleton."

"Then stop acting so foolish!" her mother said.

"I've had it." Lilly turned for the door and began walking across the room. "This discussion is over."

"Don't you dare walk out on me, Victoria!" her mother demanded furiously. "I won't have it."

Lilly ignored her.

Striding from the room and up the stairs, Lilly couldn't help but wonder if perhaps her uncle had somehow managed to deceive her father. Or worse, could he have killed his brother?

Stranger things had been known to happen, she thought. Desmond had obviously wanted his brother's wife. Desmond had never married. He had no children. He had dedicated himself to his brother and his brother's family. Or had he simply dedicated himself to his brother's wife?

That was sickening. The thought of it had her stomach churning as she stalked into her bedroom, slammed the door closed, and locked it.

Could Desmond have actually killed his brother?

God, she couldn't imagine such a thing. And knowing her mother's complete obsession with appearances, she simply couldn't imagine Angelica would have gone along with something so horrible.

That didn't mean she hadn't done it.

Pacing to the window, she stared beyond it into the shadowed, cool depths of the gardens below and fought to make sense of what was going on around her.

It was obvious Travis felt Desmond or Jared was involved in her father's death, and the attempt on her life as well.

Now, why would a "facilitator," a man who was no more than a criminal, really, care about proving whether or not anyone was involved in anything?

She frowned at the thought. That didn't truly fit the personality of the man known as Travis Caine. A bloodmonger. A man who had no problems killing in the name of his so-called job.

A mirthless smile twisted her lips at the thought. He acted more like an agent than a criminal.

But he'd made several good points. One being the fact that her father had trusted her with much more information than anyone had ever suspected.

Part of that information were the login and passwords for the Harrington financial vault that they kept on a secured server in the Harrington Manor.

She turned and stared at the laptop on her desk.

It wasn't secured. Anyone could have tapped it and could spy on any information she pulled up. She needed the ability to secure it, and she needed to do so quickly.

Was anything in this house secure though? She turned slowly, her lashes lowered, her gaze taking in the areas that could possibly hide a camera. Finding electronic bugs would be much harder . . .

The memory flashed in her mind. She had stored a secured laptop as well as a variety of devices used to detect audio or video surveillance.

She remembered wrapping them in protective pouches and placing in the cabinet that sat in the corner.

Sitting down on the bed, she pulled her boots off, careful to keep her demeanor cool. Something warned her that her bedroom was indeed bugged in some manner. She was more prone to suspect the audio versus the video, though. Not that video bothered her over much.

She almost laughed at the thought. She had visited the French Riviera more than once and made use of the nude beaches there. She had never been particularly shy about her body, just rather picky about sharing it.

She would slip out tonight and get the items she

needed. She could manage a few hours without getting caught, just not another all-nighter.

Strange, she felt no sense of trepidation about spying into her family's finances. A part of her was too determined, too intent on finding whoever had murdered Father and was now determined to kill her.

She was a threat to someone. Enough of a threat that they hadn't been convinced she had died in that car crash. They had gone looking for her, and somehow, they had managed to find her.

That had been yet another mistake on their part.

The first had been in killing her father.

The second in forcing her back here to the life she had obviously walked away from.

As she headed for the bathroom and a shower, a low knock sounded on the door.

"Yes?" Turning, she watched the door as it opened slowly.

"Fresh towels, ma'am." The petite housemaid entered the room, her arms laden with towels as she moved for the bathroom.

Lilly stepped back as the young woman moved into the bathroom. Dressed in the customary gray skirt and white blouse her mother insisted on for the house servants, she moved quietly and as unobtrusively as possible.

Servants were forced to just about tiptoe around her mother. Her mother believed that servants shouldn't be seen or heard unless there was no other choice.

"Thank you." Lilly stood back as the young girl moved from the bathroom once again.

"You're welcome, ma'am." A shy smile and the maid scurried from the room, closing the door quietly behind her.

Lilly shook her head at the girl's skittishness before entering the bathroom herself.

She laid out a towel and clothes before turning to the shower and adjusting the water. Stripping her clothes, she tossed them to the counter before pulling open a drawer for a hair clip to hold her hair out of the water.

The folded piece of paper lying on top of the clips had her pausing and staring at it suspiciously.

Pulling it free, she unfolded it carefully and stared at the words printed there.

Discretion is the better part of valor in any game.

Remember who you are, but never forget what you were, because that will be the only way to survive. Now, please, be kind enough to flush.

Her eyes narrowed on the last line before she glanced at the toilet and sighed heavily before crumpling the paper to a small ball and doing as requested.

It wasn't as though the note held surprising information. She was well aware that she needed to play a more subtle game than she was currently playing—that of learning who she was while keeping her family unaware. She hadn't been doing a very good job thus far.

For the rest, she just might be screwed. She remembered well who she had been before the past six years; it was after that that she had a bit of a problem. If her survival depended on remembering who she had been during those six years, then she was definitely screwed.

Now, if she could just find a way to force those lost

memories free, then perhaps the answer to finding who had killed her father, and who was trying to kill her, might lie there.

One thing was for certain, she was going to have to remember soon, or she would end up truly dead, rather than simply pretending to be.

CHAPTER 9

TWO DAYS LATER Travis rode his Harley into a deserted warehouse lot and eased into the old brick building with its cracked and shattered windows and decaying wood doors.

The team was waiting for him. Noah, John, Micah, and Nik were lounging on their cycles while Jordan waited in the black SUV, the passenger's side door open as he watched the entrance with narrowed, neon-blue eyes.

His driver was the red-haired little hellion who seemed to drive the commander insane on the best of days. Tehya was the jokester of the unit, the agent that wasn't really an agent but an integral part of the unit nonetheless.

As Travis pulled the bike to a stop amid the semicircle created around the SUV and swung off the seat, he wasn't surprised by the air of speculation that seemed to emanate from the group.

The three married agents, Noah, Micah, and John, were watching him warningly. They had tried to warn him over the past days about the deepening involvement between him and Lilly, but it wasn't something he wanted to hear. Warnings weren't what he needed. What he needed were solutions, and he hadn't found any yet.

"I have to get back by evening," he informed Jordan as he approached the men, who were now standing by the open door. "I've been invited to the Harringtons' estate by Lilly for a little get-together they're having."

"The French ambassador." Jordan nodded. "He's a good friend of the Harrington family. Desmond and the deceased Harold Harrington were classmates of his for several years at Eton. The party is an excuse to discuss business with their American counterparts in a setting where their wives can also participate."

"A dress-up party," Nik snorted.

The Russian knew well the type of parties the Harringtons frequented. Like Travis, he'd been to several get-togethers hosted by the Harringtons or those of their social set before his induction into the Ops.

Nik had been a member of Russia's political and social elite. He'd been a husband, a father, and a man on the fast track to a leadership position until he had pissed off the wrong political group.

Nik and Travis seemed to have that in common. Once, they had been a part of society, they'd had power, wealth, and ideals. Those ideals had been the cause of their "deaths."

"So why are we meeting here instead of at the safe house?" Travis turned to his commander, then glanced around the warehouse casually. "And I notice Elite Two's Commanders aren't here."

Santos and Rhiannon had the potential to become pains in the ass, if anyone wanted his opinion.

"This Op is under the jurisdiction of Elite One, just as their agent is," Jordan reminded him, his tone brusque. "They're only allowed in an advisory position. And we're meeting here to ensure that that status remains uncorrupted." The tight, merciless smile that pulled at Jordan's lips was telling.

Well, now, wasn't that surprising. Travis bet that wasn't sitting well with Rhiannon in particular.

"Commander McConnelly is making waves," Jordan continued. "She contacted Elite Command last night to report that she believed, based on the meeting three days ago with Night Hawk, the viability of the mission is in jeopardy. I was in a vid-conference with them this morning with my own report."

"And what was your report?" Travis asked, trying to hold back his suspicions and his anger.

"I didn't throw her to the wolves if that's what you're asking. But get Lilly under control, Travis," Jordan growled. "You and I both know she's regaining partial memories. Make sure she doesn't become a danger to the Elite Ops or the order for cancellation will go out, Travis. She's a civilian now. Elite Command won't let her walk around with bits and pieces of our secrets in her head."

That was what Travis liked about Jordan. He was a hell of a commander. He played by the rules laid out by the head of Elite Ops, Elite Command, and did the job he had taken on, but he also understood people and his men in particular.

"From all appearances he has more than a handle on her, Commander," Micah, the Israeli contribution to the unit, said. "She's been sneaking out of the estate every night and heading to Black Jack's after Travis's butler goes to bed, and strutting back into the estate the next morning as though her family weren't in a rage because of it."

And they were screaming with rage, Travis was sure of it. Desmond Harrington had demanded, more than once, that Lilly terminate her liaison with Travis, and each time, she had refused.

"Elite Command's psychologist doesn't believe Lilly's going to be able to keep that calm demeaner she has much longer," Tehya said at that point. "Dr. Lasal has been reviewing the reports sent in by each of you, as well as Jordan's and Commander McConnelly's. She believes the parts of Lilly's memories that are being repressed may be about to break free. She doesn't expect that her memories will return in full, though. Bits and pieces could be more damaging than remembering nothing, Travis."

Travis shook his head, his lips to curling in a mocking sneer. "Lasal's intentions are good, but she worries too much about things that may not happen," he growled.

"Her cover was breached, Travis," Jordan reminded him quietly. "We were lucky to save her. But Elite Command and the Ops can't risk discovery. She's a weak link. If there's any chance she'll expose the Ops, then she'll be canceled. None of us want that, but we can't allow her to become a risk to the unit either."

"I agree with Travis. She was a damn good agent," Noah pointed out then, "Personally, I think if she gets her memories back, she won't spill our secrets."

"Are you willing to bet Bella's and little Nate's lives on that, Noah?" Jordan asked, referring to Noah's wife and infant son. "I'm not certain I am." Jordan had been Noah's uncle in that life before the Ops. He still retained that blood tie with his nephew, and reminded him of it whenever he needed to.

"It's hard to bet Bella's and Nate's lives on anything, Jordan," the other man stated coolly now. "But I'm not the only one here who has had to depend on Night Hawk to pull their ass out of the fire. We owe her more than suspicion and a promise of cancellation once this is over. No matter what her commanders want."

"That also brings up a still unanswered question," Nik said. "How was her cover breached? Doesn't make sense that someone would target a call girl, no matter how exclusive she is. But they knew where to wait for her, they knew how to strike, and yet the investigation into the breach seems to have stalled."

Nik's eyes were on Jordan as he spoke, the accusation in his voice clear.

"I'm still working with Elite Command on that angle," Jordan assured them. "Senator Stanton is particularly concerned about the matter. If the Ops is compromised, then it will jeopardize his career, and possibly endanger his daughter's life."

Elite Command was a group of shadowy figures who were the financial and center of operations for Elite Ops. The only member of that section that any of them were given the identity of was Senator Stanton. A contact point, Jordan had called the senator. If all else went to hell, Stanton was a man they could depend on because his daughter was married to the team that provided backup to Jordan's team, Elite One.

Stanton's son-in-law, Kell Krieger, was one of the

former Navy SEALs that had provided backup on many of the missions the operatives were sent into. Discovery would reveal his family to the enemies the Elite Operatives had made over the years. Enemies that thus far had no idea who or what had taken them down. If they ever learned, then the SEALs as well as the operatives were guaranteed dead. And there would be no coming back.

"Then we have no idea how her identity was leaked, who attempted to kill her, or what we can expect from this operation. Right?" Travis's frustration leaked through in his voice, as well as his control. He was riding an edge with Lilly, and he knew it. Just as he knew Lilly was riding a particularly dangerous edge herself.

"We're hoping Lilly's presence with her family will draw the killer out of hiding," Jordan revealed as his gaze focused on Travis. "Have you sensed any movement or uncovered any new info?"

Travis shook his head. "All we have is the information Noah and I found the night we wired the office."

That information was incriminating enough. As far as Travis was concerned, Desmond was involved in something up to his eyeballs. He just wasn't entirely certain that something was the death of his niece.

"There's no information circulating among our contacts either," Tehya stated. "We're in the dark here. Our only hope is Lilly at this point, and that the killer is tempted to go after her again sometime soon."

"Third time is the charm," Jordan said and Travis glared at him.

"Lilly is the only operative of the entire Elite Ops organization who has been targeted in the eight years the organization has been running," Tehya stated. "Any other hit that's been attempted has always been in relation to an operation. That's not the case here, otherwise chatter would reach our contacts."

"That doesn't mean the Elite Ops isn't endangered by this," Nik said. "Whoever tried to kill her killed the plastic surgeon the Elite Ops placed her file with. Despite that safety measure, they still found her. That's not a good thing. If they found Lilly, they could find any one of us."

None of them wanted that. They had left their old lives behind and had no desire to have them resurrected.

"Morganna, Kira and I have initiated an investigation into Santos and Rhiannon as well," Tehya announced. Morganna and Kira were the wives of two of their backup members. "So far, they're coming up as assholes, not traitors."

Jordan snorted at that.

"Yeah, well, that's what we call Jordan on a good day, too." Noah chuckled.

"The responsibilities of command isn't all fun and games," Jordan drawled. "Santos and Rhiannon have responsibilities to their agents just as I do. And Lilly isn't their only agent."

"No, she's ours now," John Vincent stated, his gaze turning to Travis.

Travis turned back to Jordan. "She's always been one of ours," he stated.

And that was no more than the truth. In some ways all of the girls of Elite Two were a part of Elite One. They had trained them, watched over them. Lilly's move to the American-based operation could merely make it official. And if they survived this mission, it was a move that would definitely be made by Lilly. Travis would see to it.

Jordan shook his head. "You're making a mess for yourself, Travis." Though his tone was filled with disgust, Travis detected the smallest note of something akin to envy in Jordan's voice.

"I'll try to keep the mess to a minimum," Travis promised.

Jordan leveled a hard, aggravated look at him. "You do that, Black Jack. And let me know if she remembers anything."

Travis remained silent.

"If there's anything I need to know, Travis, now is the time to tell me," Jordan advised him. "I'm giving you the benefit of my trust by covering her ass, so at least do me the courtesy of making certain you do as much for us."

He shook his head. "Her memories aren't coming back, Jordan."

"Great," Jordan muttered. "Let's just get this over with and take care of whoever the hell has targeted her as quickly as possible. I'd like to get *my* commanders off my ass even if you don't care."

"Where do we go from here, boss?" Nik asked as he leaned against the SUV and stared back at Jordan. "That party will have most of our players there. Hell, it's just about the same invitation list that comprised the party the night Lord Harrington was killed."

"That's normal." Jordan sighed. "We've been watching the Harrington parties for years now, an operative from one of Elite's teams has always been in attendance. We've learned nothing. Whoever killed Lord Harrington did so quietly and without a trace. Except for his daughter."

"It's a damned miracle Lilly wasn't killed." Nik grunted. "If Travis hadn't been at that party that night, then she wouldn't have had a chance."

Jordan's smile was vaguely mocking as he shrugged negligently. "We were lucky."

"And now she's at risk again," Micah stated as an uncomfortable silence descended on them. "The assassin will be waiting for another opportunity. There's no doubt of that."

"Why hasn't he tried yet then?" Tehya piped up again. "He's had every opportunity, why is he waiting?"

"I'll be certain to ask him once we catch him." Travis snorted. "Until then," he checked his watch with a grimace, "I have a party to prepare for." He turned to Nik. "As do you."

Playing Travis's bodyguard was often more amusing for Nik than true work. The bastard had a morbid sense of humor and he never failed to make use of it whenever he had the chance.

"Roll out." Jordan nodded to the open doors. "The backup team has kept an eye on your exit, but we have to be careful here, too many people know Ian and Kell. Speaking of which, I believe they'll be at your little ball along with Senator Stanton."

Just what Travis needed—a member of Elite Command breathing down his neck. But if someone had to be there, at least it was Stanton. He could halfway make sense of the senator's motives. Sometimes.

Lilly was waiting for him when he pulled into his garage nearly an hour later and shut off the Harley. Lounging back on the breastplate of her own cycle, her legs crossed and dangling over the back, she pushed the dark sunglasses down her nose and watched silently as he swung off the machine with slow, lazy male grace.

Damn, he was sexy as hell in black leathers. Lean, powerful legs flexed and spread as he faced her, causing the bulge between his thighs to become more prominent. A dark t-shirt stretched over his chest beneath the leather jacket, and heavy riding boots covered his feet.

He hadn't worn a helmet and his hair was windblown, and the short, neatly trimmed growth of beard on his face gave him a sexier, more dangerous appearance. His eyes narrowed as she continued to watch him silently, and he crossed his arms over his wide chest.

"What's on your mind, Belle?"

"Leaving so soon, Belle?"

She saw the hotel room, knew where it was, saw the man, naked, sprawled out in the bed, his eyes narrowed, his expression somber.

He was her lover. He had been her first lover, and as she stared at him, she wondered why was he the only man she ached for?

"It's time to go, Black Jack." She had to fight her tears. She didn't want to leave the nice warm bed, the even hotter man, or the sense of security she found in his arms. "Nothing lasts forever, does it?"

She opened the door and stepped out. The plane was waiting for her. She had a vacation coming, just a few short days, and she wanted to go home . . .

It was gone. As quickly as the slow play of the memory began in her head, it stopped. But unlike previous memories, this one stayed. It didn't tease her. It didn't erase itself just as quickly as it had flashed in her mind.

But she remembered the emotions, the tears she had fought to hold at bay. How she had been torn between staying with Travis and going off for a few short, miserable days of hiding, of watching the family she had lost during the short vacation she had been given.

"Lilly? Are you okay?" She still stared at him as he tilted his head, his gaze so penetrating, as though he were trying to see inside her head, to track whatever thoughts were shifting through the shadows of her mind.

"I'm fine." She shot him a quick, sexy glance as she fought to cover the lapse in her control. "You have a rather odd habit of making a girl want to live in a fantasy forever."

She shrugged her own leather jacket from her arms. She hated riding without it, but suddenly, the temperature in the garage was stifling.

Not that shedding the jacket helped. As the leather fell to the seat of the cycle, Travis's gaze flared at the sight of the camisole top she wore, minus a bra.

Her nipples were tight and hard, the full curves of her breasts suddenly swollen and sensitive. They ached for his touch. She ached for his touch. There wasn't a cell on her body that wasn't suddenly clamoring for the feel of him.

As though that memory and the aching loneliness

she had felt within it needed to be soothed. She never wanted to feel like that again. She never wanted to be torn between the need to feel his arms around her and the need to spy on a family she couldn't be with.

She had to fight back the tears now. The family she had ached for, that she had missed with such desperation, barely spoke to her. There was a wall between them. Her mother looked at her and they didn't see Lilly; her mother didn't see her daughter, she saw the call girl the report said that she had been.

And her brother. She had idolized her brother, Jared, yet he had turned his back on her at the hospital and hadn't spoken to her since.

She moved closer to Travis, to the warmth and acceptance she had always felt from him. He had never asked her to be anyone other than whoever she wanted to be at any given moment.

That knowledge was there as she watched him, as he watched her, and the silence grew between them. It wasn't a memory, it was simply something she knew.

As her breasts brushed against his chest, his hands lifted, stroked from her shoulders to her elbows and back. Lilly couldn't help the slightest breath that expelled from her lungs, or the pleasure that raced through her arms at his touch.

"I missed you," she whispered as she leaned her head against his chest, suddenly seized by emotions she didn't quite know what to do with. "Why have I missed you so desperately, Travis? Were you truly such an integral part of my life?"

She asked the question, but she sensed the answer.

"Things stood in the way, Belle," he whispered, affirming what she had known to be the truth. "There are still things that stand in our way."

"Yet you're here, now." Lifting her head, she stared back at him and wondered if she should hide the emotions tearing through her. Wondered if she had done so before. Had she hid herself? Could she have given herself to him while still maintaining a shield between them?

"I'm here now." He cupped her face, his palm warm and rough, his fingers callused and so very strong. "I'll always be here when you need me, Lilly."

"I need you now." Her hands lifted to the edges of his jacket, pushed until it slid over his shoulders and fell to the cement floor beneath their feet.

Running her hands to the band of his jeans, she pulled and tugged at the t-shirt until it came free, then pushed it over the hard contours of his tight abs before her fingers moved to the snap and zipper of his pants.

He was watching her. Was he wondering what she would do? Had she always been so daring, so adventurous with him?

She must have been. She could feel a hunger that she didn't want to attempt to control, that she had no power over, rushing through her. Like a tidal wave, it washed away the protests in its path and left all but the raging hunger crumbling in its path.

Parting her lips as his head lowered, Lilly watched his eyes, watched the darkening pupils, the hunger that filled them. She wasn't alone in this need. It lived there inside him as well, almost an entity all its own and impossible to deny.

His lips covered hers, a hungry growl passing them just before that first second of contact and infusing the heat beginning to burn inside her.

Her fingers slid past the parted edges of the leather pants. The broad, heated shaft of his cock met her fingers, overfilled her palm and had her thighs clenching in need.

Her pussy rippled in hunger, as she remembered the feel of the heavy shaft stretching her, filling her, pulsing arrows of incredible sensation striking at the very heart of her sex. Her clit was swollen, her juices running thick and hot to coat the swollen, intimate folds.

Pleasure rolled over her in waves, one right after the other, as his kiss fueled an already naked hunger. His hands weren't idle either. As her fingers stroked and caressed the silk-over-iron shaft of his cock, his fingers had lifted her top, bared her breasts, and played her nipples like a master musician.

It was incredible. It was always incredible. Each night she came to him, each night he touched her with such deft, sure strokes of his hands, Lilly found herself becoming more and more entrenched in the ever-deepening emotions that roiled through her.

She was falling in love with him.

No, she had already been in love with him, she just hadn't allowed herself to realize it, or to accept it. There had always been a tie, a bond that had been unbreakable between them.

Her head tilted back as his kiss became harder, hungrier. His tongue swept past her lips, played with hers and sent her senses spinning out of control.

Looping her arm around his neck, she held on for

dear life as the kiss seemed to sear to her very soul. Flames licked over her flesh, tortured her nipples where his fingers stroked, plucked, plumped the tight tips.

The sensation of his fingers on her nipples raced straight to her womb. Electric pleasure surrounded her clit, whipped around it and shot rippling fingers of destructive need into the heart of her pussy.

Her fingers tightened on his cock just enough to drag a strangled moan from his throat as his hips shifted and fucked the hardened flesh against her grip.

The thick, heavy crest was damp with precum, sliding against her fingers, slickening the head of his cock and heating her fingers.

Lilly swore she could never live without more of him. There was a dark, hungry core inside her that consisted of nothing but the aching need for his touch. His hands cupping her breasts, his thumb and forefinger pulled at her nipple as his lips jerked back from hers and moved to her neck.

Tilting her head back, Lilly couldn't stop the whimpering little moan that came from her. His lips were so heated, his teeth raking sensation upon sensation against flesh that suddenly seemed much too sensitive.

Her nipples hurt, they needed his touch so desperately. They were swollen and hard, pushing toward him, the gnawing hunger to feel his mouth drawing on them tormenting her.

"What do you want, baby?" he groaned, his lips caressing the valley between her breasts. "Tell me, Lilly, what do you want?"

"You know what I want." Her fingers speared into his hair, gripped and pulled until his lips were poised over her nipple, so close that the feel of his heated breath over the tight peak sent shivers racing down her spine.

His tongue peeked out, licked, and then they both froze.

They moved in sequence. The training Lilly knew but didn't remember kicked in instinctively at the acrid scent of explosives flaming behind her.

She tried to turn to confront the assailants, but found herself thrown to the side, Travis's hard body covering hers, as the explosion suddenly ripped through the air.

Her motorcycle.

"Move!" Travis was scrambling, his fingers brutally tight on her arm as he dragged her the short distance to the entrance of the garage. A line of flames was licking at the sleek black frame of his own ride.

They fixed their clothes hastily, their hearts racing, adrenaline pumping through their bodies.

There was no time to get to the cycles or to stop what was coming. Wild-eyed, Lilly was on her feet, choking on the fumes as the garage door opened slowly, too fucking slowly. She watched as the greedy flames licked at the gas tank of Travis's cycle now, the interior of the garage, moving higher.

"Get out!" The garage door opened just enough to allow them to drop and roll to the other side.

They were on their feet, racing for the side entrance of the house, when the second explosion tore a huge hole in the side of the garage, catapulting debris and flames. Lilly dug her feet into the grass and sprinted for the door.

Turning at the doorway, they watched as wood, metal, and sparks rained down on the yard. The garage had little in it to burn. Thankfully the Hummer he kept in there was out for service and the Jag was parked out front or the resulting explosion would have taken out part of the house.

"Get in." The door opened and Travis was pushing her inside as he jerked his phone from the holder at his side. "It's Travis. Get the fuck over here."

He disconnected the call and turned to face her as he pushed her into the kitchen.

Nik and Henry were racing through the hallway, coming to a hard stop at the sight of them.

"Stay here, Henry," Travis barked. "The bikes just went up in flames. I've called for a cleanup crew." He turned to Nik then. "Explosives. Get out there and see what you can find."

Nik moved past her, his pale blue eyes like frozen chips of ice, his hard corded body pumped for action.

She turned to Travis, realization suddenly racing through her. "Attempt number three," she whispered. "I'm starting to get the feeling someone doesn't like me, Travis."

And that someone had to have been in her home, the only place her cycle could have been accessed. The only place anyone could have planted the explosives.

And once again she had been damned lucky. Someone didn't know what the hell they were doing obviously, or she and Travis both would have been dead.

As Lilly turned, stared around the kitchen and fought to get her bearings, she began to wonder if she would ever be safe, and if this was the reason she had deserted her home, her family, and her way of life for six long years.

To live.

CHAPTER 10

STRIKE TWO.

Lilly stood in Travis's kitchen, her arms folded across her breasts as she leaned back against the counter, one ankle crossed over the other.

She lounged, she thought, and she watched.

She especially watched the black-garbed, black-masked men that moved through the garage and the house. No law enforcement personnel were present. The situation was being carefully contained.

And that didn't surprise her. She was standing back, munching on a stalk of celery, watching, waiting, thinking.

This was the third attempt on her life. First, there had been the night her father had been killed, then a gunshot to the head, now her motorcycle. And it wasn't just any motorcycle either. That had been her baby even if she couldn't remember where she had gotten it from.

Lifting the celery stalk to her lips, she bit off another piece and listened to it crunch.

"Someone didn't know what the hell they were do-ing," a dark, slightly accented voice said.

Lilly turned her head to stare at the figure that en-tered the room. Black eyes, a peak of black hair beneath his mask. He was foreign.

It was becoming a game to stand, to watch, to let knowledge roll through her mind.

He was Maverick. She couldn't remember the name he went by, the identity he used, or the agency he be-longed to but she knew the code name.

"That, or they didn't have the time they needed to wire it right." Wild Card. Deep, dark navy blue eyes. He was different, she thought, different from the others somehow. He wasn't a killer. He was a hero.

But did that make the others killers?

No, not killers, but they were harder, more lethal, for some reason.

But once upon a time, Wild Card too had been a killer. Now, he was a lover, a man who returned to home and hearth every chance he had.

Maverick had changed over the years as well. Just as Heat Seeker had. Heat Seeker was watching her now, his dark gray eyes thoughtful, intent. As though he saw more than she wanted him to.

Could he see that she knew things she was aware she shouldn't know?

"It's been a hell of a few months for you, hasn't it, Lady Harrington?" he asked, his voice low, dark, and a bit amused.

"Seems so." She popped the last piece of celery in her mouth and crunched before smiling tightly.

His head gave a small nod of sympathy. "Seems a shame. What could a pretty woman like yourself have done to piss someone off so bad?"

She swallowed, then inhaled slowly, evenly. "Perhaps it was because of my vocation," she suggested with an edge of mockery. "A jealous wife perhaps? Who knew the life of a high-priced whore could get so dangerous?"

Silence filled the room. Every man there stilled, turned, and leveled their gazes on her. Even Travis. His gaze was dark, his jaw tight as she straightened and moved across the kitchen.

"I need a ride home," she informed him. "I have a party to get ready for, as do you."

She stopped in front of him, and for a second, just a second, her body became sensitized, her heart raced. She had been so close in that damned garage. So close to losing more of herself than she already had. She was losing more of her soul, each time he touched her. Her heart was already gone. It belonged to him, but now, she was risking the rest of her spirit to him.

For what?

What was she risking herself for? The man who loved her, or the man who would end up betraying her?

"Nik?" She spoke to the bodyguard as Travis stared back at her silently, warningly.

"Yes, Lady Lilly?" He was forever reminding her of her title.

"I need a ride to the house, please. It seems Travis is a bit tied up for the moment." Her head turned, her gaze going unerringly to the intense blue eyes and commanding stance of the masked figure that stood on the other side of the room.

He hadn't spoken much, and never in front of her.

Live Wire. His code name hinted at the dangerous personality she could be dealing with.

"Take her home, Nik," Travis ordered, but his gaze never left her.

As she turned back to him, their eyes locked and emotions surged and twisted between them enough to make her chest tight, her heart heavy.

"I'll be early," he warned her. "Make certain you can find a private spot for us to discuss this."

Lilly shrugged. "Never fear. I'll just have the butler show you to my bedroom. It doesn't get much more private than that, does it?"

She strode from the room, to the far hall and then out the side entrance of the house that they had fallen through as they escaped the explosion in the garage.

She needed to get away from the eyes watching her, the hidden thoughts, the suspicion. As though they were watching, waiting, poised to punish her for remembering whatever she had forgotten.

Memories that she hoped returned soon. The dual personalities were beginning to get on her nerves.

Travis turned back to the men in the kitchen as the masks came off and he faced the team that had come running at the first word of increased danger.

Jordan, John, Noah, and Micah watched him as he pushed his fingers through his hair and blew out a hard breath.

"That was Night Hawk," John stated, his voice decisive.

"You know, come to think of it, I haven't seen much of the woman you described as Lady Victoria Harrington, Black Jack."

Neither had he.

Once, he had belonged to England's high society. London was his playground, royalty were his peers. He had drunk, partied, and done business with the world's most elite social set.

He'd been the last of a family line that had been incredibly frugal with the inheritances that had been passed down. They had been built upon, saved, hoarded. Until Travis. Until he'd lost everything because of the deception of a faithless woman.

Travis had known Lilly then as Lady Victoria Harrington. He'd danced with her at parties, and fought against whatever it was that had drawn him to her at the time.

She had been so young, so innocent. Even then he'd found it hard to believe that her father was allowing her to participate in his activities with MI5.

"No, she's no longer Lady Victoria," he said, as the others continued to watch him expectantly. "Six years as a black op, living a double life, she's not the young girl she was anymore."

"Santos and Rhiannon are going to be at the party," Jordan informed him then. "I'll be there, as well as Ian and Kira Richards, and her uncle Jason McClane. You better get a handle on her before she enters the fray, Travis. Because the woman I just witnessed is a clear product of the Elite Ops. No one would mistake her for a silken-handed member of aristocracy, nor would they mistake her for a call girl. She was too damned tough."

"She was surrounded by the team she has been able to trust for six years," Travis argued. "Even more than her own team, Elite One was home to her, Jordan."

"Elite One has been home to all those girls," Maverick pointed out. "That doesn't change the fact that they're not a part of Elite One, Travis. She's an agent without backing now, which means her commanders are going to be hot to cover their own asses."

And that was damned hard to believe, of Santos especially. The commander had babied those girls since they had walked onto his base. Rhiannon not so much, she was cooler, but she had always seemed concerned, at the very least.

"Elite Command can't risk exposure. Santos can't risk lying to them," Jordan continued. "If she breaks, then it falls at his feet. We're responsible for our agents, no matter which commander they're working with at the time."

"You would turn on us that easily, Jordan?" Nathan asked, though they all knew the answer.

Jordan would give his own life before he'd turn on the men he commanded.

He shook his head as he rubbed the back of his neck wearily with a tight grimace.

"This isn't about me, Noah." Jordan finally shook his head. "It's about Lilly and Elite Ops. If she doesn't hold the cover and accept the background the investigator reported, then we're all fucked. Think about that. Remember what I told you earlier. If the Ops falls, we're all dead." He looked to Noah, Maverick, and John. "We fall, and our families will fall with us, when our enemies strike. I don't think that's a chance any of us want to take."

And it wasn't a chance Lilly would take. She would never risk those she had fought with, especially the girls she had worked side by side with for the past six years.

"I'll head to the Harrington estate," Travis told Jordan. "I'll meet with her and see how things stand after this little explosion. My own personal opinion based on watching her during training and over the years she's fought beside us is that at the moment, Lilly's coming to terms with the instincts she didn't know she had. She doesn't have the memories, Jordan, but she does have the instinct and intuition we taught her to listen to. We can't take that from her, it's too ingrained."

"Get over there." Jordan nodded. "I'll run interference. I have to report the explosion, but I think I can cover her reactions to it. One thing is for damned sure, this isn't going to help the situation."

But then again, there wasn't much that could help things now. Lilly had a killer after her, and whoever it was, they were slick. They weren't experienced, he had to give them that. Experience, professionalism, and she would have already been dead. A trained assassin would have taken her out with the bullet, and even barring that, there was no way they would have screwed up the explosion on the cycle.

"We need to get backup in order to protect her," Noah suggested. "This is the third attempt on her life, Jordan. The next one could kill her."

"I've already requested the backup team and have been denied," Jordan informed them, his jaw tightening. "The risk is too great. If she's going to survive outside the Ops, then she has to do it on her own."

"That wasn't Senator Stanton's decision," Travis growled. "He wouldn't have voted for that."

"All decisions made by Command are unanimous," Jordan reminded him. "It doesn't matter how he feels personally. How we all feel. The Ops has to be protected, Travis, at all costs."

Even at the cost of their agents' lives.

Travis shook his head at the thought. A part of him understood, but a part of him didn't understand a damned thing about it.

"Your agents are the Ops, Jordan. Perhaps you should remind Command of that."

He turned and left the kitchen to make his way to the bedroom. His formal wear was waiting in plastic on the king-sized bed.

He picked up the bag and threw it over his arm, checked the contents quickly for everything he needed, then grabbed the overnight bag sitting on the floor.

Striding from the house minutes later, he headed toward the back of the property and the rough-hewn shed that sat next to the back drive. Security was still active, ensuring no one had gotten to the vehicle. Deactivating the security, he raised the bay door and stepped in beside the black Viper parked there.

Sleek, powerful, like the bike that had just been blown to hell, the sports car waited like a faithful lover. Running his fingers up the side, he pulled the keys from his pocket and unlocked the car, opened the door, then slid inside.

Three strikes. This was the third time someone had tried to kill Lilly, and he was getting ready to lose his patience. He didn't know what the fuck was going on, but he was ready to find out.

And he intended to show Lilly's family, and their particular little social set, just how he would ensure her protection.

Lilly knew when he entered the bedroom.

She'd left instructions with the butler, knowing her mother wouldn't be finished dressing before Travis arrived. She and Desmond were in their suite on the other side of the house, and their house guests were similarly ensconced in their suites and preparing for one of the major business events of the year.

It was one of the smallest events, but over the years, it had become one of the most exclusive. Business deals were made or broken at this event. Company profits could be tripled or, with a spoken word, sent to hell.

It was also one of the social events of the year. For two days the women vied to wear the finest clothes, to ensure invitations to their own events, or to attend the events considered the most exclusive among this particular set.

It was a fucking bitch-fest was what it was.

Lilly kept her back to the door as the draft blown in from the hall receded, signaling that Travis had closed the door without so much as a click of the lock.

Turning to him slowly, she saw that he wore the same clothes he'd had on during the explosion. The faintest hint of dust and smoke wafted to her sensitive nostrils as she nearly smiled at the sight of a smear of soot just over his left eyebrow.

"The shower is through there." She nodded to the open doors to the bathroom. "Make use of it if you like."

He dropped the bag to the floor and laid the plastic-covered evening clothes over a chair by the door, then stared at her silently.

Vulnerability hit her like a punch to the gut. She could feel it washing through her system, tearing at the confidence she felt she had never had trouble keeping intact before.

Her fingers tightened on the belt of her robe as he stepped closer, his hands pulling at the bottom of his t-shirt and tugging it over his head before dropping it to the floor.

He paused then, sat on the end of the bed, and within seconds had the heavy boots off his feet.

"The butler turned his nose up at me," he drawled in genuine amusement. "I have a feeling he didn't think much of my dirty clothes."

"You arrived in a Viper, though." She shrugged. "His favorite car. He'll forgive you for a little soot and dirt."

"Ahh." He nodded. "So all I have to do is arrive in the correct vehicle?"

"Pretty much," she agreed. "Since I had your limo and your driver, I wondered how you would get here. Where did you have that baby stashed?"

"A small shed in the back," he informed her as he straightened, standing in bare feet as he dropped his socks to the floor beside the boots. "I see you've had your shower."

She touched her hair self-consciously. "I have to get ready. Hair, makeup, all that crap. It takes a while."

She couldn't believe she felt so damned vulnerable. Where was the smooth, confident woman she had been hours before? Why in hell did everything inside her seem to melt when Travis got that look in his eyes, the one that assured her he was thinking of doing some very naughty things to her body?

And he was doing this while standing there in bare feet with a bare chest, the soft mat of hair that sprinkled across his chest inviting her fingers to touch and explore.

"Your family's party is turning into a hell of an event," he stated as he moved closer, stopping within inches of her.

"It always does," she answered, her voice too breathy, too weak to suit her. "And the final day it becomes a complete mess, if I remember. There are dozens of last-minute requests for guests by invited guests."

"Are they often accepted?" he asked as he reached up to scissor his fingers around a curl that fell along her neck.

"Sometimes." She swallowed tightly.

She wanted him again. God, she wanted him until she couldn't think or feel anything but that need.

She swore she could feel the rasp of his chest hair against her nipples, though her robe separated them, could feel his cock pressed against her, her pussy swelling in hunger.

She didn't give a damn about the party right now.

That thought had her stilling. She had never had such a thought before, at least not before that last party she remembered, hours before her father had died.

She wasn't thinking right, she wasn't acting right. In a way she couldn't blame her mother and uncle for being so upset when they had to face the woman she was becoming. The question, though, was why wasn't she upset herself?

"Speaking of last-minute guest invitations." His lips quirked mockingly. "Santos Bahre and Rhiannon Mc-Connelly have managed to procure invitations."

She did freeze then. Staring back at him silently, unblinking, as she absorbed the information.

"How interesting." She breathed in hard and deep. "And what should I expect when my former employers arrive tonight?"

It wasn't tears that rose inside her, it wasn't depression. She hadn't been a call girl, but the world would see her as one, if that report ever became public. According to Desmond, it had taken an irrational amount of money to keep it from becoming public.

"Do you care what you should expect?" His head tilted to the side as his fingers slid into her hair, holding her in place as he gazed back at her, demanding answers.

"I don't think I care," she answered despite the tremors racing up her spine. "Would it do me any good to care, Travis? Would it make that report any easier to swallow?"

His fingers tightened in her hair for just a second as something hard and brutal flashed in his gaze. There was a glimmer of rage, carefully banked but not hidden. He didn't like that report any more than she did, possibly less.

He had been her first lover, he had been her only lover, but there was a part of her that was terrified to trust him. A part of her desperate to trust him.

Believe in me, Lilly. His voice whispered through her mind now as it did in her dreams. *No matter what, Lilly. Trust in me.* But she was terrified to trust anyone.

"The report doesn't matter," he growled. "Do you hear me, Lilly?"

"Unless the international news stations get hold of it." She felt her lips tremble and fought to stop it.

She was not a crier. Her father had taught her she wasn't a crier. She kept her chin high, a cool smile on her face, arrogance gleaming in her eyes. She was royalty. Well, distant royalty, but royalty nonetheless.

Or she had been.

Travis watched her eyes, he always watched Lilly's eyes. Once, they had been a pretty, clear hazel. They had been filled with innocence and ideals. She had been young, sweet, and lying through her teeth whenever she had played the sweet, curious little cat.

She wasn't lying now, though. He could see the humiliation that flashed in her eyes at the thought of the investigator's report, at the thought of those she believed to be her former employers showing up at her family's party.

There was no fear in her eyes, but there was pain and confusion. And a hunger for something more than sex.

"I promise you, Santos and Rhiannon don't want that report revealed any more than you do." He wanted so desperately to tell her the truth, to at least hint at the fact that she had been playing a role, that she had never been a woman for hire.

"Isn't that reassuring." She moved to pull away from him.

Travis refused to release her hair, knowing it would hold her there, hold her in place. She had never moved whenever he caressed her hair, let the tips of his fingers caress her scalp.

She stared back at him, but her gaze still had that edge of steel, that cynical distrust that gleamed beneath the still-present arousal.

"It should be very reassuring," he promised her. "Lilly, no matter what you fear, there is no one who wants to see the past become a risk to your life now."

He released her hair, let his fingers trace down the side of her cheek, to her jaw, as his thumb caressed her trembling lips. The woman he had known as Lady Victoria Harrington had been soft, gentle. She had been a true lady. The woman known as Night Hawk had built herself a new life. She had trained, she had learned. She'd gone from mission to training and back again. She had never stopped, she had never rested.

"That past is still a risk," she informed him. "If it's true, then I'll never be free of it, will I, Travis?"

If it was true. She was pressing him, asking, testing him.

"You will never be free of that past, Lilly," he agreed.

Before she could say anything more, ask him anything that could, at this moment, endanger them both, he let his lips cover hers, let his kiss steal the questions from her lips.

They weren't safe here. She had been betrayed by someone within this house.

He let the hunger overwhelm her for a few precious moments. Lips to lips, tongue to tongue, his hands caressing beneath the robe, stroking satiny flesh, tracking the few scars her body held. At her thigh, her hip, along her shoulder. He found them, caressed and stroked them, and stoked the fire beginning to rage between them.

It was always there, just below the surface, awaiting him. A fire hot enough to burn through the coldest night and to warm the hardest heart.

Stroking his hands back to her thighs, he let his palm slide between them, felt the soft, silken curls, the rain of sweet juices that slickened the plump folds.

It was like a rain of honey meeting his caress. Her thighs shifted apart as her breathing became hard, jerky. Sliding into the dew-rich slit, he found the plump swollen nubbin of her clit, so sensitive she arched and moaned in hunger as he caressed a tight circle around it.

Locking her to him, he let his fingers stroke over the tight little bud, rubbing to the side as he knew she liked, stroking the thin little hood over the delicate, sensitive bud.

Her head fell back, her hips arched forward, and Travis could have sworn her clit swelled tighter, harder, as she began to tremble in his arms.

She was so close to release. This fast, this easy, for him. She responded to him, she trembled in his arms, ached only for him.

His lips covered hers once again, his fingers parting the plump lips of her pussy further to circle the clenched, snug entrance that drew him like a magnet.

He circled the heated, slick entrance again, then dipped slowly inside.

He had to tear his lips from hers and grit his teeth as the tight muscles of her pussy gripped his finger, rippled around it and tried to milk it in deeper. It was the sweetest, hottest flesh he'd ever known in his life.

"Finish this," she moaned, her knee bending, leg lifting along his thigh, to open herself to him.

He slipped a second finger inside her, feeling the tender tissue stretching around the impalement. It was the sexiest feel he had ever known. Lilly wasn't the first woman he had touched so intimately, but damn if she wasn't the most responsive, the sweetest. She was the one that made the blood boil in his veins, in his dick. She was the one that filled his nights with fantasies and kept his hungers on a sharpened edge day or night.

"Travis, you're torturing me," she moaned, a whimpering little sound that drew his muscles tight and left his balls throbbing with the need to get his cock inside her.

She was making him crazy for her. When Lilly was around, even the mission took a back seat to the woman.

"I need you," she cried. A soft little wail had his fingers driving deeper inside her, feeling the snug flesh suck at his fingers as her hands tore at his pants.

God, if he didn't fuck her he was going to die from the need. He had to get inside her. He had to fill her, pump inside her, feel the pleasure that exploded into complete nirvana when he came inside her.

Her silken, deft fingers stroked his cock, holding it firmly as it hardened to painful intensity.

Dragging his fingers from the tight grip of her pussy, Travis gave a desperate growl as he lifted her leg with one hand, her hips with the arm wrapped around them.

"Put your legs around me," he ordered her desperately.

Whimpering cries came from her lips as he lifted her

from her feet and felt her legs circle his hips as he guided the blunt head of his dick to the sweet portal between her thighs.

It was paradise. Pure ecstasy engulfed him as he began to press inside her, taking her, possessing all that sweet, fiery heat to warm the places in his soul that had been cold before her.

Lilly felt the iron-hard, white-hot entrance of his cock inside her. Her head fell against his shoulder, her arms and legs tightening around him as he shoved inside her, sending half the length of his erection powering inside her with a stroke of violent pleasure.

She wanted to scream but she couldn't find the breath, the wash of sensations were too intense, too fiery.

She could feel the thick length of his cock stretching her, burning her, as her juices rushed to lubricate and prepare the ultrasensitive nerve endings exposed by the penetration. Nothing could have prepared them. She had to learn that. Each time he took her it was the same, so much pleasure she was lost inside it.

She could only hold on for the ride as she felt her back meet the wall, felt his hands clamp on her ass to hold her to him as he began to fuck her with hard, powerful strokes.

Each shafting entrance tore a cry from her lips and sent pleasure tearing through her as she fought to thrust back at him, her thighs tightening on him, her hands clenching on his shoulders as she let the exquisite sensation rule her.

The deep penetrating strokes stretched and burned, stroked naked nerve endings to a precipice of sensation so intense she was gasping for breath, begging, pleading.

When the explosion came, it hurled her through ecstasy. She felt as though she were a creature of pure sensation. A mass of sensual impulses that exploded over and over again, leaving her limp, breathless, and completely sated in his arms.

CHAPTER 11

LILLY PUT THE FINAL touches to her makeup and applied the last sapphire-studded pin to her hair when Travis walked out of the bathroom, fully dressed in his black tuxedo. The dark blond and light brown strands of hair that grew long at the nape had been tied back. The short growth of beard and mustache was still present, neatly trimmed and giving his face a dark, rakish look.

He was too damned handsome, and too damned dangerous. There was no mistaking the fact that Travis Caine was a man that others would be careful not to cross.

What did he have planned tonight? she wondered. She didn't believe in coincidence, and the presence of her so-called former employers at the party, as well as Travis, was a fairly good indication that something was up.

Or someone was trying to learn something. That suspicion was firmly implanted in her head now, and it refused to leave. She couldn't help but believe that Santos Bahre and Rhiannon McConnelly were hanging around for the simple reason that she was some kind of threat to them.

Rhiannon McConnelly had assured her that she and Santos Bahre weren't there to drag her back into whatever life she had lived for the past six years. There was a part of Lilly that actually believed that. So what else could they be after?

How far could she trust them? She had a feeling that trusting them was the last thing she should do.

So where did that leave her with Travis?

"Are we arriving on time, or fashionably late?" he asked as he came up behind her at the mirror and adjusted the bow tie at his neck.

For a moment, a spurt of fear washed through her, a premonition that she was going to lose him. She could almost see him walking away from her, refusing to look back, leaving her cold and alone. She had to prepare herself for that. Nothing lasts forever; she had learned that lesson already. In the blink of an eye, or the shot of an assassin's bullet, it could all be wiped away.

"You're not answering me, Lilly," he pointed out, his voice gentle. "Are you feeling well?"

"I'm supposed to be greeting guests with Mother." She breathed in deeply as she fought to pull herself back from the mist of knowledge and memories she could feel awaiting her. "It's a welcome-home party as well."

A celebration, her mother had called it. A time to celebrate with their friends the fact that Lilly had returned, that she wasn't dead.

The explanation given to friends and family had been a simple one. That she had run away, that she had hidden as she tried to come to terms with what had happened that night with her father's death.

The crash had been declared an accident. Lilly's father had been behind the wheel, and several eyewitnesses had sworn they had seen them driving from the estate together.

It wasn't possible. She didn't know who had been driving the car that night, but it hadn't been her father. He had already been dead. She knew that. It wasn't something she sensed or suspected, it was one of those things she knew without the memories to back her up and substantiated by Travis. According to him, this was what she had told him as well.

When Lilly had had no answers for where she had been or what she had been doing for six years, her mother had gone looking for those answers. She had found far more than she had wanted to find.

It was as though her mother had assumed no one else would bother to hunt for the identity her daughter had used those six years and conduct an investigation into it. And what did she think the journalists, who had been like rabid dogs after her release from the hospital, were doing? Twiddling their thumbs?

"You're worrying again," Travis stated softly as he laid his hands on her shoulders and stared at her in the mirror.

"Perhaps I have things to worry about," she retorted as she moved away from him and smoothed her hands down the hips of the sapphire ballgown she wore.

She checked her appearance one last time, adjusted the string of sapphires at her neck, checked the tips of her sapphire blue heels for any smudges, then turned back to him.

"Why are Santos Bahre and his sidekick showing up

tonight?" she asked point-blank, knowing he would at least have an idea why.

"Curiosity perhaps." He shrugged. "They could be hoping a part of you will want to return to your old life, or that any memories that resurface will give them some sort of business edge."

Her brows lifted. "I can't imagine how their business interests would coincide with my family's."

"You'd be surprised." His lips quirked in amusement. "Santos and Rhiannon are extremely astute business people. They have many more interests than that of business managers."

"Business managers?" Her lips tightened. "That's a hell of a title to give them, Travis. It's my understanding they're no more than high-priced pimps."

He surprised her.

Gripping her arms, he swung her around and glared down at her furiously. "I'm growing tired of hearing you call yourself a whore, Lilly. You were never a whore."

"What else do you call a high-priced call girl?" she snapped back.

"The title that damned investigator used was far from the truth," he growled as he swung away from her then and paced to the end of the bed.

As he turned back, his eyes seemed to flame with anger.

"You were paid for a service rendered, and that service was not necessarily sex. You were trained for combat, for covert operations, and as a companion in dangerous situations. You were not paid for sex. If you had sex with the men you worked with, then it was your choice, not your job."

Lilly glared back at him. "Tell me, Travis, once the press gets hold of that story, how do you think it will be viewed? And they will get hold of it."

He shook his head to that. "That investigator wrote his report based on accounts given by less than reliable sources," he growled. "Santos and Rhiannon operate a legitimate business. Their 'escorts' are advertised as those of a personal security nature. Do you truly believe they would risk either their reputations or their clients with anything less? They may get a hint of the trouble-making inclinations you seemed to have, or the less than savory individuals you may have worked with. But there is not a client that requested the services of Escorts Etc. that will ever claim you or the other girls to have been a whore."

Lilly's chin lifted, her lips tightening. "That is not the impression that was given while I was working," she bit out. "Don't deny it, Travis."

"Impressions and truth are two different things," he growled. "Escorts Etc. have reliable, reputable clients that will swear differently should anyone dare to accuse you of being anything less than a glorified bodyguard. Outside that, yes, you were known to deal with less than reputable individuals. Yes, the investigator may have spoken to one or more of them. But trust me, should the press actually manage to get one of them to talk, they will never dare to say you were less than a beautiful, companionable bodyguard. That cover will hold, Lilly, I swear it to you."

"Cover! You make me sound like some sort of fucking agent," she snapped back. "For both sides? Don't tell me fairy tales, Travis, because I've read the report Desmond has on you as well. You're a 'facilitator.' A man that works both sides for any country. You're no more a patriot than I was, evidently."

"I'm a businessman." His jaw tightened furiously.

"You're a liar!"

Lilly was shocked at the words that fell from her lips, the knowledge that suddenly stormed through her brain, bringing an explosion of pain to her temples.

She nearly doubled over for the brief seconds that the agony radiated through her skull, but at least this time, the knowledge remained.

He was lying. He was so much more than a businessman, and a hell of a lot more than a man that worked both sides. But what was he? That answer remained as elusive as ever.

"Lilly!" She felt him jump toward her as she stumbled, the reverberating pain lancing through her head like acid through her veins.

Pinpoints of rich colorful starbursts exploded before her eyes, nearly stealing her consciousness as the light from it intensified the pain to an agonizing level.

"Shhh, it's okay. I have you, baby. I'm right here." The words echoed through her head, as memories threatened, for the briefest second, to explode through her head.

"I have you, Lilly," he whispered again, supporting her body, holding her upright as she fought against the brutal pressure in her brain.

"I'm sorry," she gasped as his arms went around her, holding her against him as the pain slowly receded. "I didn't mean that."

His hand cupped the back of her head as he held it against his shoulder.

"I don't lie to you," he said gently, his lips against her ear. "I have no reason to lie to you, Lilly."

And that, too, was the truth. How could he lie and yet be telling the truth? The conflicting instincts inside her were driving her mad.

"I want to make sense of what's going on inside my head," she whispered, a breath of sound that she knew only he could hear. "I want to make sense of who I am, and what I know and don't know. And why, Travis, why do I trust no one but you?"

Why was her voice so low? It was a breath of sound covered by the rasp of tears she refused to shed as Travis held her close against him.

She could feel the tremors racing through her now, almost like shock, trembling through her body and rasping her voice as she fought to make sense of who she was. What she was.

"It's shock, baby." He kissed her forehead gently before swinging her up in his arms and sitting with her on the bed, holding her close. "It's just shock. You could have died today. It's finally catching up with you, that's all." There was an edge of warning in his voice, the same warning she often saw in his eyes.

Her room wasn't secure. That thought raced through her mind once again as the pain eased entirely away. There was no way, at this moment, to ensure that no one was listening.

"Just shock," she repeated as she stared over his shoulder into the dimming sunlight that glowed through the balcony doors, knowing it was more than just the shock.

She eased away from him, staring up at him intently.

The pain had left slowly, but in its place was a certainty that if she didn't figure out who was trying to kill her, quickly, then it would be too late. And perhaps it would be too late for both of them.

Travis held her tight, fighting his own demons, fighting the emotions that threatened to overwhelm him. When he had been inducted into the Elite Ops, he had been warned that his loyalty was to the team, and no one else. He no longer had a family, a country, or a lover. His entire loyalty was to the team and to nothing and no one else.

He'd had no problem with that then. He hadn't wanted to divide himself, to risk his heart, or the lives of those he loved, again.

Standing there now, holding onto Lilly, he knew that that loyalty had changed, shifted focus. Hell, it had done so six years ago and he hadn't even realized it. The team was taking a backseat to the woman, and he knew it.

Staring into her eyes as she looked up at him, Travis had to fight himself, to keep from telling her the truth. At that moment there was nothing more important than giving her the answers she needed with such desperation.

Lilly breathed in deep and hard to regain control of herself. The emotion and the needs ripping through her, the fear that battled with confusion.

I'm checking the garage later, Lilly mouthed. Someone had tried to kill her. Her cycle had been parked in the underground garage, unattended. Perhaps something had been left behind.

He shook his head firmly. He wasn't arguing vocally with her. That was telling.

They had worked together often, he had said. She was trained for covert maneuvers, personal protection and guerrilla tactics. She sensed that. They were partners in more than the bedroom games they had been playing. It was time she put some of that knowledge, those instincts to use and figured out what the hell was going on. She might not have her memories, but she still had her instincts and the bits of knowledge that were coming to her in bits and pieces, every day. She knew just enough to make her dangerous now. Just enough to possibly get her killed.

But she wouldn't go alone.

Lilly smiled at the thought.

Travis saw the smile. As John had stated earlier that day, this was pure Night Hawk. This was not Lady Victoria Lillian Harrington. This was the agent. The woman that could be more dangerous than most men could ever hope to be.

That gleam of stubbornness filled her eyes, and though he'd been expecting it, it still managed to surprise him.

She was morphing right in front of his eyes from the lady she was believed to be, to the dangerous covert agent she had been. The separate parts of Lilly weren't merging together cohesively, or better yet for the Ops, the agent persona hadn't died entirely.

No, he mouthed back at her. *It's being taken care of.*

She jerked her arm from his grip, a frown tightening her brow as her lips thinned again. She wasn't the least bit happy that someone else might be taking care of anything.

"I know how to take care of my own business," she warned him in a low whisper, the light English accent slipping away from her to reveal the cool, accentless tone of the agent Lilly Belle.

Even now, knowing who and what she was, he found it damned hard to see Lilly as an agent right now. Hell, he'd seen her in action more than once, and it was still hard to believe it all the way to his soul.

"This has gone beyond your business." He gripped her arm, keeping his voice to a mere breath of a sound. "Back off, Lilly, and let me take care of this."

"I don't need you to take care of this for me," she assured him. "I'll take care of this on my own."

She was going to make him crazy. If she remembered who she was, what she had been, he might not have been nearly so worried. But she didn't remember, and God only knew how many of the instincts buried inside her memories were still hidden.

She was adept now, she had proved that in the garage today. But he couldn't be certain, clear to his soul, that she had retained enough of her past identity to be able to protect herself effectively.

"I have guests to greet," she reminded him as she flashed him a hard look from gem-cold green eyes. "And a party to attend. We need to leave now, if you don't mind."

Damn her. Travis had to grit his teeth to keep from snapping out something he knew would cause a confrontation. Lilly didn't deal well with what she called "smart-ass male remarks." Not that he did well with the feminine kind either. Strangely enough, though, when her sweet mouth got smart, his dick just got hard.

It was hard now. As he followed her from the bedroom, along the open hall and down the elaborate, curved staircase, his cock was throbbing with an increased hunger that he was damned if he knew what to do with. Especially at the moment.

"Mr. Caine." Desmond Harrington stepped from the open doorway of the ballroom, his gaze cautious as the doorbell rang and Lilly took her place at her mother's side.

"Lord Harrington. Lady Harrington." Travis paused at the bottom of the steps and observed Lilly's mother watching her with a glimmer of silent condemnation.

Lady Harrington wasn't happy to see him.

"Why am I not surprised to see you here, Caine?" Lord Harrington sighed as the first guests began to filter into the large foyer.

Lord Desmond Harrington's expression was heavy, resigned. The deep furrows in his forehead, surprisingly, went along with his rough face. He was a man that had survived by his own wits and business sense, unlike his half brother who had been born into society and a fortune that stretched back to Cromwell's time.

"I don't know, Lord Harrington, why aren't you surprised?" he asked the other man as he kept his eyes on Lilly.

Lilly seemed too off balance. Travis could sense the fine line she was riding, the sharp edge of nerves and conflict that were tearing at her.

"You're sneering at my title," the other man growled, though there was no true heat in his voice. "It's offensive."

Travis grunted at the accusation. "Perhaps you don't understand an American's version of respect."

He was actually more English than Harrington was.

He was a Dermont, born into a long line of Dermonts, and had inherited a fortune that stretched back even further than Cromwell's time. His grandsires had married proud English heiresses and built that fortune until the present Lord Dermont could sit back and rest on the fine pillows his ancestors had created for him.

"American, huh?" Harrington's tone was singularly disbelieving. "Why do I have a feeling there's much more to you than meets the eye, or the investigator's report?"

Travis turned back to him, his brow lifting. "Went that far, did you?" He was a bit amused by the fact.

"You're not exactly on the right side of the law," Harrington muttered. "You're a danger to her now. You were a danger to her before."

No, Travis hadn't been a danger to her. They had saved each other's lives more than once. His Lilly was a hell of a lot more woman than Desmond Harrington could ever guess.

Travis turned to Lilly's uncle and stared back at him with a hard gaze for long seconds before saying, "You won't convince her to let me go, Harrington. Don't even try it."

Desmond grimaced. "I'm figuring that out, but it's something her mother isn't happy over."

"And her brother?" Travis asked. "I notice he's not here to celebrate her return to the family fold."

For a second, regret and grief flashed in Desmond's pale blue eyes. He turned away for a moment before sipping from the drink he held in his hand.

"Jared is having a hard time coming to grips with this," he finally stated as he stared down his nose at Travis. "But I have a feeling you're already aware of that."

Aware of that didn't fully describe it. He knew damned good and well that Jared Harrington had turned his back on his sister at the hospital, proclaiming that the woman lying unconscious before him was not his sister.

Her face had changed, but her relationship to him hadn't. Still, Jared had denounced her, just as he still denounced her despite the DNA tests that assured the world she was indeed who she purported to be. She had changed her looks, her name, her life, he had claimed. She had disowned her family first.

Travis stepped back as the guests began to file into the ballroom, stopping to greet Desmond, then moving to the buffet and drink bar.

As Senator Stanton greeted Desmond, Travis noticed the other man's gaze sliding toward him as though curious. Several minutes later Santos and Rhiannon made their appearance as well, their business personas firmly intact. Cool, professional. Just a hint of danger.

"Mr. Caine, it's good to see you again," Rhiannon greeted him, resplendent in a long silver and black strapless ballgown that gave her the appearance of one of the fairies she was named for.

"Rhiannon, Santos." Travis nodded as they shook hands, well aware of Desmond's interest as he watched them.

"It's wonderful to see Lilly again," Rhiannon commented with a cool smile. "Santos and I have been worried about her."

"There's no need to worry," Desmond growled. "She's safe with her family, where she's supposed to be."

Rhiannon's brow arched. "I believe that's how we came to meet Lilly to begin with," she stated softly. "The dubious protection of the bosom of her loving family. I hope you take better care of her this time, Lord Harrington."

Harrington's jaw tightened furiously as his pale blue eyes shot enraged flames Rhiannon's way. Her response was yet another cool smile before she moved at Santos's urging to join the party inside.

"I don't like your friends," Lilly's uncle informed him as he turned an angry glare on Travis.

Travis shrugged. "Friends and acquaintances are two different things, Harrington. But she does have a point."

"And that being?" he snapped.

"Lilly's family didn't protect her diligently enough. A mistake I don't intend to make."

Travis turned his gaze back to Lilly then, watching her portray the genteel English lady to perfection as she helped her mother greet the guests as they filed in.

She was sleek and well-mannered with just the slightest hint of reservation as she spoke to the guests who were once close friends.

Those friends had married in the past six years, had had children, moved away from the interests they had once shared and accepted the death of the young woman they had called their friend.

Now, they were facing her again, and sensing the changes within her. Changes that made them wary and uncomfortable.

As the line began to thin, he snagged a drink from a waiter's tray and moved closer to her.

"Thank you." There was a gleam of desperation in her gaze that he was certain even her mother hadn't seen as she took the champagne and sipped at it. Very ladylike. But he noticed she consumed more in one sip than most ladies would in the same situation.

"The band is starting up," he murmured as he bent to her ear. "Shall we go inside, snag a plate from the buffet, and dance a bit later?"

"Lilly has duties to attend." Lady Harrington turned to him with a frosty smile and a gleam of hatred in her eyes. "Do be a nice gentleman and amuse yourself elsewhere."

He felt Lilly stiffen beside him. "That's enough, Mother," she said gently. "If you'll excuse me, I believe I will take Travis up on his offer. We can talk later."

"Lilly." Lady Harrington caught her daughter's arm as she turned to leave. "Don't consort with him in public. It's bad enough you do so in private," she hissed for her daughter's ears alone.

"I love you, Mother." She kissed her mother's cheek before turning, accepting Travis's arm, and moving slowly away.

Travis felt an edge of sorrow for the other woman. She had her daughter back, but it wasn't the daughter she remembered, and it was one she was having a very hard time accepting.

"The party will wind down around midnight," Lilly stated as they entered the ballroom. "Be ready to go to the garage with me, or I'll go alone."

She kept a smile on her face the whole time.

"I wouldn't advise that," he warned her tightly.

"I'm certain you wouldn't, but it doesn't really matter." She stopped and stared up at him, ice filling her gaze. "Someone has tried to kill me twice now. I'll find out who it is, Travis, and when I do, they'll pay."

There was more than anger in her voice now, there was pain. The frosty reception she had received from her friends, the condemnation in their gazes, the unsympathetic curiosity, all were taking their toll.

She may have been one of the Ops's best female agents, but she was also one of the few that had managed to retain her heart, as well as her dreams.

"Travis, Senator Stanton wants to meet." Nik edged close, his voice pitched low as Travis watched Lilly while she listened to one of Desmond's closest friends brag about a recent business deal he and Desmond had made.

The stiffness in her body was telling. The observation of moments ago cemented in Travis's mind as he noticed her discomfort.

"When?" Travis murmured.

"It's set for now. Santos, Rhiannon, Noah, myself, and you. You have five minutes."

"Where?"

"Your limo."

Travis gave a quick nod. "Inform me I have a business call and I'll take it in the limo." Travis lifted his drink to his lips as he spoke.

Nik inclined his head before moving to stand behind Travis, taking his stance as bodyguard.

Travis continued to move about the ballroom with Lilly, listening, watching, as she reconnected with those old friends.

Their discomfort and guilt nearly matched hers.

There was no doubt in his mind that Lilly no longer fit in with the society she had been raised in. The fact that she was no longer Lady Victoria was becoming more and more apparent.

"Mr. Caine, you have a business call," Nik announced just loudly enough to allow those he was standing close to to hear.

"Lilly, dear." Travis bent close to her ear as she turned to him. "Stay in the ballroom. Keep your eyes open. Let's see who approaches you while I'm gone."

She nodded, but her gaze was filled with suspicion as he laid a quick kiss at her brow before heading out of the ballroom and then the house.

His limo was parked at the far edge of the wide circular drive. Opening the door, Nik stepped aside as Travis slid in, then joined him before closing the door securely.

"Senator." Travis nodded at the older man sitting across from him.

"Good to see you, Travis." Senator Richard Stanton reached out his hand for a quick shake before sitting back with a smile. "Jordan told me you were surprised when you learned about Elite Command. Did you think he shouldered the entire burden of the Ops on his own shoulders?"

"They're broad enough, sir." Travis grinned. "Though I doubt he'd thank me for saying so."

"Hell, no," Stanton grunted a laugh. "That boy is a hell of a commander, but politics aren't exactly his forte. He pisses off most of the members of Command every chance he gets."

"As do most of us who are unfortunate enough to come in contact with them," Santos stated ruefully, his aristocratic features mocking.

"I would guess there are days Travis wishes he didn't know about us now." The senator grinned back at Travis.

"I'm glad to know men such as you are there, if someone has to be, sir," Travis stated.

"Suck-up." Rhiannon rolled her eyes.

For all her Irish heritage she could be as rude as any American.

"Is there a problem, sir?" Travis ignored the Elite Two co-commander as he turned back to the senator.

"Elite Command has received word that Jared Harrington flew to Russia last week in an attempt to meet with one of the other agents Lilly worked with, Nissa Farren."

Travis's brows arched. Nissa had been assigned to America's embassy in Russia as one of the assistants working in the ambassador's office.

"Why Nissa?" Travis asked.

"We're not certain, but there's no doubt it's in connection to his sister. We've sent Shea Tamallen to England to connect with Harrington to learn how he found out about Nissa and exactly what he's after."

"How does that affect our operation here?" Travis asked.

"As a warning," the senator informed him. "As well to let you know that should you or Lilly find yourselves in need, then I'll be in town. You have only to contact me. Elite Command may be forced to make decisions that often seem cold or uncaring of individual agents, but we still try to do all we can to ensure not just your safety, but also your trust in us."

"Trusting shadow groups that look at the money line rather than the personal line isn't always easy, Senator," Travis stated.

"We understand that," the senator sighed. "But that's what we're aiming for."

"Thank you for the information, sir, as well as the explanations." Travis nodded. "If we're finished?"

"We are indeed." The senator nodded as well. "I have some things to discuss with Santos and Rhiannon if you don't mind us using your limo. We'll vacate the vehicle soon, though."

"Take your time," Travis offered as Nik opened the limo door and stepped out.

Moving to the house, Travis could feel an edge of wariness tightening his nape now.

"Get with our contacts in London," he ordered Nik. "Find out what the fuck Jared Harrington is up to before Shea finds her ass on the line as well."

"I'll take care of it at first opportunity," Nik's voice was a growl now. "He's moving up on my list of suspects, Trav."

"Yours and mine both," Travis all but snarled. "Trust me, Nik, yours and mine both."

CHAPTER 12

IT WAS CLOSER TO one before the party began winding down, as Lilly had predicted. The couples left were those spending the night in the guest rooms, and there were plenty enough of those to go around. The additional wings to the three-story mansion as well as the guesthouses behind it provided sufficient room for the large parties and crowds of guests who often stayed there.

He watched as Lilly quickly shed her ballgown for the black, snug jeans, T-shirt, and boots. His dick throbbed, hard as hell, as she slid a dagger into the side of her boot. Her hair was quickly released from the pins holding it, then scooped back into a ponytail that fell past her shoulders in a thick, sleek ribbon.

He was going to fuck her the minute he got her back to the her bedroom, he thought. He was going to put her on her knees, grip that damned ponytail, and ride them both to exhaustion. He should do it now, before she managed to get either of them into a mess tonight.

"I still highly advise against this," he commented as he drew his t-shirt over his head before sitting on the bed and pulling the light hiking boots he preferred over his feet and lacing them.

"I'm certain you do."

She kept patting her thigh as though she knew something was missing. The holsters she wore strapped to those sleek thighs were missing. She never went on a mission without going fully armed. The action was telling.

Santos and Rhiannon had watched her carefully after their meeting with the senator tonight, as had Ian and Kira Richards, and Jordan Malone. All eyes had been on Lilly, and everyone was seeing changes in her.

For those who had believed she had been dead, they watched her warily now, sensing that dangerous side of her. For those who knew the dangerous woman she was, they sensed the simmering volcano within her.

"Let's go then." Rather than going to the bedroom door, she headed to the wide French doors and the balcony outside.

And damned if he didn't follow her. For six years one of the highlights of his life had been watching Lilly move while she was on a mission.

"I need my weapons." She swung a leg over the iron railing of the balcony as she stared back at him. "We both know just how illegal they are, don't we?"

The two modified automatic Glocks she wore strapped to her thighs were her babies. She was beyond armed and dangerous with those bad boys. Even more, she was beyond hotter than fucking hell. His dick got harder, if possible, just thinking about it.

A sigh slipped past his lips as he followed her over the railing and dropped to the ground behind her. He let her lead this time, simply because he loved watching her ass. That and the fact that the threat of danger was minimal. No one had ever said he wasn't an overprotective male chauvinist when it came to a woman and a mission.

Slipping around the back of the house, he was surprised when she found the concealed window into the underground garage. Opening it smoothly, silently, she shimmied inside and disappeared into the darkness of the garage.

Travis followed, wedging his shoulders through the narrow opening and grimacing at the snug fit. Even wearing the black slacks and t-shirt, he found the opening was barely wide enough for him to get through.

Dropping to the cement floor, he landed as silently as she had as he surveyed the area quickly with the night vision glasses he'd slid over his eyes before leaving the room.

"Unoccupied." Her voice came through the small earbud receiver at his ear as he located her on the other end of the cavernous parking area.

The garage wasn't filled with vehicles, but it was damned close. Guests' vehicles driven personally had been stored in the underground garage for their convenience and to keep the smaller parking area outside free. Each vehicle was worth a damned fortune, if he wasn't mistaken. Not that he was surprised, just rather amused as usual.

His Viper was parked in a far slot, the valet that had parked it obviously enamored of it, as he had made certain that the spaces beside it were empty.

"How many guests were here last night?" Travis

asked, his tone soft as he flipped the night vision glasses to the top of his head and slid out the small flashlight he carried in his back pocket.

"When I left here this morning and headed to your place, the three guesthouses were already filled, and half the guest wing," she answered, her voice a breath of sound at his ear. "This garage was three-quarters filled at that time."

"Plenty of hands to do the devil's handiwork then."

A light laugh escaped her lips. "That's funny. I remember someone else who used to say that."

"I doubt they said it as well as I," he grunted, though he hoped he managed to pull off a casual tone.

He was going to have to start watching himself closer. He had known her before his "death." Not so much personally as socially. As Lord Xavier Travis Dermont, the heir to the Dermont legacy, he had attended many of the events Lilly had.

"His name was Travis as well," Lilly stated, causing him to grimace though he knew there was truly no way for her to make the connection between Travis Dermont, MI6, and the Elite Ops.

"He was a good man then."

"Yes, he was a very good man."

Travis paused, his gaze finding her shadow as she set the small motion alarm at the entrance to the garage to alert them if anyone entered.

"You knew him well?" he asked her.

"He was married to a faithless little whore," she said, sighing in regret. "The bitch was killed in the explosion that she set to get rid of him. She betrayed his mission and his cover to a particularly nasty set of criminals and actually thought she could survive it."

He didn't have to fight back the rage and pain anymore. He'd buried that part of himself long ago. His wife had destroyed him, there was no way to fight against it. Unlike Lilly, there was no going back for him. There was no rebirth.

"Was he a good friend of yours?" The hatred in her voice when she spoke of Katy surprised him, though. She'd always been cordial, friendly, despite his dead wife's ignorance whenever she was around.

They hadn't been friends, though, not she and his wife, nor he and Lilly.

"No, but I thought well of him." The reservation in her words had his gaze narrowing on her then.

"You were in love with him?" he asked, barely managing to hide his incredulity. How the fuck had he managed to miss that?

"'Love' is a strong word to use." She sighed. "I was incredibly drawn to him, though. Remember, it's been six years since I disappeared, and he died two years before that. So I was very young and he was very married."

And she had never displayed her crush, nor attempted to gain his attention at the time. Travis nearly shook his head at the thought.

"I danced with you once, you know, just before your disappearance."

"When?" She was moving along the far edge of the garage then, her own penlight trained on the ground as he moved to do the same.

"The party you disappeared from. I was there with another agent. We danced the waltz. You were dressed in a soft autumn brown ballgown with tiny silk leaves cascading through your hair."

He could almost feel her thinking. "I don't remember you." The edge of regret in her voice was stronger than the one she had used to voice her memory of his past identity. "There's a lot I don't remember of that night."

"You were beautiful that night, Lilly. You danced like a dream, and your smile was as bright as the sun."

She was silent for long moments. He'd learned over the years that Lilly didn't accept compliments as an agent nearly as well as she had as a socialite.

"Did Nik figure out the makeup of the explosive used?" she asked, ignoring his compliment as she moved closer to the slot the motorcycle had been parked in.

"He knows it misfired," he stated. "The metal explosive cap wasn't intact. If it had been, it would have exploded while you were on the interstate."

"Wow, there would have been no coming back from that one, huh?"

Travis made his way to her, sweeping the light over the cement floor as he searched for even the smallest trace of something that could have come from the cycle or the explosive.

"You have a problem taking compliments from me, or just anyone, Lilly?" he asked her as he stooped and began searching under the vehicles that surrounded the area where the cycle had been.

"Pretty much just anyone," she answered blithely, her voice muted as she bent down to check beneath a sleek, metallic red Lamborghini.

Once, she had been smooth, charming as hell. Not that she couldn't be charming as Lilly Belle. She could be, but that charm was usually layered with a frozen smile and ice chips in her gaze. And more often than not, one of those damned dangerous modified Glocks was in her hand.

"Who else beside Desmond was in the house today that could have wanted me dead?"

Lilly lay on the cement floor to shimmy as far as possible beneath the Lamborghini, which truly wasn't far, and shine the flashlight over the area, especially around the tire areas.

"I should be asking you that question. You live here." Travis slid beneath a Hummer, his own light scanning the floor thoroughly.

"Don't play games with me, Travis." She rolled to the next vehicle, slid beneath it and searched again. "Tell me what I need to know."

What the hell was she remembering?

Travis stared at the glimmer of her light as suspicion began to form inside him.

"Now isn't the time to tell you what you want to know," he finally told her. "Suffice it to say, I'm having several of your guests investigated."

"And you didn't tell me," she stated.

"I haven't yet had time."

Their voices were still barely high enough for the comm devices they were using to pick up the sound.

"Perhaps you could find the time later?" she suggested, and Travis almost smiled.

That sounded more like an order to him than a suggestion.

"Perhaps I could." They both rolled to the same slot at the same time.

The motorcycle had been parked close to the entrance to the main house. The space was currently occupied by a Lexus SUV. The four-wheel-drive luxury vehicle sat high enough from the ground that they were able to slide easily beneath it, both lights gleaming on the small spot of fluid below where the cycle's motor would have been located.

"The explosive was placed in the oil pan?" She rubbed her fingers against the fluid before bringing it to her nose and sniffing slightly.

Travis did the same, then rubbed his fingers together to test the feel of the fluid.

"That's not gas or oil," she stated.

"Nope. Not." His eyes narrowed on the spot before he reached to his front jeans pocket and pulled free a sterile bag and swab.

Tearing the swab open, he rubbed it against the spot, then pushed it into the small bag and sealed it. He was aware of Lilly watching, her eyes narrowed, her posture cautious, before she began to scour the garage floor beneath the Lexus for anything further.

Remaining quiet, Travis did the same. He was moving his light over the floor where the tires of the SUV sat when he heard her murmur a little hum.

"You have another of those bags? Tweezers?" She was tense, her light trained on a metallic glimmer as he pulled the required sterile bag and the tweezers from his back pocket.

"At least one of us came prepared," she murmured as she accepted the items.

Travis watched as she picked up the metal and slid it into the bag before sealing it and handing it to him.

"Nik gets that?" she asked, nodding toward his hand where he was tucking the bag in his pocket.

"He'll take good care of it," he promised her.

"Interesting." Her expression, from the dim light he had to see by, was equal parts confusion and suspicion.

"Interesting in what way?" Travis asked, often intrigued by the fact that Lilly was more open now than she had been during her years as an agent.

She was still Night Hawk, but not as hard, not as distrustful as he had been over the past six years.

"Interesting in the fact that he seems a jack of all trades." She shrugged. "Yet, none of those trades really ring true. Tell me, Travis, exactly who is Nik Steele?"

He grinned. "A jack of all trades, essentially. He's a mercenary, in fact. I've been lucky to purchase his time over the past six years, though there are occasions when he takes other jobs to break the monotony of working with me."

Suspicion filled her gaze now. "Sure, Travis," she finally muttered. "That's as good an explanation as any."

It wasn't a lie, exactly. That was Nik's cover, and he was damned good at playing his part.

"Remind me to be sure to check any further facts you give me on my own life, okay? I have a feeling that the line between truth and lie with you can get rather blurred."

There were times, he would completely agree with her.

He was in a hell of a position. He knew the truth, he had the answers she wanted. If she hadn't remembered who and what she was, she at least suspected there was a hell of a lot more about her than she was being told.

How could she help but resent him for not telling her the truth? The truth could kill her, though.

"Is it the explosive cap that was missing from the cycle?" she asked as she stared back at him.

"I'm not sure." He shook his head, staring back at her. "I'm into negotiations, baby, not explosives."

"I'm sure I knew that," she said as she began to slide out from under the SUV.

They both froze at the sound of the small beep of the alert Lilly had programmed that signaled that the door into the house had opened.

He hadn't thought about setting an alarm there, but she had.

That signal had most likely saved their asses.

"The cycle was parked over here," Desmond's smoothly accented voice commented harshly as the door closed. "Did you bring the flashlight?"

"I have it, Lord Harrington." Light gleamed on the floor and moved closer as Lilly and Travis quickly rolled from beneath the SUV and moved several car lengths away.

They each took a position against a tire of a Hummer, crouched and listened closely.

"When did you hear about this?" Desmond's tone was furious.

"I received the report an hour ago," his bodyguard answered. "The man we had on her lost her once she left the house, but he had a fairly good idea that she was headed to Caine's house. He arrived after the explosion and it took a while for him to learn the reason for the commotion after he arrived."

"Were the police called?" Frustration and disgust filled Harrington's voice.

"No, sir," Isaac answered as they stopped next to the Lexus SUV. "No police were called, but a team moved in. Black vans and identities hidden by black masks, no identification. The vehicles they arrived in were registered as rentals, presumably still on the lots they were registered to. We were able to get no information on them."

"Did anyone attempt to follow them?" Harrington barked.

"Yes, the investigator followed one while his partner moved in on another. They were professionals, Lord Harrington. My men weren't able to keep up with them."

Desmond cursed furiously. "Son of a bitch, what the hell is that girl going to get into next?"

"I'd be careful tempting fate by asking that question," the bodyguard grunted.

Lilly peeked around the tire, bending to see beneath the Hummer to the SUV where the flashlight gleamed on both Isaac and Desmond as they stared at the floor of the garage beneath the Lexus.

"It's a logical question." Desmond harumphed irritably.

"It appears to me that the girl was into too much before her return as it was," Isaac stated. "She should take a break."

Lilly rolled her eyes at the rueful tone of the bodyguard's voice.

"There's a fluid stain on the cement." Isaac didn't answer the obvious question. "This isn't from the Lexus either."

"From the cycle?" Desmond asked.

"I'll need to send a sample off," Isaac stated. "There's nothing else here, Lord Harrington." The light continued to sweep across the cement.

"If someone messed with that damned death machine of hers, then this is the only chance they would have had," Desmond growled.

Lilly's brows lifted. So her uncle hadn't been involved in this attempt on her life? Or maybe he was just acting in front of Issac. He could have assigned Issac to keep tabs on her, but that didn't mean Issac knew he was trying to kill her.

"Just find out what that fluid is from," Desmond ordered him. "Then see what your investigator can learn about that damned Caine. There's more to him than we have so far, I can feel it."

"What more could there be?" Issac asked. "I've worked with him. He arranges things, Lord Harrington. Is your business ally attempting a takeover? Don't want to commit murder? Call Travis Caine. Need to build an army? Call Caine. Want to take over a small country—"

"Yeah, yeah, yeah, call your bloody Caine. I get it," Desmond snarled back as Lilly turned and lifted a brow in Travis's direction.

A small country, huh?

He flashed a smile back at her. A rakish, wicked smile that had her stomach tightening and her clit swelling. He shouldn't be able to induce such a quick, heated response. There was something just not quite right about

that. Something that warned her that she was only going to end up hurting in the end.

Because she loved him.

Good God, just what she needed, to love a man that
facilitated the invasions of small countries and the take-
overs of cartels. No wonder her uncle was so bloody not
excited over this relationship.

She grinned back at him. She was going to end up
with a broken heart, there was no doubt, but damn if
she wasn't having more fun now than she had before he
showed up.

"Hell, let's get out of here." The shuffle of bodies
moving could be heard. "I need to reassure Angelica.
She's having a damned fit over this Caine situation. She
called Jared tonight and he refused to even discuss his
sister, which had only incited her further."

Lilly jerked her head back, lowered it, and steeled
her heart against the pain. What was that trick? She was
slowly learning it, or was she simply slowly remembering it? There was a way to keep it from hurting. Especially where Jared was concerned. There was a way to
block the pain, a place to put it where she could take it
out and deal with it only when she had to. She didn't
have to deal with it now.

"I have to agree with him in a way." Issac sighed
heavily as they moved away. "She's not the same woman
that disappeared six years ago. She changed."

"What created those changes, though?" Desmond
asked. "That's what I want to know, Isaac, and I want
the truth this time. That report was so pat it sickened
me. Victoria was no call girl. She was no terrorist's girl-
friend. There's something that stinks about this entire

deal and I want to know what the hell it is. And I want to know quickly."

Lilly seconded that motion. She wanted to know herself what had created her, why she had become the woman she was.

The door closed behind the two men, and the lock snapped into place.

"Jared took one look at me in the hospital and sneered," she said softly. "He told Mother, 'That's not my sister,' and he walked away."

She remembered watching the back of his head as he left the hospital room and crying. She had cried like a little child because her brother didn't love her.

She wasn't crying now.

Straightening, she kept her face turned from Travis as they made their way quickly back to the narrow window and then to her room. Sliding past the balcony doors, she came to a quick, hard stop.

"Damn, this night is just getting better and better," she stated, noticing that Travis hadn't moved in behind her. To face her mother. The coward. She had a feeling he was still hiding on the damned balcony.

"Dear Lord, you look like your great-uncle Marcus, dressed to go a-thieving." There was anger filling her tone. Angelica wasn't trying to be amusing, but Lilly couldn't help but laugh.

"I don't remember Great-uncle Marcus." She crossed her arms over her breasts and tilted her head to the side. "Tell me about him."

"He was a damned thief," Angelica snapped, her blue eyes sparking with anger. "He was arrested so many times that the shame was nearly unbearable for the family. He was royalty. We are royalty and you are dishonoring every drop of blood inside your body that binds you to the greatest history on earth."

"Oh Lord, this lecture again?" Lilly clapped her hand over her mouth, astonished that the words had actually slipped from her lips that time.

Her mother's face was a bit worse than astonished. Outraged anger filled it, darkening her blue eyes and flushing her porcelain flesh.

"This lecture again?" Angelica repeated. "Never, Lilly, never in your life have you spoken to me in such a way, with such disrespect."

"And I'm sorry, Mother." She tucked her hands behind her back and crossed her fingers. "I've just been stressed out. I haven't been feeling well."

Angelica's eyes narrowed. "Well enough to dress in black and be slipping in and out of windows. Running around riding a motorcycle like a hoodlum. What would you do if the paparazzi caught wind of this? We do not need your face splashed over the newspapers again."

"Such as it was when you found me?" Lilly suggested. "I'm terribly sorry my return has been such a hardship for you, Mother."

"A hardship?" Angelica gasped. "You believe it a hardship? No, the hardship comes in trying to figure out why the life you've been given isn't enough for you. What in heaven's name makes you think you can throw it all away for a past you seem determined to return to?" Frustrated anger filled her mother's voice, her expression.

Angelica had always loved her life, the life of an English lady. She was considered a premier hostess; she wasn't just related to the Queen Mother, she was also a friend. She had luncheons with the woman, for God's sake.

Of course her mother couldn't understand.

"It was bad enough your father had to get himself killed, he nearly had you killed as well, and for what, Lilly? For God and country? God might care, but let me let you in on a little fact. Your bloody country couldn't give a damn one way or the other, and sometimes, God has to blink. The next time you die you may not be nearly so lucky as to have the option to return."

She hadn't had the option to return last time.

Lilly caught her breath at the thought, the knowledge. She wasn't supposed to return. She was never to have returned.

"I don't want to discuss this, Mother." She sat down on the bed, lifted one foot and unlaced a boot.

"As stubborn as always," her mother snapped, stepping closer. "You were always too hardheaded. Always too determined to have your own way, weren't you? Just call you Lilly." She sneered. "Lilly, as though you're no more than a common little tart."

"Good God." Lilly rolled her eyes and let her foot fall to the floor. "Mother, have you lost your mind somewhere? One of the names *you* gave me is *Lilli*-an. And don't you think 'tart' is a bit of an outdated word to use?"

"Have I lost my mind somewhere?" her mother burst out. "You're, you're sneaking into your room at nearly three in the morning, consorting with criminals, and doing God only knows what."

"God knows everything I do." Lilly sighed, wondering if she could possibly continue to hold back the tears. The censure in her mother's tone broke her heart.

"I want this to stop!" Angelica demanded. "Immediately. You will cease to consort with that terrorist you've taken up with. You will cease consorting with anyone that you've known in the past six years. You will be Lady Victoria Harrington, Lilly if you insist." Her mother's arms straightened, her shoulders stiffened. "You will not embarrass this family further."

Lilly pulled the first boot off. As she lifted the other to her knee, Travis stepped from the balcony to the bedroom. Leaning against the door frame, he leveled a hard, silent look on her mother.

Angelica Harrington wasn't easily intimidated. She had stared down two husbands, a son, a mother, and, it was rumored, the Queen Mother at one time.

"I'm tired, Mother," Lilly said softly as she untied the boot and ignored the silent battle going on between her mother and her lover. "We'll discuss this tomorrow, if you don't mind."

She wasn't going to cry, she assured herself.

"I've tried to be understanding, Lilly." Tears glittered in her mother's eyes, and Lilly felt her own throat tightening. "I've tried desperately to be patient, to find some part of the daughter I lost six years ago." She shook her head as a tear slipped free. "Perhaps you did die that night with your father."

Lilly didn't speak. She stared at the floor as her mother turned and stalked from the bedroom, the door slamming behind her.

Lilly breathed in slowly and deeply before returning

her attention to the boot. She unlaced it, pushed it from her foot, then removed the socks she had donned with them.

Standing, she pulled the T-shirt off, then the jeans, leaving herself dressed only in the light lacy white camisole and panties she wore beneath.

She suppressed the chill that tried to race up her spine, and the sense of cold, depressive despair. Her mother had never spoken to her in such a way. She was reputed to be brutal to others, even friends. She had heard her parents argue through her life and her mother had been like sharpened steel slicing through melted butter.

Lilly could feel the wounds herself now, and they sliced to the bone.

"It must be because it's your mother," Travis stated as he moved into the room. "Anyone else and your tongue would have sliced them to the bone."

She turned and stared back at him. "If you can't respect your mother, you can't respect yourself," she said sadly. "I should have kept my mouth shut."

Why hadn't she? She used to. Lilly remembered that. The lectures were always lovingly tolerated. She had never snapped at her mother.

Travis shook his head, his hands settling on her shoulders. "She was wrong. Lady Victoria Lillian Harrington didn't die six years ago." His head lowered, and the ice that had been forming inside her began to melt. "Six years ago, she was reborn, and knowing the before and after, I have to say I much prefer the version in my arms now."

His hand smoothed down her hair, his arms held her

close. And Lilly realized that in the months since she had awakened with six lost years, no one had held her. No one had hugged her. And no one had said, "Welcome home."

CHAPTER 13

SHE WAS GOING TO break his heart. Travis had never before seen such tormented emotion on Lilly's face as when her mother had raged at her.

He'd seen concern in Angelica Harrington's eyes at other times. He'd seen love on her face. She cared for her daughter, but not to the exclusion of her pride evidently. Or the exclusion of the paparazzi.

Holding Lilly close against him, he couldn't help but wonder what the hell had truly happened that night in England at the fateful party when Lilly had lost everything important to her.

It had been by sheer luck that Noah had been outside that night and had seen the masked figures loading Lord Harrington and his daughter into the Harrington car.

They hadn't been able to stop the assailants, and by the time Travis and Noah were able to catch up with them, the car had been flying off the cliff, the explosion ripping through the darkness.

The suspects had raced away, and attempting to save

Lilly and her father had been more important than chasing after their murderers.

Hypnosis had gotten them nowhere with Lilly in her attempt to remember who killed her father. As her mother said, she was hardheaded, stubborn. She was willful, but she was a damned good woman and a hell of an agent. She was a woman that cared enough about injustice to fight against it.

"When I was younger, we dressed the same," Lilly whispered against his chest. "My mother would have my dresses made to match hers for our shopping trips, luncheons. The Queen Mother once told me that I was the perfect lady, and that she was proud to know me."

Travis bent his head over hers and held her tighter. There was such pain in her voice.

"Jared was always very jealous," she said. "But he loved me. He and Father would take me hunting and riding with them. They allowed me to go on walks with them in the evenings. We were such a close family. Before Father died. Before I died."

She pulled away from him and moved toward the bathroom. "I need a shower."

"I have to connect with Nik tonight," he told her. "Come with me."

Surprisingly enough, she shook her head. "I need to shower."

She needed to think, perhaps.

Travis didn't want to leave her alone. He could see the emotions tearing through her, feel the tension inside her.

"Santos and Rhiannon met with you and Senator

Stanton, Nik, and Noah Blake tonight as well as Jordan Malone," she stated as she moved to the bathroom. "I was rather surprised that a senator would associate with two high-priced pimps." She walked into the bathroom and closed the door behind her.

Hell, how had she known about that meeting, and who else knew about it? Travis's jaw tightened. Seconds later he pushed into the room while she adjusted the water in the shower.

Lilly turned to him, suspicion still roiling through her as she watched the set expression on his face.

"Why don't you simply tell me what I need to know?" she asked, hearing the chill in her own voice.

She watched as he leaned against the counter, his eyes narrowed on her while the water ran full blast in the shower.

It would drown out any listening device, she knew. A murmur of voices might be heard, but not the actual words they were saying.

"What do you need to know?" He crossed his arms over his chest as he watched her, his gaze flickering over her body.

Mimicking his stance, she leaned back against the shower, crossed one ankle over the other, then crossed her arms beneath her breasts, deliberately plumping them out for him.

"Are you enemy or ally?" she asked.

His lips thinned. "Don't ask me that question, Lilly," he warned her softly.

Lilly shook her head as the tears finally flooded her eyes. "Who can I trust, Travis? Tell me who I can trust and I'll go ask them my questions."

She needed someone, oh God, someone she could trust to give her the answers she needed. She felt as though she were breaking apart inside. As though she had lost something so essential that a part of her was missing now and she didn't know what to do without it.

He wiped his hand over his face as he breathed out roughly. "Lilly, you have to be patient."

"Patience is going to get me killed," she hissed furiously, shuddering at the knowledge that she had no idea how to watch her own back, or who to watch out for. "For God's sake, Travis, someone has tried to kill me twice now, and that's not counting six years ago when I disappeared. Someone tried to kill me then, and we both know it."

His jaw tightened in fury. The knowledge was there in his eyes. She could see it.

"You know what happened the night Father died," she whispered.

"I told you I knew you. You have that in the report your uncle paid for. We fought together plenty of times, Lilly. You've covered my back—"

"I've saved your ass." The tears were clogging her voice now, fighting to be free. "I know I have."

"And I've saved yours," he agreed. "You already know this."

"Why?" She just wanted the truth. That was all she wanted, and she knew she hadn't gotten it yet. All she was hearing were half-truths and lies and she was tired of it. "Why did we save each other's lives?" Her breathing hitched with the tears. "Tell me, Travis. Please, God, just tell me who I was."

"You were Lilly. You still are Lilly." But she was more, and she knew it.

"Are you my enemy or my ally?" she asked him again, feeling the pain, feeling a sense of betrayal tearing through her. "Tell me, Travis, which are you?"

"How much do you remember?"

"Pieces," she whispered. "The safe house, the storage shed where I had my cycle parked, my weapons stored. I remember what I think are pieces of what had to be missions that don't make sense yet. The memories are closer, Travis, I can feel them."

"Why can't you wait for them to return, Lilly?" he sighed heavily. "It would be so much easier for both of us."

Her hand lifted, covered her lips. She had no idea how much longer she could hold back the tears, as the pain resounded through her.

"My brother turned his back on me," she whispered, feeling her lips tremble. "He said I was nothing to him. I was no sister of his." She shook her head, fighting against that memory. "My mother hasn't hugged me. My aunts haven't visited me. The people I knew as friends stare at me as though I'm some apparition that disgusts them." She rubbed at her arms, breathed in roughly. "I changed my face, Travis. I changed even my eye color. Tell me why."

She wasn't going to cry, she told herself. She wasn't going to allow the tears to fall, because if they did, then she might never stop.

"You're my lover." She shook her head slowly, desperation clawing inside her. "Can I even trust you?"

"You can trust me, Lilly." There was a promise in his

voice, there was sincerity and emotions she couldn't define. But a part of her recognized an underlying warning as well. "You can trust me with your life."

"Then tell me what I was. Tell me who I was," she demanded roughly. "Stop stringing me along."

"How did you know where your safe house was located?" he asked softly.

She licked her lips nervously as she shook her head. "I knew the memory was just there, as though it had never been lost." Her shoulders lifted as she felt the confusion herself. "I don't know how I knew, Travis. I just knew where it was."

"You knew your weapons were missing earlier," he pointed out. "How did you know?"

"I just knew," she snapped. "I just remembered that they should be there."

Lilly ran her fingers through her hair and clenched at the strands as though she could force the information out of her brain.

She wanted the information out. She wanted her memories back. She wanted her life back. She wanted to know who she was. Lilly or Lady Victoria Lillian Harrington. Which was she, and which life should she be living?

"What else do you just know?"

"Answer my question first," she cried out. "Enemy or ally?"

"What the fuck are you doing, asking me that question?" The words tore from him furiously as he stepped quickly to her, grabbed her arms and jerked her against him. "Tell me that, Lilly. Why the hell are you fucking me if you don't know whether I'm your friend or your enemy, your lover or your assassin?"

"Are you my assassin?" Her head shot back to stare into his furious gaze. "If you were my lover, my ally, you would give me the information I need to survive," she argued, just as furious as he was now. "You wouldn't lie to me, Travis, and I know you're lying to me."

"How? If you don't remember anything, then you have no idea what is truth or lie, Lilly," he snarled back at her. "Keep it that way, damn you. In this case, trust me, ignorance is truly bliss."

"No . . ." Ignorance was going to get her killed, she could feel it.

She would have argued, but before she could get the words past her lips, he was kissing her again. He was always kissing her when there was something he didn't want to deal with. He was always stealing her senses, her resolve, by throwing her into a maelstrom of pleasure that she couldn't deny.

The pleasure was as fierce as ever, but the tears fell anyway. Silently, slowly, Travis felt the salty warmth against his lips, tasted it against his tongue.

Pulling back, he stared down at her still-too-innocent eyes, and watched as the pain built in her eyes, the tears dampened her face.

"God, Lilly," he whispered. His thumbs ran beneath her eyes to wipe away the wetness as a small sob shuddered in her chest.

Leaning his forehead against hers, he stared down at her and breathed out heavily. "I can't give you what you want. Not because I don't want to. Because I won't. I won't risk you to that point."

She had no idea how dangerous the information was that she wanted. There was a chance, a slim one in his opinion, but a chance that she could hold on to her life here.

The tears fell faster as she trembled in his arms, pain and confusion sweeping through her with a force that lanced his soul. "I'm going to die anyway, Travis. Whoever is determined to kill me will succeed eventually. Without the truth, I have no way of defending myself."

She didn't want to die. She wanted to live, to laugh, to love Travis. She wanted to hold on to him forever, but she wanted to know about the life she had lived, the enemies she had made.

She was vulnerable right now, and she knew it. She was too vulnerable.

"I won't let anything happen to you." His arms tightened around her, his hand pressing her head against his heart, where she wanted to stay forever.

"You can't stop it." She knew it. "There's so much I don't know, Travis. But I know I can protect myself." She fought the wrenching sobs trying to tear from her body. "I know I can. Just as I know . . ." Her fingers dug into his flesh as she fought to hold on to him. "Just as I know you're going to leave."

She couldn't hold on to him forever. Agony resonated through her at that realization. It was like a dagger, tearing holes in her heart, shredding her hopes. She was living day to day and she knew it, just as she knew she would be living a fool's dream if she let herself believe otherwise.

"I won't leave you in danger." She could hear the promise in his voice. The sincerity.

"Unless you're ordered to do so!" Anger was burning

inside her along with the tears, tearing at her, driving a wedge through her soul and splitting it apart.

Jerking away from him, she swiped at the tears on her face before turning to face him. "Tell me who I was. Tell me *what* I was."

Let me be able to trust him. The knot of hunger in her stomach was only building, the need to trust someone, anyone, was ripping her apart.

His nostrils flared as she watched the struggle on his face then.

"You're asking me to sign your death warrant," he finally said softly.

Lilly shook her head. "I'm asking you to save me, Travis. I can't live like this. I can't stumble around blindly any longer. I can't live without trust, without someone to turn to, and I can't live without understanding why I dream of blood and death and a fucking rifle in my hands that I know I'll use to kill." With each word her voice was rougher, more strained, the rage bleeding through until her fists were clenched, pressed into her stomach as she fought to hold back the agony resonating through her.

"Lilly Belle was trained to work with covert ops." Travis's voice was strained now, his gaze tormented. "You know that, Lilly, it was in the report provided by the investigator."

"According to that report she was a high-priced call girl trained to protect herself and the agent she was fucking." She sneered at him.

That hurt the worst. Knowing there was a chance, no matter what he said, that the world would see her as a whore.

"Don't lie to me," she whispered as his lips parted. "I

know I wasn't a call girl. I know I wasn't there to provide a little secure entertainment for whatever bullshit agent needed a friendly fuck at the time. But that's how the world will see me if that report is revealed. At least give me the truth, allow me that much."

"No, you weren't." He breathed in deeply, Travis raking his fingers through his hair and glancing at the water running in the shower.

"Then what was I?" Desperation clawed at her chest then. If she couldn't trust Travis, then who could she trust?

He moved closer. "I am the only friend you have in this situation," he warned her, his voice so dark now, so rough she flinched. "You have no other allies. You have no one else you can discuss this with, do you understand me, Lilly? To the bottom of your soul, understand me or you will die. You will die and there will be no way in hell I can save you."

Her lips parted, fear and hope slamming through her now as she stared back at him, her gaze still hazy from the tears.

"I already knew that." She tried to stop her lips from trembling. "I've known since the second I awoke in that hospital six months ago that every breath I draw could be my last."

"Only if you fuck up," he growled. "Only if I fuck up. Lilly Belle was a private contract agent that worked with a select group of agents both private and government. She wasn't trained to fuck, Lilly. She was trained to provide a distraction or to back up operations. And you were one of the best."

"I killed," she whispered as another tear fell.

His thumb eased the tear from her cheek. "You killed, just as I have, to save lives. That rifle you used covered my back more times than I can name, and each time, you saved my life. You kept me alive, Lilly. And as God is my witness, there are times you kept me sane."

"I'm not the real Lilly Belle, am I? She enjoyed killing, Travis. I read the whole report. She killed for sport."

He shook his head. "You're not the real Lilly Belle. But the real Lilly Belle was the only identity available that could be used at the time. She was killed in Beirut six months after the crash you were rescued from. That cover worked perfectly. She wasn't well known, she wasn't seen often. Many of her jobs coincided with training exercises your father sent you on while you were learning to work with MI5. So it was the identity you were given."

She shook her head slowly then. "You're not the real Travis Caine either." Pieces of the puzzle were beginning to fall into place now. Memories were slowly shifting, revealing themselves as he spoke. Bits and pieces, shards of memory not yet whole.

Travis shook his head slowly. "I'm not the real Travis Caine."

Lilly stilled. She could feel a part of herself flooding with hope now, emotions surging, demanding to race through her body at this tentative proof of trust.

If he trusted her, he loved her. A part of her knew that what Travis had just admitted would seal his own death if she ever revealed it. Not just at the hands of his enemies, but those he worked with as well.

Shadows shifted now and raged through her brain.

Pain struck at her temples as she fought to pierce the shield between herself and her memories.

She could feel them closer now than they had ever been before. As though this small measure of trust from him had weakened whatever wall had been placed inside her head to keep the memories at bay.

"Who are you?" Her hand lifted, her fingers trembling as they touched his lips, felt the warmth there, remembered the passion. He touched her as she knew no other man could have touched her, emotionally as well as physically.

She needed him to trust her completely, just as she had done with him.

She had trusted him with her fears, her knowledge; would he do the same? Would he give her a piece of himself that she knew he would have given no one else?

His head lowered, his lips moving to her ear.

"I'm Lord Xavier Travis Dermont," he whispered. "I've danced with you and once watched your eyes fill with dreams, and in that second knew I had taken the wrong woman to wife. I knew, Lilly, because that was the moment I first fell in love with you."

A gasp passed her lips a second before his covered them. Filled with life, trust, and truth, the feel of his kiss shot straight to her soul, clenched her heart, and tore away the control that held back her tears.

Her hands speared into his hair to hold him closer to her. Her lips parted, her tongue stroking against his as it sipped from her, tasted her.

For the first time, they were meeting as equals. As two people who trusted, perhaps two people who loved, she thought as his arms pulled her closer and lifted her against him.

He shielded her with his body as he had always shielded her with his protectiveness. A sense of something falling into place inside her moved through her as she heard herself cry out, felt the crumbling of the wall that had surrounded her heart.

"You're mine, damn you," Travis said as he lifted her and placed her ass on the counter behind her. "You were always mine."

She had truly always been his, because she remembered that dance. It had been her eighteenth birthday, when her hopes and dreams had been so strong. She remembered dancing with Lord Dermont and feeling the magic that had surrounded them. The same magic that surrounded them now, that fueled their kiss as his lips covered hers once more, magic that fueled each touch as he quickly removed the remainder of their clothes with desperate, eager hands.

It was as though the walls that had come down between them had released something far more than just the truth. It had released emotions held in check too long. A hunger they had been unaware had been banked.

As he shed his jeans, Lilly's hands were there. She gripped the thick shaft as she slid from the counter to her knees, staring up at him, allowing her tongue to flick out and lick the heavily engorged crest.

"Fuck. Lilly." The sound of his voice fueled this particular hunger. It began to rage through her, to boil in her veins and cause her mouth to water for the taste of him.

Staring up at him she painted the heavy crest with her tongue, flickering over it, licking beneath it, teasing him with the touch of her lips as his hands buried in her hair.

"How bloody damned beautiful you are," he whispered, the proper aristocratic English accent slipping past his lips. For her. He was giving her all of himself. In this moment, she held parts of Travis that no other woman ever had and probably never would.

The agent as well as the aristocrat. The man that had, for a few years, helped shape a nation publicly as well as covertly. The one that now only had the option of working behind the scenes.

Except in her arms. No part of him was dead now.

As her lips parted and sank over the engorged crown of his cock, Lilly knew that in this moment, she had all of him.

"Sweet, pretty Belle," he growled as the hardened flesh seemed to thicken more, to tighten until it seemed as hard as iron. Like silk covering steel, thick enough that her lips stretched around it, hard enough that they felt almost bruised as he began to thrust in shallow strokes past them.

Her hands gripped his thighs, feeling the response of his body as she sucked, licked. The muscles tightened, flexed. A heavy groan passed his lips as she rubbed her tongue against the ultrasensitive spot beneath the head.

His fingers tightened in her hair as she moved one hand from his thigh to his balls. There, her fingers played wickedly, stroking the roughened sac, cupping it, flexing around it.

Oh God, it was so good. The feel of his cock filling her mouth, thrusting past her lips and heating her tongue, was incredible. She felt every response to the

Lora Leigh

pleasure she gave him. There was no guesswork. It was
there against her lips and tongue, just as the moans were
filling the room, his as well as hers.

Travis stared down at her, watching as she sucked his
cock into her mouth and laved it with her tongue. It was
the most incredible pleasure he had ever known. Nothing could be so good as this, as watching her take him
with such intimacy, such hunger that flushed her face
and hummed in her throat with desperate moans. The
vibrations of her sounds of arousal echoed on the stiff
flesh of his dick and sent spiraling fingers of sensation
to attack his balls.

It was like being immersed in pleasure. His entire
body vibrated with it and he clenched his abdomen desperately with the effort to hold back his release.

Eyes closed, face flushed, her expression showed
such sensual pleasure that Travis could barely hold on
to his own control as he watched her.

Her silken lips, the wet heat of her mouth, the flickering of her satiny tongue combined to shred what little
control he had left after committing himself fully to her.

He was hers. As surely as she belonged to him, he
belonged to her now.

Groaning at the need to hold back just a little longer,
he clenched his teeth against the ecstasy pounding
through his body and realized that he was slowly losing
his grip on the tightly held trigger of release.

"God yes," he moaned. "Sweet Lilly. Your mouth is
so damned good."

Too good. He was going to come. Damned if he
could hold it back much longer. It was ripping through
him, tightening through his muscles, building until he

knew he wouldn't be able to hold it back much longer. He *couldn't* hold it back much longer.

His balls tightened further, the length of his cock throbbed, pounded with the need for release.

"Lilly. I can't hold back," he groaned as his hands tightened in her hair to pull her back. "I'm going to come, baby."

She moaned against the head, a soft vibration of hunger that had his cock spurting in warning release.

A cry sounded in her throat at the slight release, her suckling became harder, her tongue licking, probing, drawing in as much of the taste as possible as he lost that final thread of restraint.

Rapture washed through him. Ecstasy on a scale of complete soul-destroying pleasure tore through him as he felt the fierce, hot jets of come racing from the tip of his cock, spurting into her mouth. His body drew so tight he wondered if it would break. His head jerked back, both hands clenching in her hair as hard shudders racked his body and fed the deep pulses of seed from his balls.

And still, he wanted more of her.

Still hard, his cock so sensitive he knew he'd spill again soon, Travis pulled from her, jerked her to her feet, and lifted her to the counter once again.

"Wrap your legs around me." He lifted her legs to his hips as he gripped the shaft of his dick and found the luscious, slick entrance to her pussy.

It was like fucking into silk and syrup. Tight muscles gripped the head of his cock as he pressed inside her, and the silken feel of her flesh wrapped around him like an intimate fist and sucked him inside, inch by inch.

Lilly's back arched. Her hands gripped the edge of the counter, her legs locked around his hips, and she swore she was flying in a world of sensation so intense that even the brush of air in the room was a caress against her flesh.

Travis's erection burrowed inside her, stretching the sensitive walls of her pussy and sending her into a maelstrom of such intense sensation that it was all she could do not to scream.

In two hard thrusts he was buried to the hilt inside her, his hips pressed hard against her as the sound of their breathing became a ragged symphony of pleasure around them.

He didn't stop, he didn't pause. Once he had filled her he began moving with deep, hard strokes, shafting inside her as tender flesh and sensitive nerve endings began humming in pleasure.

The intensity of sensation began building. Electric fingers of ecstasy sizzled over her flesh, tightened her muscles and sensitized her clit until she was no more than a creature of sensuality. She could feel the ecstasy rising, brewing inside her. It built, burning through her, rushing into every cell until the conflagration hit her womb and exploded inward in a release so powerful, so deep, she knew she would feel the imprint of it for the rest of her life.

She felt Travis joining her. His cock throbbed in release inside her as he shuddered against her, his lips at her neck, his teeth rasping her flesh.

Her name was a growl, a curse, just as his was a pleading cry falling from her lips.

They were tied to each other. They were bound.

For the moment, they were one entity tied by plea-sure, by hunger. By something Lilly feared could get them both killed.

CHAPTER 14

"WE FOUND A CONTACT." Nik strode into the makeshift communications room Jordan had set up in the small house they had rented for the operation.

The samples of fluid he and Lilly had found where the motorcycle had been parked were lying on the table where Jordan sat awaiting Nik's expertise in testing it while Travis went over the reports that had come in from the other agents.

"Who?" Travis questioned him, his voice sharp as Jordan turned from the computer screen as well.

"David Fallsworth." Nik strode to one of the other computers and began typing in commands. "London. He works in the warehouse district where Lilly was shot." The file on the contact was pulled up. Picture, a rap sheet as long as Travis's arm, and a documented history of information he had supplied to the Elite Ops in exchange for immunity from prosecution in several cases.

Travis moved and stared at the screen. "What does he have?"

"What he has is a possible description of our killer."
Nik straightened with a cold smile. "But he's skittish on
this one. He won't discuss this online or on the phone.
He's willing to talk to a go-between, though. We prom-
ised we'd send one he could trust." He grinned back at
Travis.

"How do we know he actually has something?" Travis asked.

"There were two men, the day before Lilly was shot.
They were asking around about Lilly Belle, flashing
her picture. They heard she had contacts in the area
and were looking for those contacts as well as Lilly
herself. According to good ole David, he can point you
in the direction of a few people these guys talked to.
But even more important, the contact names they were
given?" He shot a look between Jordan and Travis.
"They were both found floating in the Thames days
after she was shot. We weren't notified of the deaths
because the contacts weren't ones Lilly had listed."

Travis had taught her that. She had her official contacts, then she had those that only she dealt with. The
fact that someone had found contacts that only Lilly
dealt with hinted at the fact that someone had been
damned thorough and efficient enough that neither the
Elite Ops, nor Lilly, had been tipped off.

"Do we have anyone watching him?" Travis asked
as he mentally began preparing a checklist for the flight
out.

"We have a contact watching him until you arrive."
Nik nodded.

"I'll have the plane prepped and ready to fly you

out." Jordan turned back to the computer and began typing. "Nik, you'll be flying out with him and providing backup. We'll have everything ready for you to test the fluid samples when you get back."

"What about Lilly?" Travis turned back to him, concern unfolding inside him. "Whoever's trying to kill her isn't going to stop, Jordan. If they realize I'm out of town, or unavailable, they could strike again."

"We have Wild Card on site," Jordan reminded him. "He'll stay in close proximity. I'll have Maverick move in and cover the outside of the house in case of problems until you return."

Wild Card, aka Noah, and Maverick, aka Micah, would ensure that Lilly was protected, Travis knew. They had their own women, they understood the fears riding Travis's back where Lilly's protection was concerned.

It was the best he was going to get and Travis knew it. He'd discuss Lilly's protection with Wild Card and Maverick himself.

"The jet is prepping as we speak," Jordan announced. "You fly out in an hour."

Travis's jaw tightened. There would be no chance to talk to Lilly, and calling her wasn't going to happen. He couldn't be certain the calls were secure.

"Fallsworth will be waiting at the Wharf Tavern, two blocks from the warehouse district at noon tomorrow," Nik told them. "He's usually pretty reliable. Let's hope he is this time as well."

"Find Lilly's killer and we have a damned good chance of finding her father's killer, as well as the person or persons who's been targeting the savings, pensions and trust funds of the rich and famous," Jordan grunted.

"And we hopefully shut down a major contributor to a nasty little terrorist organization at the same time."

But he was leaving Lilly without so much as a warning. That didn't set well at all with Travis, but at the moment, his choices were limited.

"Let's roll." Nik nudged his arm as he passed by him. "Faster we get there, faster we get back."

He wouldn't have a chance to warn her he had to leave, but he could leave additional protection. He wasn't comfortable leaving her alone. Her memories were returning slowly, and only in pieces. There was too much she was still fighting, too many memories that were still evading her, leaving her vulnerable.

"We have her covered, Black Jack," Nik said, his voice low. "Let's find the bad guys, then you can figure out the rest of it."

Travis gave a brief nod before turning and leaving the room. Stepping from the house, he pulled the phone from its holster at his waist and quickly keyed in the speed dial.

"What's up, gorgeous?" Raisa, code name Raven, picked up the other end.

One of the remaining three Elite Two agents, she and the others were on standby in Hagerstown, waiting in case Lilly needed them. They were there unofficially; neither Elite Command nor their commanders were aware they had ditched their fact-finding missions and headed there to help Lilly.

They were a unit. They were family. Sisters, they called each other. They were Lilly's sisters.

"You and the others have night watch. Be careful, though, because Wild Card and Maverick are on watch

as well," he ordered her. "I have to fly to London to meet
a contact. Keep your eyes open and make sure she stays
safe."

A slight harrumph came over the line. "You think
we're not doing that anyway, hotshot? You taught us to
be family, Travis. That hasn't changed just because she
doesn't remember us."

Travis's lips quirked into a smile as the door behind
him opened and Nik stepped out.

"Take care," he told Raisa softly. "I'll call when I
land."

Disconnecting the line, he shoved the phone back
into the holster, disconnected the leather carrier, and
handed it to Nik as he accepted the mission sat phone
the other man tossed to him.

Any calls into the cell would be directed to the satellite phone. The satellite phone was more secure and reception more dependable.

"Let's roll, Black Jack," Nik sighed. "I'll contact
Fallsworth that you're on your way in and see if we
can't get this over and done with as soon as we land.
Hopefully, we can fly back and get the arrest warrant
processed for our killer as a nice little present for Night
Hawk."

Travis had a feeling it wouldn't be nearly that easy. It
was a nice thought, though.

Rubbing at the back of his neck, he strode quickly to
the Hummer and moved into the driver's seat as Nik
opened the passenger-side door and slid in.

Leaving like this wasn't setting well with Travis.
Something felt damned wrong about it.

* * *

The dull throb of a headache in her temples was becoming irritating. Lilly walked slowly down the curved staircase of the house that her mother and uncle, well, her stepfather now, she guessed, had taken for the summer, and headed for the kitchen.

Coffee might have a chance of easing it. She had developed a taste for the rich brew in South America during training exercises.

Pain seared her temples as the memory slowly filtered through her mind. It wasn't a flashback, it was something that was just there when it hadn't been before, and with it was heavy pressure and sharp pain at the sides of her head.

This could become a definite distraction, she thought as she extracted a cup from the cabinet and moved for the filled, heated coffee pot at the end of the counter.

Things had changed, not just with her, she thought as she filled the cup and moved to the heavy walnut table that sat in front of the bay window in the breakfast nook of the kitchen.

Things had changed with her family as well. Six years didn't seem that long, unless one was dropped into the situation rather than easing through it as they lived daily life within it.

Her family had changed. Her uncle was now her stepfather. Her brother had disowned her, and without the steadying influence of her father, her mother was more neurotic than ever before.

Lilly almost grinned at the thought.

Her father had commented many times that perhaps her mother needed a vacation in the south of France. The wording in reference to her mother's friends who checked themselves into the clinic, or forced their children in for whatever transgressions they had committed.

Her mother didn't deal well when she perceived a threat to her social standing or the appearance of perfection that she strove to project where her life and her family was concerned.

Lilly could just imagine the nightmares Angelica Harrington had when it came to that investigator's report being released to the public or the paparazzi.

And then to have Lilly herself projecting the very appearance of the wild, unconventional life she had lived those six years? No doubt her mother had been trying to convince Desmond that the south of France was the best place for Lilly right now.

Desmond and her father both had had a strong dislike for the Ridgemore facility, thank God. Unlike some families who sent their children for a stay there over the smallest of reasons, Lord Harrington and his brother had expressed their disapproval of it often. Several times they had stood by other fathers who had been forced to fight their wives over the tradition of using the facility as a form of punishment.

How many times had her mother threatened to send her there? Lilly knew there had been more times than she wanted to remember. As much as she was certain she had missed her family and her life here, wouldn't there have also been a sense of relief at having to no longer live by the rigid guidelines her mother had set for the family?

Wouldn't she had loved the adventure, the easing of the restlessness that had always filled her?

"There you are." Her mother stepped into the kitchen,

moving for the teapot at the side of the stove. "Would you like more tea, dear?"

Lilly lifted her cup. "It's coffee, Mother."

Angelica grimaced in distaste. "You were raised on tea, dear."

"I enjoy the coffee." Lilly sipped at the warm drink before setting the cup back on the table and crossing her arms on the table top as she watched her mother.

"Your manners have seriously deteriorated." Angelica nodded to Lilly's arms crossed on the top of the table.

"I know, Mother," Lilly agreed as she left her arms in place. There was no polite company present, so there was no need to worry about it.

"Do you now make gross noises in public as well?" Distaste marred Angelica's face.

"Not hardly, Mother."

Silence fell as Angelica made her tea and moved to the table.

"Desmond and I are heading to D.C. for an early dinner with friends; would you like to join us?"

Lilly shook her head. "I might lie down for a while. I woke this morning with a headache."

She might take the opportunity to snoop around Desmond's office a bit. She hadn't had a chance before now. It seemed either Desmond or her mother was constantly around her if she left her bedroom.

Her mother finished her tea, an uncomfortable silence falling between them.

"Lilly, you need to make a choice." Her mother set her empty tea cup to its saucer and stared back at her coolly.

"What sort of choice, Mother?" she asked as she leaned back in her chair, laying her hands politely in her lap.

"Whether you're Lady Victoria, or the hoodlum Lilly Belle." Angelica rose to her feet, her eyes glittering damply though her expression was willfully set. "Both cannot coexist. You must be one or the other. Decide quickly which it will be."

"Or what, Mother?"

"Or I'll have to make the decision for you."

With that, Angelica moved from the kitchen, her head held high, her shoulders straight.

Lilly sighed. It seemed her mother was perhaps a bit more irritated with the situation than Lilly had assumed.

Covering her face with her hands, she inhaled slowly and fought to bring her own emotions under control.

Once, she had fought daily to please her mother and to still live the life she had wanted to live. That had worked, to a point, until she had turned eighteen and her mother had introduced Lilly to the man she had expected her daughter to marry.

Hell, Lilly could barely remember him. She certainly couldn't remember his name. Lilly had taken one look at him and escaped the room on a pretense that her father was expecting her in his study.

She had, as far as her mother had accused her, shown her contempt for her mother that day.

Lilly had, in her own estimation, showed her mother that she wasn't a child who needed her friends, or in this case her husband, chosen for her.

Living with her mother had not been easy, but Lilly

had loved her. Just as she had loved her brother. She had adored her father. And through the six years she had been away from them, she had missed them to the point that at times, it had felt as though the pain would kill her.

Her eyes widened.

That was a memory.

She remembered that now.

She had ached to go home, to play with her niece and nephew, to watch them grow up, to protect them from her mother's neurosis and to even argue with her mother when she had to.

She hadn't missed the threats of being committed to the Ridgemore Clinic, though.

She almost smiled. Well, maybe she had missed the threats.

As she heard Desmond and her mother leave the house, Lilly rose from her seat and walked to the foyer to see Isaac trailing out the door behind them.

The house was eerily silent now. With her family gone, the servants were prone to congregate in the basement servants' quarters and relax.

That left Desmond's office deserted.

And locked.

Her eyes narrowed as she remembered the small, seemingly innocuous leather case in the items she had grabbed from her storage shed.

Making her way upstairs, she quickly extricated it from the luggage she had hidden it in.

Her lock-picking set.

And she remembered how to use it.

Getting into the office was simple. The electronic

keypad security was bypassed and the key lock simple to get through once Lilly began working. Within minutes, rather than the seconds it used to take her, she was sliding into the office.

Once there, she looked around, wondering at first where the hell to start.

Instinct was an incredible thing, though.

She moved to the computer, powered it on, and as she stared at the request for the passcode, that memory as well slowly emerged.

Once she was in, she was able to begin the download of the hard drive and the online vault into an account she had set up that morning herself.

As the information uploaded, Lilly turned her attention to the files in the room. The file cabinet contained mostly financial information that she was certain would be easy enough to find in the electronic files she was downloading. It appeared to be printouts of specific information used for business purposes.

Desmond, as her father had before him, did quite a bit of business while taking the yearly trip to the States.

There were other files scattered around the room, though. Going through them, Lilly found something she hadn't anticipated finding. Tucked into a long, slender yellow envelope were pictures of her.

Those weren't investigator's reports.

She stared at one, her brow furrowing as she tried to remember.

Her hair was several shades darker, but her features were clearly the ones she was growing accustomed to now. She was dressed in a long, silken evening gown, her hair pulled to the crown of her head to cascade to her shoulders. It was a party of sorts, the older male she was standing with recognizable.

The leader of a Colombian drug cartel, Diego Fuentes. His hand rode low at her back, his smile clearly flirtatious as she laughed at something he said.

Her eyes narrowed as the ache in her head became stronger.

He wasn't just a cartel leader.

A double agent.

Diego Fuentes was a CIA asset into the drug world as well as the terrorist influences invading it.

She had been on a mission.

There were other such pictures, but the one most telling was taken in the area where she had been shot. The picture had been taken in the winter. There was actually snow on the ground. Lilly was standing outside a warehouse talking on a phone. In the background she could make out a small sign that proclaimed the building holding the offices of Secure Escorts Etc.

This picture was taken before she was shot. Someone had been watching her, tracking her jobs, tracking her, until she had nearly been killed.

She slid the pictures inside the envelope, folded it, then shoved it into the waistband of her slacks at her back.

What was her uncle involved in?

She moved quickly to the computer, checked the progress of the files downloading to find they had finished, and quickly covered her tracks and shut down the computer.

As she was moving around the desk to make her way from the room, the slight beep of the security pad outside had her racing for cover.

It was daylight; hiding behind the curtains wouldn't be wise. Just before the door opened, Lilly slid behind the ornate couch along one wall, flattening herself against the wall as she lay on her side and watched as the door opened.

Her mother entered the office and moved to the file cabinet.

"I can't believe he forgot the files," she muttered as another set of legs followed behind her.

"Do you need any help, Lady Harrington?" one of the security personnel that Lilly remembered her father employing when she was sixteen asked softly.

"I have it, Samuel," she sighed. "He should know how important this is. Simply because he doesn't agree with them, he thinks we should just toss it away. There are days I simply don't understand that man."

"Yes, ma'am," Samuel answered noncommittally.

Lilly's brow arched at the irritation in her mother's voice as well as the fact that she was bitching so vociferously to what she would consider a servant.

"Something simply must be done about him." Angelica's voice sharpened, "It's as bad as trying to deal with Victoria and her insistence on being called Lilly. Have you ever heard such nonsense?"

"No, ma'am," Samuel answered.

Angelica sighed heavily again. "Shall we leave then? I imagine this is something else we'll have to deal with ourselves."

"I'll take care of it, ma'am," Samuel promised.

Lilly's eyes narrowed as her mother and the bodyguard left the room, locking the door behind them.

Sliding from behind the couch, she dusted herself

off, then stared at the door and shook her head in aston-
ishment. Perhaps she should have paid more attention to
her mother when she was younger. Spent more time
with her or something. Never had Lilly known her to
speak so familiarly with help. Not that she disapproved
of it, she just knew her mother did disapprove of it.
Highly.

The changes six years had wrought blew her mind.

CHAPTER 15

TWO DAYS LATER LILLY moved through the house, her hands jammed in the pockets of the violet silk slacks she wore, a heavy frown on her face as her hand gripped the silent cell phone in her pocket.

She hadn't heard from Travis since the morning he had left to take the metal and fluid samples he had found to Nik. She'd gone to the house, only to find it silent and empty. Even Henry the butler hadn't been in residence.

There had been no voice mail, no letter, no text, no message sent via anyone to let her know where he was or what was going on.

"Lilly, there you are." Her mother stepped from the sitting room, looking concerned. "I was wondering if you might like to go shopping?"

"Not today, Mother." Lilly gave her a soft smile, hoping to soften the rejection, although she could see the edge of hurt and anger in her mother's expression.

"You're ghosting about this place like a restless spirit," her mother accused, propping her hands on her hips and facing her with a frown. "Really, Lilly, perhaps you should see that psychiatrist the doctor recommded."

Lilly rolled her eyes at the suggestion.

"I don't need a psychiatrist, Mother," she assured her. "I'm fine, just tired."

Angelica crossed her arms over the tan and cream print blouse she wore and tapped her sandaled foot as she stared back at her daughter. The light, honey-brown above-the-knee-length skirt was a perfect complement to her mother's legs just as the cream-colored pumps were.

"You wouldn't be so tired if you slept at night rather than sneaking out at all hours," she retorted. "Really, Lilly, you can use the front door, you know. You are over twenty-one and hadn't had a curfew for several years before you disappeared. I doubt I'd try to enforce one now."

"How do you know I've been slipping out of my room at night, Mother?" she asked.

Lilly had a very well-developed intuition and she knew she hadn't felt prying eyes watching her. She had been aware of the investigator her uncle used to spy on her. He normally watched her balcony window. As though that were the only place she could sneak from the house.

"Does it matter how I know?" Angelica advanced further into the foyer. "I'm simply curious to know why you feel you must. What are you doing, Lilly, that you feel you have to hide it?"

"Perhaps I've just needed to get out," Lilly said. "I don't sleep well."

"And the doctor gave you something for that." Angelica frowned in concern. "You're out with that Caine person, aren't you? Do you think I hadn't noticed he hasn't been slipping into your bedroom lately?"

That Caine person, as though he didn't matter enough to actually have a first name.

"Does it really matter what I'm doing?" Lilly finally sighed. "As you said, Mother, I'm a big girl now, I don't have curfews and I know how to make my own friends."

"I used to think you knew how," Angelica said sadly. "I'm not so certain anymore, Lilly. I don't think I even know who you are anymore."

That makes two of us, Lilly thought.

"I don't want to argue with you, Mother."

"I do have a suggestion, dear," her mother said. "Dr. Ridgemore has suggested that perhaps you need to rest more. You know he has a fine facility in southern France. It's the perfect place to relax. You'd be well taken care of."

Lilly stared back at her in incredulity. "Ridgemore's facility is a joke," she burst out. "Surely you're not serious, Mother!"

Angelica's face tightened. "You're not acting well, Lilly, and your uncle and I are extremely worried. Even Jared agrees that might be the best choice. And Ridgemore is *not* a joke. It's a very well-respected medical facility."

Her mother wanted to have her committed? Did she really think that Lilly would allow her to do such a thing?

But her mother was serious, and Lilly knew it. Angelica had decided several times when Lilly was younger that she might need therapy or counseling. Both of which meant that Lilly wasn't doing as Angelica wanted and might need to be convinced by a harrowing stay in Ridgemore's clinic.

Lilly had heard rumors of the clinic, and she had seen the few friends she'd had who had been sent there. They returned much too quiet, too restrained. They no longer trusted their friends, and made choices on what their parents considered acceptable rather than what they themselves wanted.

"You've obviously been through a very trying time, dear." Angelica touched her arm gently, her blue eyes darkening with remorse and sadness. "Whatever happened during the six years you were away was traumatic enough that you chose to block it out of your mind. I only want to help you to become better. Jared thinks—"

"Jared thinks, my ass," she snapped. "What's his problem? Is he scared he's going to have to share the Harrington inheritance or something?"

"My God, Lilly, listen to your language!" Her mother gasped. "You sound like a street tramp rather than a lady."

Lilly pushed her fingers through her hair and fought for a way to tamp down her frustration. She had no doubt her mother was looking into having her committed. It was popular among the upper classes to force children into asylums for drug or alcohol addictions, even for something so minor as consorting with people the parents considered too common. Defiance was often diagnosed as a mental problem that needed advanced psychiatric help. Such treatment did nothing more than create greater problems than before.

"Mother, there's nothing wrong with me, mentally," she said as she stared at her mother in disbelief. "I'm perfectly fine, I promise you."

She tried to pass her mother, to put as much distance between the two of them as possible right now.

"Lilly, we need to discuss this." Her mother's fingers tightened on her arm. "This is a serious issue, and one that must be addressed."

"And does Uncle Desmond agree with you?" Lilly snatched her arm back. "Tell me, Mother, how long do I have before Ridgemore's 'friendly' assistants arrive to drag me to his asylum?"

"How common you sound," Angelica said. "You are not the child I raised, Lilly. You need help and you know it. As always, you have Desmond wrapped around your little finger, just as you had your father. Neither of them dared to disagree with you then, and Desmond wouldn't risk it now."

As far as Lilly was concerned, Desmond was anything but "wrapped." As normal, her mother did love to exaggerate.

Lilly shook her head in disbelief. She couldn't comprehend this. Her mother had been strict when she felt it was necessary, and Lilly knew Angelica had often agreed with her friends when they sent their own children away. But Lilly had never believed, never even imagined, her mother would seriously consider such a thing for her own children. She had threatened in the past, often. She and Lilly's father had argued over it. But a part of Lilly had never thought she would actually do it.

"You made a mistake warning me, Mother," Lilly assured her. "Trust me, there's not a chance in hell I'm going to allow you to have me committed."

"No one allows it, dear," Angelica promised her. "You may think you can make such disastrous decisions on your own, but you are a member of royalty, which means you can be forced to adhere to our rules."

And she was right. Angelica could very well force her daughter into an asylum, unless her uncle Desmond blocked the move. As head of the family, Angelica couldn't force Lilly into anything without his help.

She had to fight the tremors threatening to rush through her body now, the fear that her mother would do something so horrible tearing through her. This was the part of her mother that her father had always shielded her from.

Lilly shook her head, disbelief still warring with fury as she stared at the mother she had always loved.

"Father would have never let you do something like this," she whispered painfully. "And you would have never truly considered it when he was alive."

"Oh, really, Lilly," her mother spat. "Surely you remember the arguments your father and I had? The screaming matches? They were all about you. He treated you more like his lover than his daughter."

Lilly recoiled in shock and disbelief. That hadn't been true! Her father had loved her. He had taught her to protect herself. He had trained her to protect the Crown. He had trusted her. But there had been nothing indecent in her father's love for her.

"You're crazy!" Lilly stared at her mother in horror. "You're the one who needs to be committed, Mother, not me. You've lost your mind if you think you can make such an accusation or that I will allow anyone to lock me up. I'd kill them first."

"You should see yourself," her mother sneered. "You're at the edge of violence and unable to control yourself in the least. I'll be damned if I let you destroy yourself or the Harrington name further."

"That's enough, Angelica." Lilly swung around to face her uncle as he glared at her mother, the battle of wills heating the foyer with tension.

"You know it's the truth as well as I, Desmond," Angelica snapped. "Harold spoiled her atrociously. She believes she can do whatever she chooses now and embarrass her family. She's not some common little whore ripping around the countryside. She's related to the Queen, for God's sake."

"I'm sure the Queen really doesn't give a damn what I'm doing at this moment or any other," Lilly snapped back. "I do know I've had enough of this conversation."

Turning from her uncle and her mother, Lilly headed for the winding staircase.

"Dr. Ridgemore will be here tomorrow to speak with you." Her mother's words had her freezing in her tracks. "Please try to look presentable, if you don't mind."

Lilly turned and looked at her uncle. "Are you going to allow this, Uncle Desmond?"

His expression was filled with disbelief as he stared at Angelica. "Hell no, I won't allow it." He glared back at his wife.

"You think you're the only one who has the right to make a decision here." Angelica's head lifted arrogantly. "Jared can overrule you, Desmond, as you are not her legal father, and I promise you, he will."

Jared. Her brother. Oh God, the brother she had known and loved all those years ago would have never allowed her mother to do something so heinous.

"We'll see about that," Desmond said. "I'll call Ridgemore myself, Angelica. You don't have the power to stand against me on this."

Angelica was nearly shaking with rage as Lilly quickly moved up the stairs. Her voice lifted furiously.

"You think I have no power? Do you believe I will spend my life arguing with you over that child's destructive tendencies? I'll be damned if I will. She will learn to behave like a lady once and for all. Nothing else will be acceptable."

Lilly knew she had to get out of here.

She hurried to her bedroom and the large walk-in closet. There, she jerked the hidden backpack from inside one of the heavy pieces of luggage she had stored it in and threw it to the side. Pulling a change of clothes from the racks, she quickly dressed in jeans, a T-shirt, and hiking boots. She threw a light leather jacket over the backpack, slung the strap over her shoulder, then went quickly to the balcony.

Within seconds she was over the railing and hurrying toward the garage. But rather than enter the cavernous parking area, she moved past it, sprinted into the heavy foliage surrounding the stone wall, and within minutes was jumping lithely to the sidewalk beyond.

She had no idea what the hell was going on, but one thing was certain—she had seen too many of her former friends become casualties to their parents' determination to force them into a certain mold. They had married men they hated because of the threat of disinheritance or worse. They had turned away jobs, turned away friends.

Nowadays such enforced confinement was supposed to be illegal. Yet it wasn't. Lawyers and doctors conspired with parents. They drugged, rehabilitated, and mercilessly berated young women, and sometimes men, until they did as they were ordered. Until they became robots no longer searching for happiness but seeking only to stay out of that brutal, medicated environment.

Fear sent a chill of horror racing up her spine at the thought. She had to get away. She had no vehicle, and it would take forever for a cab to arrive.

Before she knew what she was doing she dialed a number. She stared at the phone, listening to it ring. Who the fuck was she calling?

"Where are you?" The young feminine voice was cautious.

Lilly gave her the location quickly.

"Get out of sight. I have a tracking beacon on your cell phone, leave it active. Someone will be there soon. Disconnect now."

The line went dead.

Lilly flipped the phone closed before ducking behind a stone fence, using the hedge that bordered a vacant property for cover. And she waited.

She glanced at the phone and the number she had dialed. She had no idea who it was, but she recognized the voice on the other end. It was familiar. It was someone she could trust. She hoped.

God, where was Travis?

She tried his cell phone number again. His house number. Voice mail was the only option she was given.

"Travis. Help me," she whispered into the phone.

She had no idea who was coming for her or how much they could be trusted. All she knew was that at this point, she would prefer to fight her way free of terrorists than to go against her mother and Dr. Ridgemore.

Cynthia Danure, the stepdaughter of one of her mother's friends, had told Lilly years ago exactly how she herself had ended up under Dr. Ridgemore's care. How her mother had assured her he was just there to talk to her. He had come with several assistants and a medical van. Cynthia had been taken away sedated and hadn't returned for six months. By then, the young man she had been in love with had been framed for stealing and incarcerated in a prison for two years.

The young man had been bright, with big dreams and a will to see them through, but he'd been unfortunate enough to be stubborn. He'd gone looking for Cynthia, certain his lover wouldn't simply run away.

Lilly wouldn't be caught in that trap. She had no idea how firmly Desmond would stand up to her mother, or whether her mother was right when she said that Desmond couldn't stop her. She knew she was being betrayed by her mother and her brother. Whatever they were after, whatever they had in mind for her, it was definitely something she couldn't survive. Something she wouldn't allow.

The phone rang. The display showed the number she had dialed nearly twenty minutes before.

"There's a white Ford Taurus pulling around, Lilly," the voice on the other end informed her. "Get in the car."

She waited until the Taurus eased in closer, then stepped from behind the bushes and ran for the passenger door. The car didn't stop. The door flew open, though, and Lilly jumped inside, slamming the door closed as the vehicle accelerated.

"Well, it's bloody damned time you remembered us, bitch." The bright smile, dark brown eyes, and easy affection on the other woman's face at least gave her a measure of hope that she hadn't stepped from the frying pan into the fire.

Lilly sighed heavily. "I'm going to assume I know you. And I'll assume I've not just fried my ass by calling. But could you please at least give me your name?"

The other woman's wide, almond-shaped eyes became wider, gleaming with concern as she shot Lilly a quick look.

"Raisa McTavish," she introduced herself. "Code name Raven. We've been waiting for your call. I assumed all your memories had returned when you contacted Shea."

Lilly shook her head before checking behind them quickly.

"We're not being followed," Raisa assured her. "Besides, Nissa is behind us a fair ways to ensure no one even tries. So, what made you desperate enough to remember the number if you haven't remembered us yet?"

Lilly pressed her fingers to her forehead and fought the pain building there. "I have no clue. I haven't been able to contact Travis and things were getting a bit insane in the Harrington household."

Raisa gave a light laugh. "Your mother is such a witch. I never understood how a person as compassionate as you actually came from the same genes."

"Perhaps Father diluted them." The pain was beginning to build. Lilly had never seen her mother as an evil person until now.

"Well, your father was definitely a hunk," Raisa purred. "For his age, he was damned fine-looking. It was a shame he died. You once said he taught you most of what you knew."

"He was a good man." He would have never betrayed his children. Never would he have suggested for a second that Lilly be committed for opposing him, or for seeing Travis. He would have raged, given her the cold shoulder, perhaps disowned her. But something so cruel as to have her placed in an asylum? He would never have done such a thing.

"So what's the wicked witch of the Thames up to?" Raisa continued good-naturedly. "I imagine she's screaming bloody raging murder over your association with Travis."

Lilly shook her head as she swallowed against the pain building in her head. "She's not raging. She's trying to have me committed instead."

Silence filled the car. Several more turns were made before Raisa blew out a hard breath. "Do you remember your cousin Elizabeth? She was committed just after your death."

Lilly lifted her head and stared back at the other girl, horrified. "Elizabeth was a child."

"Fourteen when your aunt and Angelica went against her father to have her committed for claiming her brother's wife had tried to touch her. She was in Ridgemore's establishment for over a month before you managed to find a way to get in to check on her but you couldn't get her out. They had her for two years before she was released. She hasn't been the same since, you told me once. You secretly checked on her often."

Her cousin Beth? Little Elizabeth, who had been such a gentle, sweet child. A vague disassociated memory eased through her mind then. Little Beth, medicated, staring at Lilly vacantly. How she had wished she could have helped her.

Lilly swallowed back the bile rising in her throat. She shouldn't be so shocked, she thought. Perhaps a part of her had always known how her mother was. That was why she had been so close to her father. He had protected her against her mother's rages when she was much younger.

Lilly wanted to wipe the image of Beth out of her mind, but it refused to leave. She had slipped into the clinic and tried to speak to her cousin. She remembered that. She had sat with the girl, whispered her name, and Beth had stared unseeingly at the wall.

When Lilly had turned her face to stare into her pretty brown eyes, a single tear had run down Beth's cheek.

She had been placed in the clinic because the bitch her brother had married had tried to molest her, and Lilly remembered that she hadn't doubted it was the truth.

Lilly had known the woman Beth's brother had married. She had been a perverted little tramp who hid behind polite smiles and innocent protests. She had done as her parents wished to their faces, and behind their backs had lived a life that would have given her father a stroke and her mother a nervous breakdown.

Lilly reached up and rubbed at her head. The head-ache was growing progressively worse, each new mem-ory, no matter how slight, sending shards of pain ripping through her head.

"Where's Travis?" she finally forced herself to ask. "I've been calling his cell for days."

"Travis is OTC," Raisa stated as they pulled into a winding gravel road. "He was called out the other day. He contacted us when he left and we've been on watch since. We didn't expect you to call, though."

"On watch?" Lilly asked, shaking her head. "Why you? What about the team he's with?" And she knew there was a team.

Raisa frowned at her. "Do you remember anything?"

She shook her head. "Bits and pieces."

"Damn. That sucks," Raisa murmured sympatheti-cally. "That's okay, darling. You're back with your sis-ters now. We're here to help. And 'on watch' means we were watching the house at night, keeping our eyes open for any bad guys that might be coming your way and following up leads on who blew up those lovely cy-cles Shea souped up for you. She's rather upset over that. Said she was castrating the bastard who did it the moment she knew who it was. Travis's team has been watching out for you as well, but Travis knew we wanted to be a part of this."

A face flashed in her mind. Long blond hair, dark blue eyes, a sad face, a melancholy air. Someone who had been horribly hurt. She had cried once in the dark. She had whispered someone's name over and over again. Shea. Shea Tamallen.

Lilly shook her head, grimacing at the increased

ache in her head. It was becoming agonizing. The pain in her temples was beginning to radiate through the rest of her head.

"Here we are. Home sweet home." The Taurus pulled up in front of a charming two-story farmhouse. Rose-bushes grew along the side of the wraparound porch while tall oaks and pines sheltered the house on three sides.

"Nice," she whispered, forcing the words past her numb lips.

"Let's get inside, see what's up with your mother." Raisa opened the door and jumped out. "Come on, we have something for that headache too. I know it has to be a bitch—your face is nearly white."

Lilly stepped slowly from the car.

She knew where she was. She remembered the house. She had been here before. She had hidden here before. It was a safe house, but for what?

"Come on, Night Hawk, let's get you all better." Raisa steadied her by gripping her elbow and leading her to the house.

God, she needed Travis. She needed to know what the hell was going on and she needed a sense of balance. She could trust him. She might want to trust the overly cheerful, willful woman leading her to the steps, but she had no idea if she could.

She knew Travis would protect her. Right now, she didn't have a chance in hell of protecting herself.

The front door opened and two other women stepped out. They all ranged between the ages of twenty-six to perhaps twenty-eight. They stared at her with eyes that were too knowing, too filled with secrets and shadows.

They were her sisters. Not by blood, but by war. And they had a pact.

Travis stepped off the plane to see the black SUV that pulled up on the darkened tarmac. As the vehicle came to a stop, Jordan stepped out of the driver's side and watched silently as he moved across the distance to the vehicle.

"We have a problem." Travis threw his pack into the back of the vehicle and turned to face Jordan.

"What kind of a problem?" His stomach was clenched, a sense of foreboding raging through him as he stared back at his commander.

"Lilly's disappeared. She left the estate twelve hours ago and hasn't been seen since. Her family is searching for her, but no authorities have been called in as of yet. Santos and Rhiannon are screaming at Command to pull in unit four to find her, and Command is refusing to answer the summons."

Travis froze. "What do you mean, missing?"

"She walked out of the house and disappeared. The last time she was seen she was arguing with her mother over you. Wild Card was in house at the time and reports Angelica has made arrangements to have Lilly committed to an asylum in the south of France because of her refusal to stop seeing you."

"Fucking bloody bitch!" Travis quickly circled the vehicle and jumped in on the passenger side as Jordan put it into gear. "Any leads?"

"All we know is that her family hasn't found her," Jordan reported. "Things went from bad to worse real fucking fast, Travis. We've contacted Senator Stanton but he's refusing to give us any information on any damned thing. Command is silent. The only response Santos and Rhiannon have had is to take care of their own house-cleaning. And I'll be damned if I like the sound of that."

"Have you heard from Elite Two?"

Travis needed his cell phone. The sat phone had been damaged just after arriving in England. Lilly would have called.

"MIA," Jordan responded. "They can't be found."

"That's not unusual." Travis stared straight ahead, forcing himself to be patient until he could retrieve the cell phone. Lilly would have left a message. He knew she would.

"Give me a break here, Travis," Jordan grunted. "I'm not Santos. I know how close this unit is to those girls. You know where they are, and I bet you anything they know where Lilly is. Thing is, if she doesn't contact myself or her commanders soon, if she doesn't make the right moves, then her mother will have the power to get her committed, just as she wants to do. She's already making arrangements to have the case heard in England. And we both know how that goes."

"She'll make contact," Travis informed him. "I need a cycle and a communications helmet as well as my cell phone. Keep Santos and Rhiannon in the dark until I find out what the hell happened. I don't want to spook Lilly or the girls."

Travis shook his head. "The girls are watching her, Jordan. If they had her they would have contacted."

Jordan shot him a surprised look. "You're certain?"

"I'm positive."

There was a chance she had made it to the safe house she owned. He would look there after contacting the girls and learning what they might know. He was praying they were with her.

"Wild Card didn't follow her when she left?" he asked.

"No one knew she was gone until it was too late." Jordan shook his head. "We have a serious situation here, Travis. An Elite Op on the run, her memories compromised, her ability to protect herself hindered." His voice became angrier. "And didn't I warn those fucking fools this would happen? The minute Lilly stepped out of line, her mother was ready to ship her ass to Ridgemore. Exactly where we can't risk her being."

The drugs and advanced shock therapy Ridgemore would use could possibly destroy Lilly. The psychiatric drugs Ridgemore was known for could be disastrous.

It was a problem Jordan had indeed warned Elite Command of. Angelica Harrington's circle of friends knew only one way to deal with children determined to lead their own lives. That was by enforcing their wishes through restraint and drugs.

It was no damned wonder those same kids were becoming drug addicts, and many of them were eventually taking their own lives.

"I'll find her." He would find her, or there would be hell to pay.

CHAPTER 16

"TRAVIS GATHERED most of the information over the past few months." Raisa spread the hard-copy files and maps out on the long kitchen table two days after Lilly had arrived.

Lilly had spent most of her time at the farmhouse sleeping. The headaches were bad; the shots Shea had given her had barely touched them. It had taken the medic more than twenty-four hours to find a combination of medications that would help and to acquire them.

She was finally headache-free, though, and able to figure out exactly what was happening to her, and to her life.

"Here's what he's been working on." Raisa drew her attention back to the table. "This is the warehouse where you were shot six months ago." She pointed to the top of a warehouse across from another unmarked warehouse. "You were parked here." She pointed to the Land Rover parked between the two warehouses. "The shot was fired perfectly, but you turned at the last second. That's all on video but we can't access the video file from here yet."

"We're still uncertain why you were targeted or by who." Nissa Farren, the communications whiz kid of the group, turned from her equipment to look at the rest of them. "Travis has been running down leads the past few days—that's why he's not here. We didn't expect your mother to try to have you committed. But never fear, Black Jack will take care of everything."

Black Jack. His code name. She was Night Hawk. She was part of a group of women trained to provide backup and distraction on missions conducted by the male counterparts of an elite covert operations group. The name of which the other women still refused to give her.

"It seems Black Jack can take care of everything," she murmured.

"Travis and the others are our big brothers," Shea Tamallan said, her smile somber as she looked at Lilly. "They've always watched over us, along with Santos."

"And Rhiannon?" she asked. "What about her?"

Nissa shrugged. "Rhiannon is harder to figure out. I've been working with her for a few months longer than you were with us. None of us have ever figured her out. She's very compassionate, but she's also very by-the-book. It makes it harder to work with her."

"She would have never approved our deployment," Shea stated. "She and Santos argue often over us, and the missions we're given. They didn't want you returned to your family, but Elite Command needed you for this mission."

"How nice," she murmured. "But Santos has always watched over us, right?"

"It's hard to explain without telling you more than we should," Raisa stated soberly. "We have to be careful, Lilly. And you especially have to be careful. If there's the least suspicion that you know as much as you do, then Elite Command will have no choice but to order your death. They can't afford the risk to the other agents."

There was a lot of information she still didn't have, but she had acquired much information in recent days. She knew she had been specifically trained to work with a certain group of agents. A group Travis was a part of. The call-girl cover had been created to keep them above suspicion as agents, and the troublemaking personas were intended to allow them to move freely as needed and to lend them an air of danger that made it logical for them to be in the company of the agents they were trained to provide backup for.

"What information do we have, if any, on the latest attempt?" Lilly asked.

"We have the explosives cap and the fluid," Raisa said. "Both of which were used in the bomb makeup and have been used before. Surprisingly enough, your father was tracking the maker of that bomb before he died. It's the same bomb tied to an explosion at one of his offices four months before his death."

Lilly nodded. "I remember that. It happened around four in the morning, so no one was hurt, thank God, but we never did find out who was behind it. We couldn't even figure out why they would have wanted to do it." She shook her head. "it's just an office building. There was nothing to be gained from blowing it up." A frown creased her brow. "So whoever blew up Father's office in London used the same bomb to try and blow me up here in Maryland?"

Shea shrugged. "We're hoping that Travis's trip to England will shed some light on all of this," she told her. "We need to wrap this up, hopefully—in Santos and Rhiannon's opinion—before you remember anything about the six missing years. They truly wanted you to have the chance to return to the family you missed so desperately once they were ordered to allow it, Lilly. We all wanted that for you."

Because they had all lost so much as well. Family, friends, careers, and lives, as they continued to fight for a world that didn't give a damn about them.

Lilly turned away from the table and paced over to the window. "When does Travis return?"

"We believe he flew in before dawn this morning. He'll be debriefed on his mission, which normally takes close to twelve hours, then Jordan should release him. He'll come looking for you."

"Does he know where I am?"

Shea nodded. "I left a message on his cell phone. I asked him to call with an update, which isn't unusual in itself."

She gripped the phone in the pocket of the light hoodie she wore. The girls had made her turn it off, telling her that she could be tracked if it was active. It was how they had found her. She knew they were telling the truth, but . . .

But if Travis did call her, she wouldn't know it. Wouldn't be able to hear his voice.

She raked her fingers through her hair and turned to the window again. Waiting. Watching.

Travis hadn't called Shea yet. Why hadn't he called?

"You know, it's so odd to see you without those Glocks you wear on your thighs." Nissa gave a light laugh as Lilly ran her hand to her thigh. "Would you like to have them?"

Lilly turned to her. "You have them?"

Her smile was wide, bright. "We have some of your things here. We brought them just in case you needed them."

Nissa rose from her chair and motioned Lilly to the back of the house. The bedroom she went into was the one she shared with Shea. The two half-beds were placed on opposite sides of the wall. One side of the room was neat as a pin. The other side, as though an invisible line ran through it, was a complete shambles.

Of course Nissa moved to the messy side of the room.

"Here you go." She pulled a large bag from the nearby closet and tossed it to the unmade bed. "Two changes of clothes, your guns and knives, and plenty of ammo. There's also an unregistered sat phone, but please don't call Travis yet. There's also cash, credit cards, a few disguise aids, and some fake IDs. Everything a girl needs to survive in the deep dark underground."

Everything she needed to survive, but not to live.

"You were ordered to contact Santos and Rhiannon if I called, weren't you?" Lilly sat down on the bed, pushing the mussed blankets behind her as she began to go through the bag.

"Of course." Nissa shrugged. "At least that's what their commanders told them to do. Santos's exact words were, 'We were told to order you to do this'." She laughed. "We rarely pay any attention to orders from Command."

"And if Santos had given the order himself?" She looked up at the other woman.

Nissa shrugged again. "We would have ignored it. Lilly, we only have each other to depend on. One of these days you might be covering my ass again with that rifle of yours. I don't want you pissed off with me if that day comes."

"Where's my rifle?" She remembered it now. The lethal sniper rifle that she had used to cover the asses of the agents she worked with. There was another in her storage shed, but it wasn't her favorite.

"That I don't know." Nissa shook her head. "Santos retrieved it from the Land Rover when you were shot. I haven't seen it since."

But . . . There was another safe house, she thought as yet another piece of memory broke free. And that safe house was fully stocked.

"Company's coming. Move!" Shea yelled from the kitchen.

Lilly moved. She didn't stop to question anyone or ask for directions. She grabbed the holster and pouch of clips before racing to the next room and the window that looked out on the driveway.

She had time to buckle the belt and strap the holsters to her thighs. She checked the Glocks quickly, shoved the clips in and stood ready.

"No one called and warned us of a visit." Shea raced into the bedroom and slapped a comm device in Lilly's hand. "If we're attacked, get out, hit the woods, and head for Friendly's Tavern. Know where it is?"

Lilly nodded. "I know."

"Someone will be there."

Shea raced from the room as Lilly slid the device in her ear.

"Comm check," she murmured.

"Comm check," each woman answered in reply before Nissa reported. "We have a van moving in, dark panels, dark tint. Looks like we have a masked driver. Be prepared to jump and run. We don't fight this out unless we have no other choice."

Lilly pulled the Glocks from their holsters.

Her jaw tightened as the van moved slowly into view. She watched, silent, eyes narrowed as it came to a stop behind the Taurus.

A second later, all hell broke loose. The back doors flew open as four dark figures raced from the back, two from the doors, and all began firing.

The Taurus exploded.

The house shook, windows imploded, and shards of glass rained around Lilly as she tore through the bedroom for the back door, joined by the other four women.

"Stay to the trees!" Shea ordered her as they moved out the back door at the same moment the front door burst open in a rain of fire. "Run!"

As Lilly and the other women raced for the tree line only feet away, Lilly saw the shadows moving there. Dark, masked, though diffrent from the others. Her guns cleared her belt as she ran, keeping the trees between them. Suddenly those dark figures rushed past them.

"Take cover!"

Travis.

Lilly stared, shocked, into his furious eyes as he paused to bark at her. "Stay back with the others! Cover our asses and make sure no one gets hurt."

He shoved a rifle at her.

It wasn't her custom-made rifle, but it was close enough.

Lilly holstered the Glocks, grabbed the rifle then ran up the rise to a tree that would give her the best possible view. As though she'd been born to climb, she shimmied up it as Nissa followed her.

"Spot," she ordered the other woman.

"I'm an excellent spotter," Nissa answered as they moved into position. "You have ammo for that bad boy too in your bag." Nissa nodded to the bag Lilly had slung over her shoulders.

Lilly took aim.

"Our boys have the narrow gray stripes on their shoulders," Nissa hissed. "Don't hit one of them. We enjoy the hot, lurid fantasies we have about them. Even though most of them are married now."

Lilly gave a quick smile, then braced the rifle on a limb of the tree and took aim.

"They have a sniper at three o'clock. Looks like a spotter searching for you, sweetie." Nissa pointed out the slightest disruption among the branches at the three o'clock angle.

Lilly aimed, checked the wind, calculated her distance and fired.

The first body fell. With the second shot his spotter followed suit.

As she narrowed her eyes and surveyed the trees for an additional threat, the whiz of a bullet slamming into the tree next to her head had Lilly freezing.

She calculated the direction, checked the distance, and waited.

"Where is he, Nissa?" she growled. "Sometime before he takes our heads off."

"To the right of the first, third tree, halfway up at the seven o'clock limb. He's going to be hard to hit with this wind, though."

"See his spotter?"

"Haven't seen him. Caught a leaf trembling at nine o'clock, though, if you want to take a chance."

"I'm feeling lucky."

She found the position, watched the leaves, and took the shot.

The body fell, but she didn't track it—she watched the seven o'clock limb, waited, caught a gleam of black, and took the next shot. Another body fell as she quickly swung the rifle to the battle raging in the front yard. Somehow snipers had been in place before the attack. Someone had sent ten men to take out four women. They should have sent more.

She had taken out the snipers while the team below made quick work of the assailants that had rushed the house.

Below, the four shadows with their little narrow gray stripes were kicking some serious ass. Within minutes there were only two left, lying flat on the ground, hands raised in surrender as the dead bodies were being gathered.

Lilly watched as the team worked with perfect precision while the four women covered their backs. This was one of the reasons they existed, what they had been trained for.

She and Nissa watched for snipers, while the two

women on the ground kept the perimeter clear and watched for any breaks or surprises.

"We have a clear." Raisa's voice came over the link. "I repeat, we have a clear. Two live ones on the ground. Stay in place and I'll bring you your masks."

Lilly and Nissa waited until they saw Raisa below them. Jumping to the ground, they took the dark masks, pulled them over their heads, and tucked their hair beneath.

"Stay clear of the live ones," Raisa told them. "Black Jack and Live Wire want a clear field with no distractions." She looked amused. "Live Wire seems to think you might be a distraction for Black Jack. Now, what would give him that impression?"

Lilly shook her head, her lips thinning. "They weren't here to take out Live Wire, they were here to kill me. I think I have the right to know why."

Moving quickly to the front of the house, the rifle cradled in her arms, Lilly strode straight to where the two men were restrained and laid out in the grass.

The four men standing over them moved aside as she came closer. Staring into the dark, furious gazes, she handed her rifle to Travis, reached down and, with a quick jerk, revealed their faces.

She wished she hadn't.

She stared into faces she knew. Into the eyes of men who had been hired by her father. Men she had known before her "death."

"Do we need to interrogate them?"

Her head jerked to Live Wire. Jordan Malone.

She gave a quick nod. She didn't remember the rules,

but she knew not to speak, not now, not here. They knew her, knew her voice, knew their target. She wasn't taking chances.

Jordan jerked his head to Travis. "Get out of here."

She backed up, still staring into the malevolent gaze of the bodyguard she knew as Ritchie. He wasn't one of her mother's most trusted, but he was still a part of the Harrington staff and had been for years.

The other, Samuel, was also well known. He'd been hired by her father and well trusted. He'd flirted with her several times. Laughed with her mother, played poker with her uncle.

"Ritchie James and Samuel Mayes," she murmured to Travis. "Bodyguards working for my mother and uncle. I need to see the others."

Travis nodded, his body language showing his fury as he led her to the others and quickly stripped off their masks.

She stared at them icily.

"We have files on them," Travis said quietly. "Enemies, Lilly. All four of these men were with a private mercenary group we went against in Berlin three years ago."

"I know them." She heard the complete emotionlessness of her voice, felt it inside her. "But not from Berlin. In the past six months I've seen them either speaking to Desmond, Isaac, or one of the other bodyguards. This was an orchestrated hit. I was set up."

"We don't have reports on them," he stated quietly. "We've been watching the family. We've not seen them or we would have put a better circle of security around you."

She shook her head. "It would have been easy for them to get past you. One at a time, coming in quietly. They met inside the house here or in England. I saw this one." She kicked the balding blond in the shoulder. "This one was at the hospital several times when Desmond's bodguard Isaac came in."

Travis lifted his hand and motioned one of the others over.

"Burn the bodies," he ordered them. "We need to interrogate the other two, but get a team in to clean this mess up. Let's keep this quiet. I'm sure Lilly doesn't want to deal with her mother's concern over a hit when she returns to the house."

Lilly turned to him in shock. "Are you crazy? Do you know what she's planning? I'm not going back to the house. She's having me committed, Travis, and Harrington bodyguards just tried to kill me."

A hard, cold smile formed on his lips. "Does she know what *I* have planned, sweetheart?" he asked her. "Trust me, neither she nor Ridgemore will dare to defy me once I show up with you. And this time, trust me, I won't be leaving until this is settled, baby, and you're safe."

Her lips curled mockingly. "Strange you say that." She stared at him now, so damned happy to see him that she could barely stand it. So furious that she hadn't been able to find him, that he hadn't been there when she needed him. "You didn't tell me you were leaving."

His eyes narrowed on her. "I left security."

"I didn't need your damned security," she hissed as she moved closer, staring up at him, her body shaking she was so damned mad at him. "I needed to know you would be gone. I needed to know to watch my own ass while you weren't here."

"You should know that anyway." He reached out, grabbed her arms and jerked her closer. "I left security, Lilly. I would have never left you unguarded."

"Then where the hell were they?" Her finger stabbed into his chest. "What am I supposed to do, damn you? Kill the whole fucking family while I'm waiting on your damned security? Or just hope for the best as the guys in white suits drag me off?"

"No one would have gotten you out of that damned house. I had men in place. If you had given them time, they would have gotten you out and gotten you to safety."

"Well, excuse me for not twiddling my thumbs while I wait on you to take care of poor little ole me." She tried for American Southern, it came out rather mangled. She blamed it on her anger. She was certain she had pulled it off before.

"Don't push me right now," he snarled back at her. "Do you have any idea the hell I've gone through while trying to find you? Do you have any idea how close I was to not getting here in time?"

"Do you have any idea how close I was to blowing them all to hell and back?" she snapped back. "I might not remember jack shit but don't think I don't know what I'm doing. And don't think I will ever tolerate you disappearing like that again without one word of warning. Not while you're sleeping in my fucking bed."

"Wow. He's sleeping in your bed. Do I get details now or later?" Raisa laughed behind her.

Lilly ignored Raisa. She glared at Travis. "Find a place to talk. Fast. We have things to clear up, love, and we'll do it rather quickly. Or you'll wish you'd never seen me, met me, or touched me. I promise you that."

She turned on her heel and stalked away from him. It was all she could do to keep her hands away from her guns.

That way, she didn't shoot him just for being a man. For leaving. For not letting her know. For making her fear he would never return.

CHAPTER 17

IN A PERFECT WORLD, she would have known there was security in love. There was a mother's dedication, compassion, and devotion as she had once believed. There was a family's loyalty. In a perfect world, there was the knowledge that tomorrow would bring another day to add to the vault of memories and love.

Where had her perfect world gone?

Lilly sat on the bed in the darkened bedroom of another safe house, this one a large apartment in the heart of Hagerstown only a few blocks from the bar she had often met Travis in.

She stared into the dark but it was memories she saw. Her father's laughter, his gentle voice, and his loyalty. She saw their walks, remembered their talks. She saw her mother, always distant from them, always appearing amused, yet accepting of the bond they had had.

She'd been wrong.

Jared had often stood with Angelica, quiet, intense. Her brother had always been very intense, very studious, but she'd believed he was being protective.

Where had her family gone?

Looking down, she could barely make out the dim outline of her fingers as they picked at each other. A nervous habit she'd had all her life. Her mother had often lectured her over it. Lilly had seen those lectures as loving, as a mother's concern. But she remembered now the times that her mother had commented that perhaps it spoke of a deeper problem. That perhaps Lilly would feel better if she spoke to a doctor about her problem.

Lilly stared at her fingers. Perhaps it hadn't been her problem that had needed to be addressed.

She remembered, although she hadn't wanted to remember before, the horrible fights her parents had once had. Not that she had known what the fights were about at the time. All she remembered were the sounds of the raging arguments that had come from their suite.

They had argued over her often.

How many times had her mother tried to have her confined during those years that Lilly had believed she was safe and secure with her mother's love, with her brother's loyalty? That it was all simply threats.

She nibbled at her lower lip as she felt the pain gather in her soul before bleeding through her spirit. Where was that perfect world she had believed existed?

This was why she had chosen a far different life when she'd had the chance. But still, how desperately she had missed her family.

She had forgotten the monsters that existed in that perfect world.

"Lilly." A soft knock at the door heralded Travis's arrival.

She wiped the tears quickly from her face as the door

cracked open, allowing a slender ray of light to pierce the darkness.

"You have a very bad habit of disappearing when I don't want you to, Travis," she told him quietly as the door closed behind him, enclosing them once again in the darkness.

"Can I turn the light on?" he asked.

"I'd much prefer you don't."

She watched as he paused, his dark shape shifting slightly before he moved to the bed as though he needed no light to see by.

"Whoever is trying to kill me is someone associated with, or within, my family. Isn't that right?"

He eased down on the side of the bed. "That's what we suspect."

She nodded slowly. "How would they have found me after the first attempt to kill me? A new face, new hair, new eye color, plastic surgery." She rubbed her fingertips together. "No fingerprints. How did they find me?"

"We don't know." He sighed. "That's one of the things I've been trying to find out. So far though, all signs point to the Harrington camp."

She gave another slow nod. "The first attempt was during the party. Father was in a meeting when I came to the office. I remember that much. He'd been investigating the embezzlement from several companies Harringtons owned or had shares in. The money was going into an account proven to fund terrorism. I had been helping him for months, but those final months, he pushed me out of it. We argued over that."

"He was trying to protect you?" he asked.

"I think perhaps he was," she said as she looked

down at her hands to realize she was picking at her fingers once again. "Do you think it was Uncle Desmond?"

Her father and uncle had been very close, but she remembered that Desmond hadn't known that her father worked for MI5, and he had cautioned Lilly against letting anyone in the family know that she was as well.

Even her mother hadn't known what Lilly was doing.

"Let's say he's at the top of the list," Travis answered. "We're focusing on him."

Lilly felt her heart clench at the thought. "Father trusted him. He loved him."

"The ones we trust the most are often the ones who will betray us first," he said, gently. "Whoever it is, Lilly, whatever their motive, they meant to see you dead. Today made the fourth attempt on your life, and this one was professionally contracted."

"How did they find us?" She frowned in confusion, still trying to figure that one out. "My cell was turned off. I didn't contact anyone. How did they find me?"

"You could have been followed," he answered softly. "Several of the assailants were in your uncle's employ. Any one of them could have followed you to the safe house, then returned. It could have taken time to call the others together, to plan a reasonably successful assault. Two days isn't much time to plan the assassination of four women. One of whom was known to be able to take care of her herself quite well."

"You could have planned and executed that one within hours," she pointed out.

"But I'm better than they are." He chuckled.

Lilly allowed a small smile to touch her lips, but she couldn't bring herself to laugh.

"They're my family," she whispered. "My mother and brother, my uncle. They're all I've ever known for love and security. What the hell happened, Travis?"

He breathed out heavily. "As long as you were the child you were supposed to be, then you were well loved," he told her. "Perhaps it's that society, that generation, or just that small clique. I'm more inclined to say it's a very small clique that believes in committing a child for daring to have free will. Most parents suffer the minor embarrassments and disappointments as a part of life."

She let her head fall back against the wall behind her and stared up at the dark ceiling.

"Mother never showed me this side of herself. Not to this extent."

"Or your father never let you see it?" Travis suggested. "He tried to protect you."

"Maybe." She moved to swing her legs off the bed but he stretched his arm across her thighs and held her in place.

She was suddenly very conscious of the thin robe and her nudity beneath it. The shower she'd had earlier had done nothing to still the nervous tension racing through her.

She'd wanted to run. She wanted to fight. She wanted to find a place to expend the fury inside her before she was forced to return to the house her uncle had rented for the summer.

"Travis, now isn't a good time." She still hadn't managed to forgive him for his absence.

He chuckled lightly. "Bullshit, Lilly. You have all that energy dying to burst free and I'll be damned if I didn't miss you like hell."

"Oh yeah, you missed me so much," she mocked him. "All those phone calls, checking up on me, phone sex at one in the morning. It was so much fun."

She pushed against his shoulder, but not really with enough force to dislodge him. When it came to Travis, saying no wasn't an easy thing to do.

"There was phone sex? Was it good?" Dark, roughened by arousal, his voice whispered across her senses like a velvety caress.

"It would have been if it had been more than simply in my dreams," she bit out, clearly remembering the anger and fear that had torn through her when she realized she was only days away from being committed.

"I wouldn't have allowed you to be taken from me like that, Lilly," he said gently, as though he knew exactly what she thought, what she felt.

"You couldn't have stopped it. You weren't here, remember?" she pointed out angrily.

"Lilly, I didn't leave you unprotected."

"I protected myself." She pushed at his shoulder harder this time. "Let me go, Travis. This discussion is becoming boring."

"Then get unbored." His voice was harder, though no less sexy. "I didn't betray you, Lilly, nor did I let you down."

"You weren't there," she snapped furiously. "You didn't even tell me you were leaving, Travis."

"Dammit, Lilly, it was a quick trip out. I should have been back before the next night. My sat phone was damaged or I would have gotten your message and returned faster."

"So what is this relationship then? Or is it not even a

relationship? Friends with benefits? Fuck buddies? What, Travis? Tell me the rules now so I at least know what to expect the next time you decide to disappear for however long."

"You want to know what the hell this relationship is?" He came over her, looming above her like a dark shadow of sensual wrath.

"It would be nice." Her voice was weak and breathy. She sounded like a damned sex kitten or something. Hell, she was starting to feel like one.

"This relationship is completely monogamous," he growled as his hand smoothed down her shoulder, her arm, gripped her hip. "And I'm a possessive bastard, Lilly. Did I ever mention that?"

She shook her head. No, he hadn't mentioned that at all. Perhaps he should have; she would have melted far sooner.

"So that would make this relationship fairly exclusive, wouldn't you say?" He jerked the hem of her robe to her thighs. "That makes you mine, baby. No friends with benefits. No fuck buddies. Simply fucking mine."

"Call next time," she snapped.

"Fine." His other hand gripped her neck, held her still and kissed her with enough force, enough hunger, to curl her toes.

It was like this with him. Like a fire blazing through the darkest night, stilling the rage and the pain and re-placing it with hunger and a sense of emotional security. There was no true safety, not in their lives, not in their line of work, but there was this.

Deep, desperate kisses filled with hunger and heat

branded her lips and her senses as pleasure began to wash over her in heavy, heated waves. Travis jerked her to him and Lilly found herself being lowered to the bed as he came over her, his hands tearing at the belt of the robe, at his own clothes. Through drugging tastes of her lips, his head tilting, his tongue thrusting against hers, he managed to divest himself of his clothes and to tear aside the edges of her robe.

She was all but naked now. The dark surrounded them, white-hot hunger and needy groans mixed with his own male growls of arousal. It was like having those ragged edges of her soul slowly repair themselves.

She wasn't alone any longer. Travis was here. He was touching her, holding her. There was nothing, no one, that could harm her as long as she held his heart.

Heavily muscled shoulders flexed beneath her touch as his hands cupped her breasts, sending surging pulses of sensation rippling through her nipples when his thumbs stroked over them.

Lilly could feel the invasive pleasure throbbing through her pussy, swelling her clit. Her juices gathered on the intimate folds as her nipples swelled, ached, and lifted to his touch.

"I missed you, my Lilly," he groaned as his lips moved to her neck. "I dreamed of your touch. Of tasting you, having you."

His lips moved lower, his tongue stroking over a tight nipple as brutally hot fingers of sensation struck at her womb, her clit. Arching against his thigh, Lilly felt the desperate hunger unraveling inside her. This moment in time was hers alone. She didn't have to share it. No one could invade it. There was no danger here, there was only this. His lips covering her nipple to suck it inside his mouth as his tongue flicked over it.

He drew on the tight bud, suckling it deeply, almost roughly, as she arched to the incredible sensation. From one nipple to the other he moved. The excruciatingly sensitive tip rioted with such extreme pleasure that she couldn't hold back the whimpering little cry that tore from her lips.

It was incredible. Her head thrashed against the pillow as he licked the hard nubbin, swirled his tongue around it, then sucked it inside his mouth again and fed on the arousal rising inside her.

Lilly's hips arched as Travis's thigh wedged between hers and pressed firmly against the mound of her pussy. Her clit swelled tighter, throbbed with pleasure. Her juices spilled from her clenching vagina, her body desperate for his possession, preparing it for the intensity of touch that she needed.

She wanted more than gentle touches, and that was what she was getting. She wanted more than easy kisses and slow caresses. And he would give it to her.

"Sweet Lilly," he growled as he pulled back, reaching out with one hand to the bedside table and flipping on the low light there.

The soft glow washed over his naked, bronzed flesh. Muscles rippled beneath the skin, perspiration dotted his brow, his shoulders.

Easing back, he stared down her body.

"Touch your breasts," he ordered, his eyes focused on the swollen mounds as he lifted her hands to them. "Show me, baby, what you like, what you want. Make me crazy."

Make him crazy? Oh, if this was what he wanted, then she had a lot of experience in touching herself.

She cupped her breasts, her fingers clenching on the mounds teasingly. With her index fingers she raked her nipples, gasping at the pleasure of having him watch.

"Oh yeah," he breathed out roughly, his eyes narrowing on her now. "Is that how you like it, baby? Slow and easy?"

A teasing smile curled her lips. With thumb and forefinger she pinched at the distended nipples, her breath catching at the thought of Travis touching her so firmly, with his fingers, his teeth.

She bit her lower lip to hold back another moan as she tugged at the tender tips, her shoulders shifting against the bed as pleasure tore through her.

"Ahh, so that's how you like it, love," he whispered. "Shall I do that for you, while perhaps you show me other things you might like?"

He moved, sliding behind her as he lifted her before him. Lilly gasped as she found her head resting on his thigh, the heavy width of his cock at her cheek as it rose proud and flush along his stomach.

"There, love." His hand stroked her breast, cupped it, petted it. "Show me what else you like while I play with your pretty nipples."

Lilly could feel the perspiration gathering along her neck, her breasts. Fighting to breathe, Lilly felt his thumb and forefinger surround her nipple as he placed one of her hands on her midriff.

"Show me, Lilly," he growled. "Show me what you want, sweetheart."

What she wanted? She wanted his touch. She wanted his fingers stroking her, touching her, possessing her.

She stared up at him as his fingers worked her nipple, rolling it, plumping it, and sending electrical flames of sensation tearing to her womb.

Her fingers slid lower, ruffling the border of curls just below her abdomen. She could feel the folds of her pussy swelling, her clit pounding, as her fingers feathered against it.

"Beautiful," he breathed out roughly. "Part those pretty folds, Lilly. Let me see your little clit. Let me see how you pleasure yourself."

Lowering her other hand, she parted the plump folds of her pussy as she used the other to circle the tight bud of her clit. Pleasure was racing through her, excitement sizzling through her nerve endings, as she touched herself with her fingers, while Travis tormented her nipples with exquisite pleasure.

As she looked up at him, her gaze locked with his, and she watched his eyes narrow, darken, as her fingers circled her clit. The pleasure was incredible. It was like nothing she had ever known when she'd touched herself before. It was brutally intense, whipping through her system and sending her nerve endings rioting with exquisite pleasure.

Her fingers stroked through her folds, dipping into the slick dew, returning to run around her clit as his fingers sent waves of pleasure surging through her nipples to her pussy, clenching the intimate folds with brutal need.

Her hips writhed beneath her own touch as her head turned, her lips parting, her tongue licking along the shaft of his cock as it rose before her.

She needed the taste of him. The touch of him. She needed him.

She moved her fingers faster as a hard groan tore from his chest. Her head lifted, her tongue touching the head of his cock, licking over it, tasting it.

She felt as though she were dying of excitement. It was racing through her bloodstream, pounding in her heart. She couldn't survive this. She was going to die from the intensity of the sensations, but she would die happy. She would die knowing no pleasure could ever be so great.

As her fingers dipped inside her pussy a gasp of tormented pleasure passed her lips. Her lips parted, surrounded the engorged head of Travis's cock, and sucked him inside her mouth. She milked the hard, throbbing flesh, sucking it deep, laving it with her tongue.

Driving her fingers deep inside the hot depths of her own flesh, she angled herself higher against his chest, kept the hard crest in her mouth and slowly came to her knees. Her thighs tightened on her own hand for long seconds before slowly withdrawing them.

Lifting her head, she felt his hands tighten for a second in her hair before he allowed her to straighten. Licking her lips, Lilly lifted her fingers, still wet from her juices, and painted the heavy dew across his lips as they parted and he sucked two of her fingers inside.

The feel of his lips suckling her fingers had her pussy rippling in impending orgasm. She had never been so close to coming without actually being penetrated.

"I needed you," she whispered as she straddled his thighs, staring into his eyes as he released her fingers, his hands moving to clench the mounds of her ass.

"God. Never again. Swear." His expression twisted into lines of tormented pleasure as she gripped the shaft of his cock and rubbed it against the tortured knot of her clit.

"So good," she moaned, her hips shifting, her pussy clenching.

"Fucking good," he groaned. "Fuck me, Lilly. Stop teasing the hell out of me."

She smiled back at him, shifting the engorged crest until it was poised at the entrance of her pussy.

Ecstasy began to pound inside her then. Moving her hips, shifting, pressing down, as she felt the wide, heavy length of his erection stretching her wide.

Pleasure-pain enveloped her, sending sizzling, heated currents of rapture racing across nerve endings so sensitive, she whimpered with the building exaltation. She couldn't stay still. Her hips jerked against the hold he had on her ass, her need to race to completion beating inside her.

"Easy, baby," he groaned, his fingers bunching in her ass, pulling the rounded flesh apart, sending additional sensations assaulting her nerve endings.

Sensations she had never expected to enjoy. The feel of his fingers dipping into the extreme wetness flowing from her pussy, around his cock. The feel of those fingers smoothing the slickness back, rubbing against that once forbidden, untouched area.

It was untouched no longer, because she didn't have the willpower to stop him. Hell no, she wasn't stopping him. She was pressing down, making the touch firmer, more invasive.

Her eyes flared open as his fingertip penetrated that

hidden entrance. Heavy-eyed, intense, he watched her with increasing hunger as his finger continued to slip slowly inside as she pressed down, taking his cock deeper, his finger deeper.

The dual penetration was exquisite. Her fingers clenched on his shoulders as she rode him slow and easy, taking all of his cock, all of his finger, and milking them as she felt the pleasure burning over her nerve endings.

"God, you're beautiful." His voice was whiskey rough, dark and hungry. "So fucking sweet and hot, Lilly."

Sweat eased down his temple, drawing her gaze as she felt his finger ease from her rear, gather more of her juices and penetrate once again.

"Travis. What are you doing to me?" Shudders of pleasure were tearing through her as she felt her muscles ease, relax, and welcome a second finger.

"Travis." His name was a plea, a cry of such incredible pleasure she didn't know if she could bear it.

His hand eased on her hip. Rather than holding her back, he let her free. She couldn't hold still. She couldn't stop the need to ride him hard and fast, to feel the fiery burn, the desperate sensuous rise of ecstasy.

Lilly felt her head tip back on her shoulders as it began to build, to tighten through her. She tightened her hold on him, her nails digging in, desperate mewls rising from her throat as electric intensity, white-hot fingers of sensation, began to radiate outward from both penetrations. His cock filled her, stretched her. His fingers fucked inside her rear, sending flames shooting along previously untouched nerve endings, triggering a flame that built, that rose, that overtook her in an explosion so sudden, so blinding, she screamed his name.

He was thrusting hard and deep beneath her, one arm wrapped around her, holding her close as his fingers drove deep, his cock drove deeper, and he groaned her name and stiffened beneath her.

Fiery bursts of release erupted inside her. She felt it, throbbing, pulsing, filling her as her pussy clenched around him. Her head fell to his shoulder as she felt herself crying, shuddering, hard tremors raking through her body as the pleasure tore through her over and over again.

She couldn't contain it. She couldn't fight it. She had lost any measure of restraint when it came to Travis long ago. So long ago. When he was bound to another woman, when she was barely a woman, on a dance floor surrounded by others, she had given him her heart.

He had always held her, and she had never realized it. He had filled her fantasies as Lord Dermont. Then he had filled her deepest desires as Travis Caine.

And now, now he filled every dream, every emotion she had thought she would never be filled. The lover she had never believed would be in her life.

Breathing heavily, she collapsed against him, shudders still racing through her body as the aftershocks of pleasure continued to pulse through her. The wildly exciting penetrations of her body left her exhausted, left her mindless. She could do nothing but hold on to him now, to pray that for this moment, he would continue to shelter her, that he had the strength to hold her as she fought to catch her breath.

As she felt his fingers ease slowly from her a small moan escaped her lips. The pleasure was still brutal. The feel of his fingers retreating caressed those nerve endings, so sensitized she could barely catch her breath from the added caress.

"Easy, baby." He sounded sated, relaxed, as his hand smoothed down her back. "Give me a second here and I'll carry you to the shower."

She had to laugh at that. A low, weak sound, but one filled with a deep satiation. "You'll drop me."

"Right now," he agreed, his lips smoothing over her shoulder. "No breath right now."

He gave a deep sigh, one that assured her that he had been just as satisfied, just as fulfilled as she was.

"That's okay." She snuggled closer. "I like being right here."

"I like you being right here." His lips pressed against hers gently. "Right here in my arms, Lilly. It's where you belong."

And it was exactly where she wanted to be.

It was still dark and Lilly lay pressed against his chest when Travis's cell phone rang. Travis picked up his phone and looked at the display. He frowned when he saw "Harrington" on the screen.

He sat up in bed, careful not to disturb Lilly. She turned over with a soft murmur. "Hello."

"Caine," Desmond said. His voice sounded grim. "We have things to discuss. You, me and Lilly. If I make sure Angelica is not here will you both meet me at the house around noon? I really think you both need to hear what I have to say."

Travis was silent for only a moment. Then he looked down at Lilly and said, "We'll be there."

CHAPTER 18

THE LIMO PULLED into the stately, oak-tree-lined drive that led to the house her family had taken for the summer. After pulling to a stop, Nik got out from the driver's seat, came around the car, opened the rear door, and stood aside as Travis stepped out.

His eyes narrowed as the door opened, and rather than the houseman at the entrance, he instead saw Isaac, Desmond's personal, chief bodyguard.

The dark silk suit he wore almost hid the bulge of the weapon he wore beneath his arm, but not quite. He was a formidable figure, if one wasn't confident in their ability to stand against him.

Travis was rather confident.

Isaac's dark brown eyes flicked to where Lilly stood beside him, resplendent in a soft, light blue camisole and matching skirt. Strappy flat sandals covered her feet. Her shoulder-length brown hair was pulled back into a casual ponytail and she even carried a small clutch purse rather than a rifle.

She looked every inch the perfect little lady.

Travis held his arm out to her, and almost grinned at the arrogant little tilt of her head as she laid her hand on his arm.

"Lady Lillian. Mr. Caine," he greeted them as they moved up the steps. "Lord Harrington is awaiting you."

"I'm certain he is," Travis responded. "And Lady Harrington? She's gone?"

"Lady Harrington is in D.C. shopping, I believe," Isaac informed them as he stepped aside. "Lord Harrington may have neglected to pass along the information that her daughter had been found and was returning."

"Her daughter was never lost," Lilly informed him coolly as they stepped into the foyer and waited for Nik to step in before Isaac closed the door behind them.

"So I see." He inclined his head in approval. "Follow me, Lord Harrington is waiting in his study."

Travis placed his hand on Lilly's lower back as they followed the bodyguard. It was hard to believe Isaac McCauley was involved in anything nefarious. He had been with the Secret Service, served a short stint with the CIA, and had then gone private. His reputation was sterling and above reproach.

Isaac paused at the study doors, gave a brief knock, then opened them and stood back as they entered.

Desmond Harrington stood in front of the cold fireplace, his leather-shod foot propped on the hearth as he leaned an elbow casually against the mantel. He'd shed the suit jacket he usually wore. The sleeves of his white, fine cotton shirt were rolled to his elbows and the dark blue silk slacks were still perfectly creased.

At first glance he was the epitome of professionalism, until Travis looked closely at his face. He looked like an exhausted thug. The red hair closely cropped, the lines on his face. Desmond Harrington was a hard man, and it showed in every line and wrinkle of his face.

In his free hand he held a short glass of what appeared to be whiskey. Watching them, he remained silent as he lifted the glass and sipped from it before nodding to Isaac.

"Can I offer anyone a drink?" Isaac asked as Travis, Lilly, and Nik came to a stop in the middle of the room, facing Desmond.

"I'll have my regular, Isaac," Lilly answered, her voice smooth and sweet and so ladylike it was hard to believe she could wield a sniper's rifle as easily as she held that glass of Crown and Coke.

"I'll take the whiskey straight," Travis answered as he pressed his hand into Lilly's back, urging her to the love seat despite the fact that they hadn't been invited to sit.

Nik stepped back, crossing his arms over his chest as he leaned against the wall beside the door and watched everyone with narrowed eyes.

Silence filled the room as Isaac poured the drinks, then moved across the room to hand Travis and Lilly theirs.

"Isaac, would you mind stepping outside now?" Desmond asked.

"I do, Lord Harrington," Isaac answered firmly. "You know that's not a very good idea at the moment."

Desmond sniffed disdainfully as he turned his head, threw back the rest of his drink, and grimaced tightly. "There are days, Lilly, when I wonder what the hell made me think I could handle the legacy your father left behind."

He slapped the glass to the mantel, raked his fingers over his head, and blew out a hard breath before glaring back at her.

He looked tired, she thought. Tired and filled with regret and grief.

His gaze focused on Travis Caine for long, intense minutes.

"It's damned hard to trust you," he said, sighing.

"I'm a man of my word, Lord Harrington," Travis reminded him. "You know that as well as anyone."

Lilly looked at him in surprise. He sounded as though her uncle actually knew him.

Desmond shook his head as he turned to her. "Six years ago I contacted Mr. Caine to negotiate an agreement between Harrington Translation and Dictation and a much larger company intent on taking it over. Your father was buried in an internal investigation at the time and I agreed to handle the attempted merger. I contacted your Mr. Caine to aid in that."

"A legal negotiation?" she murmured as she turned to Travis.

He grinned, sliding a look at her from the corner of his eye. "I do stay within the law occasionally, my dear."

Desmond grunted at the comment. "We would have lost the company if it hadn't been for him. With your father's death, and what we believed was your death, the family was in chaos for months."

"It appears to me that the family is still in chaos," she stated sadly.

Her uncle shook his head before lowering it for long moments. Finally, he heaved another sigh before moving to a nearby high-backed leather chair and taking a seat.

"Mr. Caine contacted me with the information that you had been found," he stated as he leaned back. "He told me then that he had known of your existence for years and had remained quiet. With your injuries, though, he was afraid you wouldn't make it, and he wanted your family close if that were true."

Lilly remained silent. That didn't sound like the truth to her; it didn't feel like the truth, though she had no doubt it was what he had told her family.

"Why are we here, Lord Harrington?" Travis finally asked. "You sent Lilly's mother away and were rather intent on this meeting. I will assume there's a reason for it."

"Of course there is." Desmond glared back at him irritably before turning back to Lilly. "Returning may not have been a good idea, child. Perhaps when Mr. Caine called I should have simply gone to the hospital alone and advised you to continue hiding."

"Why would you do that?" she asked, wondering herself why her intuition hadn't warned her to stay away.

"Because this family is more fucked up than any dysfunctional American family that you'll find," he stated roughly. "Jared rather surprised me, though. I didn't expect him to disown you."

"Perhaps he doesn't like losing the additional inheritance," Travis suggested.

Desmond shook his head. "Lilly's money is in trust. Nothing could be done with it until you turned twenty-six—if you were still alive, that is. And upon Lilly's death it wouldn't go to Jared anyway. It would go to a charity chosen in Lilly's name. Your brother's trust was set up the same way."

Yet another surprise.

"When was that decided?" Lilly asked. "Father told me nothing of this."

"And he wouldn't have until you were old enough to begin drawing from the fund," he answered her. "Unfortunately, you 'died' before you reached the age that you could touch your inheritance."

"What is the point of this, Uncle Desmond?" she asked.

"Someone tried to kill you six years ago, and then three times in the past six months. It's hard to believe it isn't personal, isn't it, Lilly? And now you know there's less reason to suspect your brother. So tell me I haven't risen on your list of suspects."

Lilly looked to Travis, then back to her uncle. "I don't know who to suspect," she finally stated, wondering what the hell was going on here.

"You were helping your father on that investigation," Desmond said then. "You were working with him and MI5 before you disappeared."

Now, she was shocked. Her father had made her swear to never reveal anything about the investigation. She stared back at Desmond silently, trying to figure out what he knew, and what he simply thought he knew.

"She has an excellent poker face." Desmond nodded toward her. "She always did have."

"What do you want, Harrington?" Travis sat forward now.

"I want my brother's killer. And I want the person trying to kill my niece stopped," he said, his voice soft. "I want the slow, steady embezzling of Harrington funds to stop, and I want my life back."

"And I'm to facilitate this, how?" Travis asked.

"Better yet, why should you be drawn in?" Lilly rose to her feet, tipped her drink to her lips, and finished it in one hard swallow before moving slowly to the bar.

She needed a moment to think, to figure out what the hell was going on here.

"You argued with Mother when I left?" she asked as she moved past Isaac to pour herself another drink.

Desmond chuckled. "Oh yes, my dear. Your mother and I argued quite loudly and for well through the next day. When Ridgemore showed up, we argued quite a bit more. You know how it works. She screams until she gets what she wants, and if she doesn't get what she wants, then she makes your life hell. Correct?"

Lilly poured herself another drink before turning back to him and leaning against the bar. "Mother never screamed at me. Not when Father was alive, anyway."

His expression softened, turned gentle. "No, she didn't scream at you. Because whenever she did, she had to face not just your father, but also your uncle. We did our best to shelter you. Sadly, it seems it was in vain."

He was gazing at her as though he held some affection for her. The way he watched her when she was a child. He had spoiled her just as her father had.

"Your father and I had hoped that by combining forces we could compel your mother to allow you to have your dreams," he said quietly. "You wanted to join MI5. You wanted to be adventurous. She wanted you to marry well, have children, and become a replica of herself. To her, that was her measure of success. Unfortunately, it seems to be how she and her friends measure their success. By how well they can turn their daughters into younger versions of themselves. She had your husband picked out, the sex of your children and their names. She had already decided where you would live, close to her of course, and who your friends would be. It would be her way, or no way at all."

"You make her sound crazed. I mean, more than usual." She needed another drink just to hold back the anger that she was only now seeing this. And not because he was telling her it was the truth, because she had witnessed it herself.

"Not crazed, simply arrogant, and certain of her own power." He shook his head. "She's royalty, remember?"

It was coming together so slowly, too slowly. Lilly felt the heavy weight of agonizing knowledge as it began to settle into her heart, to slice at her soul. She wanted to scream in denial, but she couldn't. She had to hold it back, she had to focus on the truth rather than the fantasy world she had lived in as a child.

Desmond wiped a hand over his face as Lilly kept a careful eye on him, as well as Isaac.

"I was helping your father." He stared at the whiskey in his glass for long moments before gazing back at her. "God, he loved her." He leaned his head back against the chair and stared at the ceiling. "He loved you better, though, and she knew it."

Lilly's lips trembled for a brief second before she controlled it. Instead, she met Travis's gaze, saw the compassion in it, the regret.

"How did she manage it?"

Once again Desmond shook his head. "I don't know. Harold had figured it out. He told me that night, but he didn't tell me it was Angelica. He was going to fill me in the next morning. The next thing I knew, you were both supposedly dead. I only figured out it was Angelica about six months ago and have been trying to pin her down with hard proof ever since."

Lilly swallowed tightly as Travis moved from the loveseat to stand beside her, to lend her his support, his warmth.

"How did she find me? I changed everything about myself."

"Everything but certain mannerisms," Desmond pointed out. "You attended a party in Bangladesh a few years ago for the ruling family's oldest son. We were there, along with Jared."

Lilly flinched at the pain that struck her temple, as well as the memory. She remembered it. Clearly. She had been forced to leave the party early when Jared had kept hitting on her. He'd danced with her, flirted with her. Her own brother. It had been more than she could bear.

"Your mother commented several times that Lilly Belle was so similar to her Victoria." He gave a harsh laugh. "Hell, I didn't even catch on."

"The pictures found in Desmond's files were taken by Samuel," Travis revealed. "Your mother had him following you." He turned back to Desmond. "I'm guessing you stumbled across the pictures in Angelica's files and made copies."

Lilly watched as Desmond pinched the bridge of his nose and fought back the dampness in his eyes.

"I hired Isaac for his reputation and his ability to keep his employers alive," he finally stated harshly. "We've been trying to catch her embezzling the money.

We've tried to find a way, especially since your return, to get the proof we needed."

"She's smart, and she has the money to hire others to do her dirty work," Travis said coldly. "She sent a hit out on Lilly yesterday. They found the safe house she was staying at. Ten men arrived to kill her and the three young women she had taken refuge with."

"My God." Desmond sat forward, swallowed tightly, then looked to Isaac. "I may need another drink."

Isaac turned to the bar just as the large glass window of the room shattered.

Travis pushed Lilly to the floor as Isaac was thrown against the bar by the bullet that slammed into his body and jerked him around. Another tore into his shoulder and he landed on the floor unconscious or dead, she wasn't certain which.

The doors to the library flew inward and four assailants rushed the room, automatic rifles drawn and leveled on them as Lilly stared up in horror.

Her gaze went around the room quickly. She couldn't see Nik. Where had he gone? Had he been in on this? Had he betrayed the Ops?

She had to swallow against the bile in her throat as pain pierced her head. Memories were swarming her now, racing into her brain with a speed she couldn't fight.

She was an operative. A highly secret operative, one whose very existence depended on the agency that had saved her. An agency whose survival depended on their ability to never be revealed.

"Well, Desmond, it looks as though you're as stupid as your brother." Angelica walked into the fray.

Resplendent in cream silk, she wore slacks, a matching top, and heels, which, combined with her light hair, gave Angelica the angelic appearance her name implied.

She appeared innocent, unthreatening, untouchable.

She stopped in the middle of the room and stared down at Lilly. Her head tilted to the side, and for a moment, regret flashed in her gaze.

Desmond sat down slowly in his chair, his hands resting casually on the arms as he leaned his head back and obviously fought with the realization that they may have failed.

"You always were a nosy little bitch." Angelica sighed as she glanced at Isaac's fallen body before turning back to Lilly. "You should have returned as my daughter rather than some little whore determined to destroy what I've built over the years. Really, Lilly? A call girl?" She shook her head. "I truly hope the money you made whoring was worth the loss of your life now."

Lilly eased up until she was sitting on the floor, partially shielded by Travis's larger body. "Anything would have been worth escaping you," she told her mother quietly. "I only wish I had remembered why I decided to remain dead to begin with. Tell me, what did happen the night you killed father?"

Angelica just glared at Lilly for what felt like hours, then sighed. "Well, I guess it doesn't matter now if you know since this will be over soon."

Lilly swallowed in relief, hoping that she had just bought them all a little more time.

"The night of the party, your father had been acting very strange. Actually, he had been acting strangely for several days before that. He had been very distracted and he claimed that he had been tied up in work, but I had a feeling that it went deeper than that. I knew he had been looking into the embezzlement of funds from our and other families' accounts, and up until that point I hadn't been the least bit concerned that he would trace anything back to me. Nothing could be traced back to me, after all. When Jared began working for Dunnolly & Dunnolly, I had gotten access to his password during a lovely family visit, and that's how I got the passcodes to the accounts of some of the other families. My accountant got the rest. He made it look like the accounts had been hacked from the outside, and after that, the money was difficult to trace, and even if they did trace it, none of the accounts were linked to me in any way. If any suspicions were to fall, it would probably fall on Jared. I suspect MI5 had him in their sights for quite some time. And besides, who in the world would suspect Angelica Harrington of pulling off such a crime? Really, it was the perfect setup."

"And you were just computer savvy enough to make it work with just a little help," Lilly said, her eyes narrowed. "I always was impressed with the skill you've managed your own wealth."

Angelica pursed her lips in annoyance. "Your father managed to trace one of the offshore accounts back to my accountant—the idiot." She looked scornful. "Once he matched that up to the fact the other families who were targeted were all represented by Dunnolly & Dunnolly, it eventually led him to suspect me. I had noticed that he was missing from the party that night and I went looking for him. He was in his study, on the phone. He sounded agitated, so I listened, trying to find out what he was talking about. Apparently he was on the phone with his MI5 contact and he told him or her that he knew who was behind the embezzlement and that he wanted to come in with the information. I couldn't let that happen.

"While he was finishing up his call, I slipped into my office next door, got the gun I kept in the safe there, and went in to confront him." She laughed. "Actually, I should say that he confronted me. He asked me if I had overheard his conversation and I told him that I had. He asked me to turn myself in, which I found hilarious. Really, why would I want to do something like that?"

"So you killed him," Lilly said, her tone tight with fury.

"Yes," Angelica said, coldly. "That would have wrapped things up nicely. The party was still in full swing and the study was far away enough that no one heard a thing. I was just about to call one of the associates here and tell them to dispose of the body when you came knocking. I hid behind the door, and when you came in, I knocked you unconscious."

"And your so-called associates put Lilly and her father in the car and sent it over the cliff," Travis said. "You were hoping that the explosion from the car crash would disguise the fact that your husband had been shot."

"So clever," Angelica said mockingly. "Yes, that's what I was hoping. And I was sure that I could move the process along quickly enough that no one would look at his body too closely. Who wouldn't try to accommodate the grieving Lady Harrington who had just lost her husband and daughter in such a tragic accident?" She looked at Lilly. "Well, almost lost. I had been convinced that your body had been washed out to sea." Angelica shook her head. "Well, we'll see if we can't make your death a fact this time around."

Lilly laughed. "Oh, and how will you manage it this time? That bullet to the brain wasn't exactly fun, Mother."

"You're such a disrespectful little bitch," her mother sneered. "Do you think I'm not aware that you spied on us? Sitting in the trees watching the family from afar? You would have never stayed away. Eventually, you would have returned. And we couldn't have that. The trust fund your uncle watches so closely is too important. The charity." She smiled slowly. "Well, it needs your money far more than you do."

The charity. Lilly felt her heart speed up further, a sense of realization flooding her senses.

"The charity is a terrorist fund," she whispered, her hands beginning to shake as the weapon tucked at the small of her back began to burn against her flesh with her need to use it.

"Of course." Her mother smiled. "Those quarterly donations of the interest ensures that I have a steady supply of men to do what needs to be done. The world is in horrible shape, darling. It needs some discipline."

Discipline. The world needed discipline.

"Lilly Belle has such enemies as well." Angelica clucked. "Such a shame. They broke in while I was shopping and killed you, your lover, and your uncle and his bodyguard." She looked at Isaac's still form. "Handsome man. It's a shame he had to be so damned ethical."

A movement at the front of the room, behind the men

surrounding Angelica, caught Lilly's attention. Nik. He was slowly easing along the edge of a heavy armoire to assess the situation.

"Poor Mother." Lilly sighed. "You can't get your way, so you kill. But do you truly believe we're the only ones who know this?"

Angelica laughed. "You have no proof, darling. What you do have, however, is the ability to irritate me and to take the money I promised my friends." She glanced to one of the hard-eyed men beside her. "Truly, there's nothing you can do. It's over, darling. You'll die for good, you'll be mourned, and I can grieve the death of yet another husband who died trying to save you from the people you managed to tie yourself to. Whores such as yourself do manage to create bad situations. It's a proven fact."

"You watch too much television." Lilly followed Travis as he eased to his feet. "It's not going to be that easy."

Angelica stepped closer, her expression hardening. Her hand lifted and she slapped Lilly across the face. Lilly didn't even try to avoid it. She took the blow. When her mother was dead or in prison, then Lilly wanted no doubts in her own mind as to the choices she had to make.

Nik was now in position. Desmond was slowly sliding his hand into the side of his chair. Lilly prayed he was moving for a weapon. She realized that Isaac was conscious, as she saw his good hand slide beneath his body.

This was the only chance they were going to have.

"Your weapon, Mr. Caine," Angelica demanded as she turned to Travis. "Your reputation is far too good. I think I'd prefer you not keep it."

Travis's hand slid beneath his jacket, slowly.

Desmond's hand gripped something at his side.

Lilly, using Travis's body for cover, slid her hand to her back.

It happened quickly. Too quickly.

Nik stepped out. Travis drew his weapon, Isaac rolled to his back, and Lilly dropped to her knees.

She fired at her mother. Tears filled her eyes and ran down her cheeks as the bullet slammed into Angelica's shoulder. It wasn't a kill shot, but as everyone acted at once, two more bullets took her from Desmond's and Isaac's guns.

Nik and Travis made quick work of the others. Lilly stared into her mother's eyes, watched as realization surged through the other woman.

Angelica dropped to her knees, blood soaking the cream color of her top, dripping to her slacks, as she held Lilly's gaze. Held it. Hatred flooding it, twisting her expression.

"Fucking whore," Angelica wheezed as she slowly melted to the floor, her eyes losing that brilliant glitter, dimming, and slowly becoming lifeless.

Her mother.

Lilly crawled to her, lifted her head in her lap, and slowly brushed the hair back from her face as the gunfire eased and the smell of death began to invade the room.

There were other men there now. Elite Ops One. Black masks covered their faces, but Lilly knew who they were. She didn't bother to look up. She watched her fingers touching her mother's brow, her hairline. She looked composed and peaceful in death.

She looked innocent. She looked like the mother Lilly remembered.

"Good-bye, Mother," she whispered as the tears continued to fall. "I loved you."

She had lost everything. Everyone.

"Lilly." Travis was behind her, easing down, his hands settling on her shoulders as she realized she was sobbing. "It's over, baby."

She shook her head.

"It's okay, Lilly." He sat beside her and eased her into his arms. "I have you, baby. It's over."

"I love you, Travis," she whispered as she laid her head on his shoulder. "I love you."

"I love you." He laid his cheek against the top of her head.

"You'll have to leave me now," she whispered. "I know that."

"Shhh," he shushed her gently as he whispered. "Keep the memories inside, sweetheart. You don't remember anything. Keep it that way." He turned her face to him. "Keep it that way, and I'll hold you forever."

Forever? Could she truly have a forever now?

With Travis?

She felt the smile that touched her lips, felt the pain and loss as it eased from her heart.

"I'll have you forever?"

"Forever," he swore.

She turned her head to him, her lips touching his as she whispered. "Then I don't remember a damned thing, Black Jack."

He smiled against her kiss. "That's the way, Night Hawk. Now, let me hold you forever."

His arms surrounded her. There, amid her past, all the death, and the things she thought she had lost, Lilly found love.

A love she could hold on to forever.

EPILOGUE

IT WAS OVER.

Lilly stood aside, Travis's arms wrapped around her, as agents of Homeland Security arrived at the house and began taking over the situation.

Senator Stanton was there, as was Jared Malone. The Homeland Security agent assigned to the case didn't question Travis's presence too deeply, though he questioned Lilly extensively.

But it was over. Her mother was dead and the threat that had followed Lilly since the night her father had died was gone.

"Lilly, come sit down," Travis urged her as the agents continued to question Desmond. "Let me get you a drink."

She nodded shakily. She felt as though she were in shock, though it wasn't exactly shock. Or perhaps it was. She couldn't make sense of the grief tearing through her.

She had lost everything. Her entire family.

"Here, baby." Travis pressed a glass in her hand. "It's your favorite."

Her favorite. Whisky. She had never been a champagne girl. Another disappointment to her mother, she remembered.

She wiped at the tear that escaped and wanted to huddle into herself and wail like a child. She had no family.

"Let me in there."

Lilly's head jerked around at the sound of her brother's voice.

"Damn you, I bloody well don't care what kind of a crime scene it is, let me see my sister."

The shock was building.

Lilly stood to her feet and watched with a sense of complete disbelief as her brother pushed past the agents standing at the door and stalked into the room.

And he wasn't alone.

The glass in her hand dropped to the floor, the sound of it shattering at her feet, ignored at the sight of her brother.

"Jared," she whispered, the tears falling now, shudders racing through her body at the sight of her brother, older, his eyes filled with remorse as he opened his arms to her.

Lilly pressed back against Travis, her hands gripping his arms now as she stared at him. Stared.

He had disowned. Her he had been such an important part of her life yet he had turned his back on her. There was a conversation behind her, Travis ordering someone to get him another drink.

"Lilly." He stopped in front of her, his gaze tormented.

She stared at him, unable to understand why he was here now.

"You look just like grandmother's pictures when she was younger. It's no surprise Mother knew who you were at that party."

Lilly stared back at him painfully. "You disowned me."

He shook his head wearily as he raked his fingers through his overly long hair. "I had no choice, Lilly. I had to stay away, and I had to have a reason for doing so. I was working to uncover the truth of what she was doing; I couldn't do that if I was here, allowing her to draw me into her machinations."

Lilly shook her head, as she tried to make sense of everything. "You were going to help her have me commited."

"Lilly." Desmond moved beside him. "He would have never done such a thing. But she had to believe he would. We needed every moment to gain the proof we needed against her. She wasn't working alone, though she did, I believe, like to convince herself that she was smart enough to steal the funds she'd embezzled without any help. We had to learn how deep it went."

Lilly shook her head as she turned to stare at her uncle.

My God, things were out of control here. There was no way she could make sense of this.

"Desmond and I knew what she was doing, but proving it wasn't nearly as easy. She may have been crazed, but she was damned intelligent. Too intelligent to catch easily."

Lilly shook her head again. "Did you know?" she

asked Travis as he held her close to his chest, his arms holding her steady.

"Travis didn't know, Lilly," her brother said gently. "Just Desmond and I knew, and I was actively working the case, which made it impossible for me to allow Mother to believe I was in any way convinced that you were truly alive. Or even cared if you were."

She flinched.

Lilly could feel her breath tight in her chest, the dizziness that filled her. Memories were crashing inside her now. Six years' worth were flooding her senses as she fought to breathe.

"Lilly, we did what we had to in our attempt to try to gather enough proof to have her arrested," Jared stated. "She was always one step ahead of us. When you were shot in England, we knew you were her weak spot. She couldn't accept you had possibly become an escort. From the conversations I overheard, she was enraged by your cover, and determined that if you didn't fit into her idea of the life you should live, then she would kill you. Returning you home was the distraction we needed to force her to mess up."

"You used me?" What hurt worse, six years of lies, or learning the truth simply because they had needed her to trap her mother?

"You weren't safe any longer," he sighed. "At least here, within her sight, your memories erased, you had a chance of surviving long enough for us to finish what had to be done. Isaac and Desmond watched out for you, just as Travis did. It was the only way to keep you alive once she knew who you were."

Lilly lifted her hand to cover her mouth. She was going to scream. She was going to sink to the floor in madness as she stared at the father she thought she had lost and the brother she had believed disowned her.

"Lilly Belle," her brother whispered. "Do you remember how Father used to call you that, when you were a child?"

She did remember. Just as she remembered how her mother had hated it.

"You shouldn't have done this," Travis snapped behind her, fury filling his voice. "For God's sake, you could have gotten her killed. You nearly did."

Jared frowned darkly over her head. "What would you have me do?"

"A hell of a lot different than this," Travis growled back.

"Lilly, I love you, sister," Jared whispered as her gaze sliced to him. "Give me a chance now. The danger has passed, let me try to make up for it now."

A sob escaped her lips.

"Lilly," her brother crooned, his eyes flashing with grief as he stared back at her now. "There's no way to make up for the past six years, or the pain you've suffered. There's no way to make up for the lies. But I love you."

Desmond moved in beside him. "He loved you enough, Lilly, that he let you go to save you. Something we all know couldn't be easy."

The tears were flowing now. She couldn't hold them back. She couldn't stop them from falling.

Travis released her as she stepped into her brother's embrace.

Travis watched as her brother sheltered her in his arms, as he bent his head over hers and his own tears fell.

"Travis." She turned to him, throwing herself back in his arms, tears and joy filling her voice as his arms went around her. "I'm finally really alive."

"I know, baby." He held her close to his chest. "I know."

I won't let her go. He mouthed back at the senator, the only man who could spoil Lilly's happiness.

The senator shook his head. *I always knew you wouldn't.* His response surprised Travis.

Lilly was in his arms. His woman. His lover. The holder of his heart.

She had her family, her true family. The men who had stood aside and allowed her to do what she had to do to survive, while they had fought to clear her way home.

She could truly go home now, as the woman she was rather than the woman her mother would have forced her to be.

Lilly leaned back in his arms now. "You'll hold me forever now?"

He smiled down at her. "Always, Lilly. I'll hold you always."

And there, in front of her brother, her uncle, Lilly reached for his kiss. Slow, loving, her lips touched his as her hands clasped his face. She leaned into him, leaned against him, and Travis knew nothing mattered, nothing would ever matter as much as Lilly did.

He held his Night Hawk in his arms. The woman he had loved far longer than he should have. The woman who had held his heart far longer than she should have.

She was home, but he was home, too.

Right there, in her arms.

Midnight Sins

Cami lost her sister in the brutal murders that rocked her hometown so many years ago. Some still believe that Rafe Callahan, along with his friends Logan and Crowe, were involved. But how could Rafe—who haunted her girlish dreams, then her adult fantasies—be a killer?

Deadly Sins

A newcomer in town, Sky O'Brien is a mystery to Logan Callahan. Like him, she is a night owl. Like him, she is fighting her own demons. Like him, she hides a secret in her eyes—a fire that consumes him with every glance. Could she be the one to heal him?

Secret Sins

Sheriff Archer Tobias has watched the Callahan family struggle to find peace and acceptance in the community—despite the murders that continue to haunt them. But he is torn between duty and desire when Anna Corbin becomes the next target.

Ultimate Sins

Mia, left an orphan after her father's death, was raised amid the lies and suspicions against Crowe Callahan. But nothing could halt the fascination she feels for him, or the hunger that has risen inside her.

St. Martin's Paperbacks   St. Martin's Griffin